C000214515

Watcher 22

Sue L. Clarke

Grosvenor House
Publishing Limited

All rights reserved
Copyright © Sue L. Clarke, 2019

The right of Sue L. Clarke to be identified as the author of this
work has been asserted in accordance with Section 78
of the Copyright, Designs and Patents Act 1988

The book cover is copyright to Sue L. Clarke

This book is published by
Grosvenor House Publishing Ltd
Link House
140 The Broadway, Tolworth, Surrey, KT6 7HT.
www.grosvenorhousepublishing.co.uk

This book is sold subject to the conditions that it shall not, by way of
trade or otherwise, be lent, resold, hired out or otherwise circulated
without the author's or publisher's prior consent in any form of binding or
cover other than that in which it is published and
without a similar condition including this condition being imposed
on the subsequent purchaser.

This book is a work of fiction. Any resemblance to
people or events, past or present, is purely coincidental.

A CIP record for this book
is available from the British Library

ISBN 978-1-78623-605-0

For my wonderful daughters

Acknowledgements

Thank you to Frosty and my family for all your advice and encouragement and especially for listening to my endless ramblings

A very special thank you to Sarah and Emma for all of your ideas, particularly with explaining developments in technology, introducing a playlist and giving me advice on the design of the front cover.

I am very grateful to all the Dinner Party Crew with a special mention to John, for his endless patience with proofreading and Michele, for her clarity and positivity.

Thank you to everyone at Grosvenor House Publishing Company for your dedication and expertise.

Watcher 22 Playlist

1. *Over The Rainbow* - Eva Cassidy
2. *Let's go round again* - Average White Band
3. *Everybody Hurts* - REM
4. *Sweet Dreams* - Eurythmics
5. *Watching the detectives* - Elvis Costello
6. *Don't Fear the Reaper* - Blue Oyster Cult
7. *I am the passenger* - Iggy Pop
8. *For your eyes only* - Sheena Easton
9. *China in your hand* - T'pau
10. *Do you know where you're going to?* - Diana Ross
11. *Return to sender* - Elvis Presley
12. *Firestarter* - The Prodigy
13. *Sweet little mystery* - Wet Wet Wet
14. *More than this*- Roxy Music
15. *The first time ever I saw your face* - Roberta Flack
16. *Somebody's watching me* - Michael Jackson
17. *If I could turn back time* - Cher
18. *Stuck With You* - Huey Lewis & The News
19. *Red light spells danger* - Billy Ocean
20. *Bridge over troubled water* - Simon and Garfunkel

Over The Rainbow
Eva Cassidy

My dad had always told me that he found my mum at the end of a rainbow which, as a child, seemed quite plausible. Stranger things have happened.

The party was over and my friends, who had dressed up as *Wizard of Oz* characters, had finally gone home. The kitchen was piled high with plates and there were CD's scattered all over the floor. I poured myself a Bacardi and coke. Bacardi is truly the nectar of kings and queens, I thought to myself as I leaned forward and loaded Eva Cassidy's version of *Over The Rainbow*. Life had at last settled down after the trauma of the previous year.

I saw the headlights sweep across the living room and thought nothing of it, that was until I heard the rattling. One thing has never changed, when it comes to Fight or Flight, I was definitely in the new category, Freeze. As a child, I had always pulled the blankets over my head when scared of monsters under the bed. As an adult, this had developed into staying stock still and holding my breath. I convinced myself that it was the wind, but turned down the music just in case. Charlie would have checked of course, always happy to face things head on. I remembered when burglars came into our house when we were actually in and wrecked the kitchen and stole our car keys. Without a second thought, Charlie strode out into the night to try and chase down the villains. On his return I was still sitting in the same position, feeling terrified as he had left the house. I'd watched too many scary films and was frightened that there was someone in the house, in the loft maybe or at the back of a wardrobe. There wasn't, not then and not now I told myself. I turned the music back up and was just starting to relax when I heard the back door slam and immediately lost my rhythm on the rocking chair. I had made sure that Charlie, my partner, was having a night on the town and it had been a good half an hour since my friends had left. My stomach clenched and liquid fear crept through me. The mellow glow of the alcohol disappeared immediately. I was instantly sober. If there had ever been a serious incident in my life or my children needed me, I became almost immediately sober, not in the 'driving a car' sense you understand. My heartbeat pounded inside my head, marking time. I managed to lean over and grab my phone just as the shouting began.

'Hallo, hallo are you there? Don't panic! Your doorbell doesn't appear to be working and it is rather an emergency. Did you get the letter? I'm guessing that if you didn't then right now you are probably terrified and haven't got a clue...'

'Freeze!!!' I shouted at the shadow behind the frosted glass door. I tapped my cheek just to check I was awake. I aimed my mobile phone like a weapon, hopeful that the prowler would be threatened by its form in shadow.

Deep down I knew that the voice was familiar but adrenaline had finally kicked in and I sprang into action, well I left the rocking chair.

'Helena, are you aiming your phone at me? For the love of Mary – it's me Brown from *XP*!!!! Did you hear me Helena? Do you remember the debriefing? It was me and now well now something's come up and it is rather urgent. The letter explained it and...'

'Brown! Brown from *XP*? What the hell? What letter? Oh no, I'm not going back to *XP* Brown!! Please don't tell me that you've found part of my soul in one of your dreaded machines and I'm going to become unhinged or find out that this party was really part of Plenni and we never really escaped!'

'Good Grief Helena!!!! Slow down there. It is unfortunate that you didn't open the letter as you would have been prepared and less, well less frightened. No matter, I am here to ask a favour – nothing more and there will be a considerable financial reward. There's no need to let the old paranoia out of the cage. Berni said that you hadn't opened the letter and she thought a personal visit may be more...'

'Terrifying, is the word Brown!! You scared me half to death! And what could be so urgent and why didn't you call me?'

'I'm coming through into the room now Helena, please lower your weird phone weapon.' Brown pushed open the door and I lay down my phone on the coffee table. Brown smiled, but made no comment, his eyes were drawn to my ruby slippers. "Wizard of Oz night?'

"How did you guess? Now then back to business Brown, I think you should tell me about the emergency.

3

Couldn't Berni deal with it? After all, she works for you doesn't she?'

'Yes she does, we called her straight in, after your party, of course. We were hoping that you would also join us. '

'Are you offering me some work, a proper job with training and a pay cheque and ...'

'Yes, yes, all that – the details are in the letter, there would be a short induction and then there's the Official Secrets Act to sign. Our program, *Watcher 22,* is now also used by the military overseas and so forth. All very hush-hush.' Brown paused and coughed, clearly wrestling with an inner confidentiality demon. 'Look, all of those things can be sorted out but we need you right away, we didn't anticipate things progressing so quickly. This is serious Helena – one of our clients is stuck in the program and we think that you may be able to bring her back or at least give us some idea about how the client is feeling. Our experts and tech guys are working hard to pull her out, but any ideas or insights you can offer will be well received. This has never happened before, but there was one occasion when you crossed the line. You have the most experience and you may be able to help. Please...'

'OK. OK. I'll come, but right now? I'll need to phone Charlie.'

'Yes of course, please do that from the car.'

'I do have a job you know.'

'Yes we do know, but it's a job you can go back to as I'm sure you'll agree.'

'Yes, that's true. I'm assuming you have made the necessary contacts and organised my cover?' I hesitated before answering my own question. 'Yes of course you have.

I never really had a choice did I Brown? I will try to help the poor soul trapped in the program. How awful to be dangling in the stratosphere, stuck between worlds, of course I'll help if I can. Do I have time to get changed or must I come dressed as Dorothy?'

'You have five minutes Helena and we'll pull the car around to the front.'

'Thanks Brown.'

'Just one last thing, this isn't some newfangled interview technique is it, to test my coping skills under pressure?' I asked cautiously.

Brown just glared back at me.

'I'll take that as a 'no', sorry, five minutes should do it.'

I changed quickly into nondescript jeans and a jumper, grabbed my phone and some essential toiletries and locked up. *XP* must be really worried to come and get me this late at night. I left Charlie a voice mail message – just explaining that I had been asked to help out in a crisis at *XP* and I would be back in the morning. The sleek black BM cut cleanly through the night and reminded me of our so-called 'escape' just one year earlier.

'Have you asked any of the other members of the team to come?'

'No not as yet, but they have been alerted, just in case. Let's hope it doesn't come to that Helena. We need you to read and sign the paperwork, so we can get you straight inside.'

Brown handed me a thick folder and a silver Papermate pen. I sat back, knowing that I had a two hour journey ahead of me. I would read the paperwork more thoroughly this time around. Sympathetic as I may be, I didn't want to get stuck in someone else's nightmare or weird memory. Anyway, I had decided this would be a purely advisory role, re-entering my own past had been bizarre enough. I would insist on being a bystander this time and helping from the touchlines. This was my plan, but we all know about best-laid plans…

Let's go round again
Average White Band

I was signed, sealed and about to be delivered. I had sent Charlie a text and we both agreed that the job offer seemed reasonable, with a favourable financial package. Due to the high importance of the case, the college I had been working for would be provided with an immediate replacement and I could return to my job as soon as my work with *XP* was complete. On the face of it, I had nothing to lose. I would also have a break from the routine of teaching and work with my friend Berni. All in all, it was a great opportunity. I began to wonder what had happened to the poor soul I was going to try and help. It must be serious if their experts were struggling and Berni hadn't managed to resolve it.

I began to think back to the last time I was at *XP*. Each member of our team was a participant in the experimental *Watcher 22* program. We had all been searching for answers to very different kinds of questions. Conventional counselling and therapy had either been avoided or unsuccessful. The program had been advertised as 'an interactive counselling experience.' where memories could be rewound (similar to rewinding a videotape). The idea behind it was that hindsight could be a valuable tool in the healing process. *XP* provided each of us with our own Pod and by combining *Watcher 22,* hypnosis and Twilight anaesthesia, we became ringside spectators of past events, unable to interfere or alter anything, simply observe. The process could become very isolating and welcome relief came at team meetings (Plenni). We had all selected two Guides and I smiled as I remembered mine, Alan Rickman (nicknamed Flint) and Dame Judi Dench (nicknamed Pink). The voices of the Guides are heard in the client's head and dialogue between them is instant. We were lucky as our team had escaped and each team member had gained something different from the *Watcher 22* program.

I brought myself back to the present as the BMW swept noiselessly up to the entrance of *XP* and two military types whisked me into the main building. Berni was waiting for me which was very reassuring. There was only the faintest whisper of her Glinda the good witch make-up from the party and some silver sparkles in her hair.

'Brown, get Mason. We need to get Helena up to speed and the clock's ticking.' instructed Berni. Berni looked unusually stressed and it made me realise just how serious this situation was. She smiled weakly and handed me a bottle of chilled water. We were then directed towards the impressive glass staircase, which would take us up to one of the debriefing rooms. Brown hurried us into one of the rooms and we both sat down at the smoked glass table. I shuddered, remembering how distressed we all were last time we were here. Berni sensed my trepidation and patted me lightly on the shoulder.

Brown tapped a silver stylus onto the glass table and it became a transparent computer screen. Berni and I were unphased by this impressive technology, as we had seen it before. An image appeared, a woman, middle-aged, possibly in her forties. She was lying flat on one of the pod beds attached to all the machinery that made visiting the past possible. The camera zoomed in on her face, she wore the white suit and visor that had been the uniform inside the pod. We could see that the woman's eyes were fixed, unblinking as she stared aimlessly ahead.

'She's stuck in one of her past life events. We can't seem to bring her out of it and we risk damage if we jolt her back.' Brown explained.

'We need the details of her background and a summary of her situation and which past event she is re-visiting.' Berni said firmly

'I'd like to know who her Guides are, in case we can use them to help in some way.' I added.

Brown clicked his stylus and two transparent screens appeared in front of us. Information cascaded down the screens, at what seemed like the speed of light.

'Wow!' exclaimed Berni.

'Amazing!' I added.

Then came the voice, a calm soporific voice with just a slight edge of urgency and an Irish lilt. He read gently read through the details in a measured, yet slightly agitated tone. (It was the voice of Liam Neeson) I smiled to myself, good old *XP* and the fantastic range of Guides on offer. We discovered that the poor soul stuck in the program was Joanna, aged 44. She had been working as a Personal Assistant in the retail industry. She has two children, who are now grown-up and reasonably settled, as much as grown-up children can be. Joanna had approached *XP* as she needed to try and gain some closure, after the death of her sister, Francesca. Life had thrown its usual bag of tricks her way and although she had always been a coper, the death of her sister had proved unbearable. She was searching for some form of acceptance, to regain a sense of control over her day to day life. Joanna had also been suffering from insomnia and was finding it difficult to cope. She believed that the special connection between her and her sister could not be broken and she was desperate to find a way to communicate. Joanna was provided with medication and counselling, but couldn't seem to move forward, especially as Francesca had committed suicide.

At this point, Berni wiped away a tear as did I and even Brown's bottom lip seemed to quiver. In time, Joanna did manage to return to work, mainly on automatic pilot as she dragged herself through the long days. Her main focus had been to save up enough money to enter the *XP* program, which she had achieved in a record six months. Joanna had been accepted onto the program and had successfully revisited many past events and up until now things had been going well, Joanna appeared to be making good progress in coming to terms with her past.'

Brown then cut in, just to speed things along. 'This is the first serious incident that has occurred with Joanna's revisits.' We were both surprised that such a serious case would have been accepted by *XP*.

'Did anyone consider just how dangerous this program could be for someone like Joanna?' Berni asked, with a note of annoyance in her voice.

'For God's sake Brown, don't you do a risk assessment or something before you agree to take someone on?' I asked.

'Of course we do, it's a very professional service. Joanna had to satisfy a team of highly qualified counsellors and psychologists that she was competent and understood the risks... But, after failing to respond to both medication and therapy-she felt that she had little to lose. She could no longer see a future and desperately wanted to find a way forward. Francesca's suicide was five years ago and Joanna felt this was her last chance to accept her death and make a fresh start. It was Joanna's choice. It is always the client's choice, just as it was the choice of each one of you.' Brown added somewhat huffily.

'Well, Brown I still feel it was ill-advised. But it is what it is and we're here living in this moment. Could you tell us where Joanna is stuck and which point of her life we are up to?' asked Berni, in a business-like manner.

'Of course, the sisters are just 16 and 18 years old. This revisit must have been emotionally charged for Joanna. We have taken her back to an incident when she was arguing with her father. It was a vicious argument about Joanna and Francesca staying over at their friend's house overnight. Previously their mother had agreed with the arrangement, but this was only in the early sixties when the patriarch always had the final word.'

'Thank you for the historical context Brown, where does Joanna fit in?' I asked, well aware that minutes could feel like hours in revisits'

'From the notes, it appears that Francesca was the more adventurous of the sisters and often took risks, which Joanna knew about and kept secret. In this particular scene, Joanna knows that Francesca will really be staying with her boyfriend and Joanna feels responsible for carrying this knowledge but is tied by loyalty. I think we may be able to send you there now, but only for a few minutes. If you could just pop these visors on and sit back and relax. We nervously did so. Both of us had been convinced that our time with the *Watcher 22* program was well and truly over. It was very strange to be asked to be a voyeur to such a very private family altercation. The screen crackled in such a familiar way that Berni and I felt the need to link arms.

We were thrust into a room full of shouting. The atmosphere felt heavy and laced with the threat of violence. Joanna was stood in front of the fire, holding onto the mantelpiece as though her life depended on it. Her father was sat in his favourite armchair, a glass of whisky in his hand. The whisky glass was filled to the top and the light glinted on the smooth surface of the golden liquid belying its' dark reputation. I looked to my right-hand side and saw Francesca kneeling on the settee with her back to the fracas. She was facing the window so that she could see outside. Berni and I hesitated for a moment mesmerised by the similar countenance of the young sisters. As the shouting intensified we were brought back to the unpleasant present. We hurriedly looked around for the older Joanna and found her out sitting on a footstool in the far corner. The adult Joanna looked frozen, only her eyes winced with pain. Berni also noticed and we exchanged a worried look. We needed to act and quickly.

Tempers were starting to rise and we could see that both Joannas, from past and present, were flinching at the same time. Suddenly, young Joanna grabbed her father's half-empty whisky bottle and threw it against the wall. As the glass shattered and the liquid crept down the walls, its cloying, intoxicating odour seemed to spread through the air. The room felt as if it was closing in. There was an agonising vacuum of silence, more terrifying than the shouting could ever be. The sisters' father rose, almost in slow motion, and started unbuckling his belt. Everyone in the room knew exactly what was coming. Young Joanna didn't flinch, she moved her head to one side, a sign of acceptance, and braced herself for the beating which would inevitably follow.

This was sickening, what on earth could be learnt here? This was a scene from the past that could not be changed. We moved in front of the adult Joanna in an attempt to block her view, it was all we could do. I turned and watched Young Joanna, as she adopted the position for a beating.

Young Joanna was now facing us, she frowned and her eyes flickered as though she was trying to make sense of the situation. She raised her head and seemed to be searching for something or someone. Another connection, was this another imbalance in the program? Berni and I blocked her glare, then Berni gently laid the ravaged Joanna's head on her shoulder and nodded to me. I made the necessary contact with Brown and Joanna slowly closed her eyes on this sad scene. The tension drained out of Joanna's face and we were transported back from whence we came. Joanna was returned to her pod and monitored closely. I hoped that they wouldn't sedate her to heavily, as she needed to avoid any medically enhanced respite in order to heal.

Berni and I were sent back to the debriefing room. Brown seemed relieved and there was just a hint of nerves, as he handed the pack of paperwork to us both.

'Thank you for bringing Joanna back to us. Our greatest concern is that the *Watcher 22* program may have developed some serious glitches and as it is being used to protect our national security, all our findings are important. We have grave concerns regarding the time we have been allotted, to bring all our clients back from past events, I'm sure you can understand how important this is to our military friends who have been using *Watcher 22* in covert operations. We would have preferred more time to test it thoroughly, but in cases of National Security, you simply do not argue. The implications of this newfound problem are far-reaching. Joanna's case is traumatic enough without her being stuck in a disturbing life event. You both seemed to act instinctively and almost automatically. It was almost as if you both knew that the only way to bring Joanna back, was to block the connection between Joanna and her past self. It could be that certain events should remain untouched, unless we have either a direct request from the client, as they are unable to move forward because of it. Either way, it is complicated despite having many advisers and psychiatrists working together on each client's program. Why did you instinctively break the glare between Joanna and her younger self? You could have gone for Francesca or her father, or asked for an emergency withdrawal.'

Berni and I looked carefully at each other. She nodded for me to go ahead.

'I think that our experience of actually being in that position, rather than just observing, has given us an insight into what action to take. Joanna is only eighteen. How many revisits has she done? For that matter how many Plenni's has she done and how did they go?' I asked tentatively.

Brown muttered something to Mason and he hurriedly left the room.

'It's time for some refreshments whilst we wait.' Brown poured tea and handed out Danish pastries.

'Why couldn't you just pull her out using your amazing computer program and brilliant science geeks?' I asked with just a hint of sarcasm. 'I remember when Brian got pulled out when he was panicking about a revisit before Toby died.'

'Simply flicking a switch or yanking her out may have caused even greater damage and even more distress for Joanna. We want her to be aware of her surroundings and help her to regain some control in her life, not take it from her.'

'Helena, do you remember when you had to be retrieved when your past self appeared to see you?' asked Berni.

'Yes yes,' interrupted Brown somewhat impatiently, 'but those were events which, although emotionally charged, did not have the deep-rooted connection that these sisters appear to have. And we diffused them before they became a real threat or the client became 'locked in'....' Brown's voice began to fade and he looked uncomfortably at his shoes as Mason shook his head in despair.

'What did you say?' I asked as Berni grabbed my arm. 'Locked in?'

'Seriously Brown. Has that really happened? People can get locked in? I think that now is the time for truth.

We do work for you now and we have both signed the Official Secrets Act.'

Brown stood up and looked distinctly uncomfortable and there was a very slight flush on his cheeks. He pressed his right ear and nodded. Of course, he had an earpiece in and it became obvious how closely we were under surveillance. Berni and I exchanged glances, the seriousness of the situation beginning to make an impact.

'We need to just focus on Joanna now. My hands are tied. I am unable to tell you more at this stage. It has been a long night for us all and we have a positive outcome. Mason accompany the ladies to their sleeping quarters. Oh and just for tonight I must ask you to relinquish your mobile phones.'

'What? Why on earth would we do that?' I asked, finding it difficult not to raise my voice.

'Messages have already been sent to your homes and partners were advised a while ago about the erm... circumstances. I realise that this is an imposition, but we need to keep things secure and...'

'Thanks for the vote of confidence, we get the idea. I've seen *Killers* so I know that mobile phones can be tracked and conversations can be listened to.' One look at Berni and I realised that 'we' didn't know. Berni looked horrified. We both handed our phones over to Brown. Mason opened the door and we were escorted to our rooms. As we walked silently up a spiral staircase, my mind was working overtime and I wondered what on earth Berni and I had gotten ourselves into. Then something strange happened. The voice of Flint (Alan Rickman) suddenly came into my head. This hadn't happened since I had left the program. Not once. My time with *XP* was very definitely in the past, or so I had thought.

'Dear sweet Helena, I feel we taught you nothing. You may have gone, but you have not been forgotten. Nothing ever really 'goes'. You still have such a lot to learn. You didn't honestly think that it would be so final, just like flicking a switch, did you? Poor dear Helena, always the dreamer.' There was a click and a fizzing sound and then nothing. I froze on the staircase. Berni could tell that something was wrong, but knew better than to ask me until we were alone. We linked arms as we walked down the corridor and I'm sure I could make out the unmistakable sound of Flint's laughter somewhere in the distance.

It was only faint, but I could hear the Eurythmics. I shook myself awake and then checked again, but the music had stopped. Maybe it was just the ghosts of this place reminding me not to hang around for too long. I reached across for my phone to ring Charlie, my hand searching impatiently on the glass surface of the bedside table. And then I remembered, we no longer had our mobiles. Berni and I had only spoken a few hurried words last night, due to the lateness of the hour. Neither of us felt that it was safe or wise to try and analyse what had just happened. Berni had hugged me and told me to try and sleep.

In the crisp light of morning, my heart began to beat just a little bit faster and my stomach tightened. How dare they? I had been whisked away from home late at night and dragged into a complete stranger's life. *XP* was taking liberties; confiscating our phones was pushing it a little too far. I vaguely remembered Brown telling us that our loved ones had been informed, but this case isn't a wartime incident or a matter of national security or is it? After all, we had already signed the Official Secrets Act. I looked around the room searching for clues, anything to give us an edge. It was a standard room with an en suite bathroom and noticeably no landline telephone on the bedside unit. A tap on the door broke my thoughts, I hoped it was Berni. It was. I let her in checking down the long, red-carpeted corridors. I'd watched far too many films.

'What's going on Berni?' I asked hopelessly.

'I don't know, I really don't. This glitch they have found in the program. It's serious. Some of the clients are midway through their revisits, which would make it difficult for them to suddenly stop. I have no idea what the military or the government are using it for and I don't think they will ever tell us. I worry more for the normal clients, people like you and I who were just looking for some kind of closure. This could easily have been us Helena. Do you remember just how frightening it was? And that was without this cross patching. How strange it would be to sense your older self in the room or even look yourself in the eye.' Berni shuddered. 'How has it come to this Helena?'

'I don't know Berni, but I think I've seen enough. I'd like to go home now AND I want my phone back. We're not prisoners here are we Berni?'

'No, no, at least I don't think so... The last few days have made me feel quite disturbed and there's a stream of messages flowing through my head. It's like having uncontrolled access to a radio frequency and to be quite honest it's overwhelming at times.'

'I'm sorry Berni that sounds really tough, being psychic must be a nightmare in this situation. We need to find out what they want from us and some sort of time frame. I think *XP* must have unleashed the beast by altering the space-time continuum. Einstein's theory of relativity referred to this many years ago. Having the past and present person in the same room at the same time is surely a very dangerous thing to do....' I was interrupted by the sound of a siren screeching loudly through the building. We could hear footsteps pounding down our corridor. Berni and I froze for a second. Then we sprang into action. I dragged on a pair of jeans and forced on my sweatshirt. Luckily Berni had dressed before coming to my room. We could hear the sound of banging and doors slamming. I opened the door and saw the security men checking each room.

'Time to go Berni.'

I didn't like the look of the security men. They weren't suited and booted FBI types, more like bouncers and one of them had a dog, which I hoped was a sniffer dog rather than an attack dog. We ran down the hall towards the lifts. A guard stood in front of the lift doors and pointed impatiently towards the staircase. We began our descent and as my heart pounded in my ears, I could just make out the distant strains of *Run for Home* (Lindisfarne) and a static crackle. I stopped for a second and Berni turned around and gave an order in a clear yet definite tone.

'Helena, don't stop!'

I shook away the sounds in my head and we carried on down the stairs. We were both a little out of breath when Mason came over to us and escorted us out of the building. It seemed as if a whole fleet of shiny BMWs were outside *XP*. Mason kept holding his ear and speaking into his sleeve in true secret service fashion. He hurriedly opened the car door and bundled us in. I frowned at Berni and she just shrugged her shoulders. The car moved away at some speed and I decided to wait before asking if we could both go home.

I waited a little while before posing the question. I tapped on the tinted glass which separated us from the driver. Before I could begin, a pre-recorded message started to play through the speakers. We wouldn't be going home. Everyone was being relocated for safety reasons and apologies were made for the inconvenience, blah blah.

'Bloody great Berni! I thought we would just be consultants, friendly guides to help our fellow inmates. What the hell is going on here?'

'I don't know Helena. Until you arrived it was all plain sailing. A few minor upsets but nothing that couldn't be sorted out through discussion or further flashback visits. It seemed a little mundane actually, that was, of course, until you arrived.' She raised her eyebrows as she repeated herself.

'Thanks Berni. Do you think my presence has disturbed the Gods in some way? Altered the equilibrium perhaps?'

Despite the seriousness of the situation Berni let out a stifled chuckle and put her arm through mine. And then the tone changed as she whispered in my ear...

'I don't think your presence commands such biblical representations. And by the way Helena, exactly when were you going to tell me that you'd started hearing the music again?'

'How did you know...?' One look at Berni and it was obvious. Of course she would know and especially in such an emotionally charged situation.

'I was going to tell you. But it's only just happened and then with all this....'

'Do you hear the Guides as well? No, let me guess, you hear only Flint.'

It was a rhetorical question of course. I nodded. Berni patted my hand and gave a resigned sigh. 'Of course, that may have been the catalyst.'

Before I could respond the car screeched to a sudden halt and the door was hurriedly yanked open. Berni and I tried to make out where we were, but it seemed a pretty remote location somewhere deep within the countryside. We were rushed inside the building through an oak doorway. An interior door was then unlocked and unbolted and we were herded into a room, dimly lit by old gas lamps. The door slammed shut before we were noisily locked in. Charming I thought to myself before trying to get my bearings in this strange half-lit world. We were herded into a rather cosy kitchen, with an Aga range and chintz armchairs. It would have been a lovely country retreat in different circumstances. As I turned to face Berni, I could see why she was distracted.

(An unknown location)

Watching the detectives.
Elvis Costello

5

Chapter

Barry was whistling as he toasted crumpets over an open fire.

'Good evening ladies, I was wondering when you'd be putting in an appearance.'

Barry's cut-glass accent seemed strangely at home in this country pile. His tone was relaxed and calm probably a skill learned working in a highly stressful business environment and dealing with the highs and lows of the Stock Exchange. Berni and I plonked ourselves down on the floral covered armchairs, both stunned by the events of the last twenty four hours.

'Why are you here Barry? What the hell is going on? Are all the team members being brought in?'

'Take a few deep breaths Helena, one needs to simply keep calm. I myself have no idea what's going on.'

Berni sighed. 'Something awful must have happened Barry, Perhaps a security leak?'

'Or a terrorist threat!' I added rather dramatically. Barry winced slightly before putting another crumpet on a blue, willow patterned plate.

'I don't know much, but I feel confident that things have not escalated to DEFCON 3 yet Helena.' He drew his hand across his brow and a faint sliver of silver paint reminded me of happier times.

'I was sound asleep, a natural sleep I might add, when I was extracted from the comfort of my cosy nook by a rather a gruff gentlemen, wearing body armour. They did have the courtesy not to smash their way in by using a glass cutter and Bob's your uncle. The familiar BMW brought me to this rather lovely country abode. I was told little on the journey except for there been some kind of breach and I was being taken to a place of safety as a precaution. I'm sure I know nothing that would be of any use to anyone. However, things are starting to fall into place now that you have both arrived and perhaps it's our little group that needs to be protected.'

'We'll soon find out.' I added wearily.

'I think Shauna's arrived.' Berni stated in a flat tone.

'Brace yourselves ladies, the volume is about to go up!'

'Barry could I ask you, before Shauna arrives – do you hear them?'

Barry looked across at me and shrugged his shoulders.

'I hear a lot of things Helena, my mind is just recovering after being awash with the bubbly stuff for way too long.'

'Helena means the Guides Barry, do you hear the Guides?'

'Hell no! And I'm rather glad. I haven't heard the sound of Alan Rickman's rasping sarcasm or the soft lilt of lovely Aneka's voice since we left. Don't tell me they're back and you're hearing them again?'

'Just Alan.'

Barry grimaced. 'And you think that may have some connection to what's going on here?' he asked.

'I don't know, but it's a hell of a coincidence.'

'There is no such thing as coincidence...' Berni murmured to herself.

'Are we safe here Barry?'

'Yes,' he paused, 'at least I think we are, for now, at least.'

'*Watcher 22* is a dangerous tool in the wrong hands.' Berni stated and then pursed her lips, shaking her head before continuing. 'We all know how real it can be and when you are in a flashback observing the past, you can see many things that you would never have remembered. It is much more effective than regression therapy and has many more possibilities. Having said that, in the outside world if it replaces torture, then I must admit I'm all for it.'

'Heavens Berni. That was deep, but I do agree with you there. I was thinking more along the lines of industrial espionage. This is an innovative new program that would be very attractive to all the major powers, even though it is somewhat experimental. I would imagine that globally the program would have great appeal, not only with the military but also with the world's biggest companies such as Apple, Microsoft and Google. Remember that *Watcher 22* is a computer program and marketing the software could be extremely lucrative. It would gross a massive revenue if it was released into the open market, which was, of course, never the intention.'

There was a reflective silence. Barry's ideas made sense, but where did that leave us.

'It was designed for use as an advanced counselling program, to be monitored and strictly regulated by a responsible overseer such as XP.' Berni said quite sternly.

'Yes it was, but when profit and national security are put together this software becomes a very attractive package. This could be a program that is highly desirable not only to the world's armed forces, but for corporate espionage purposes. Do you think that the Official Secrets Act and *XP* as a company would be able to protect their program and keep it from falling into the wrong hands?' I asked.

'I think that the success of the program, albeit in its experimental stage has somehow leaked and the security that was put in place for the trials has been insufficient. This is a very sophisticated and powerful program that could instigate massive change in espionage and psychology, due to the possibility of direct intervention and may influence the way that memory is perceived. Let me explain using an example. If someone is suspected of spying or causing a terrorist incident, then *Watcher 22* could take the person back to the incident and if this was viewed by an audience then their guilt or innocence could be ascertained.'

'So it could impact how the Judge and Jury view guilt or innocence?' Berni asked frowning.

'Potentially there are no limits. And as we have experienced the program first hand, we are in effect, the guinea pigs. This makes us a valuable commodity. Our anonymity appears to have been compromised. We were not the only group to have experienced *Watcher 22*, but most of us are visible and working in the public sector.'

'You mean once they have our identity, we are easy targets....'

The door slammed.

'Jesus Christ! What the hell's going on!! And what do you mean by easy targets?' demanded Shauna as she bounced into the room. Shauna had always been the most outspoken of the team members and was not one to mince her words.

'We don't know anything yet Shauna. But we really **should** be concerned about Brian and Andy.'

'Why, is this some sort of witch hunt? We paid to use that bloody program and we were guaranteed anonymity. What on earth could we offer as individuals? We all had our own soddin' reasons for doing it and our own very different problems!'

'I don't think they are after us to chat about our issues, it's the program and the process they're after. We've experienced the program and although we're clearly not IT geeks, we have first-hand experience of its capabilities and potential.'

'Bleedin' hell. Are our lives in danger? Are we safe here? What the fuck is going on!'

Shauna began pacing the room. Berni gently guided her to an armchair. Shauna began clenching her hands, a telltale sign of her distress.

'And through all this, you're toasting bloody crumpets Barry? Seriously…'

Barry smiled. 'A man's got to eat! They did drag me out of bed at 3.30am!'

He then produced a large silver flask of coffee. 'I know it's not Plenni, but I requested this when I arrived. It might help us to keep calm until the others arrive.'

'Yeah. Well, I'm a bit fuckin' jumpy now as you can tell. A caffeine hit might do the job. As long as it's not drugged! What if it's poisoned? Can we trust these idiots?'

'I don't think they're the enemy Shauna. These are 'our' idiots, as far as I can tell and they're trying to protect us.' I added.

'We need refreshments so that we may gather our thoughts. I'm convinced that it's safe. For now at least and as we have no idea how long we will be staying here, I suggest we tuck in. It will help us to concentrate.' Barry said firmly handing around plates of freshly buttered crumpets while Berni poured the coffee.

'It's just fucking weird! And they locked us in. Cheeky bastards. Give us one of those crumpets Barry, I'm half starved.'

Don't Fear the Reaper
Blue Oyster Cult

'Can anyone else hear that?' I asked as everyone was busy devouring a most welcome snack and caffeine hit. Berni shook her head silently, with a wistful look in her eye.

'I feel he must be targeting you. Some sort of residual connection from the program, a bit like a lost sound wave or confused signal.'

'If that's the case, would you like to explain to me why the songs that Flint has chosen are relevant to our current situation? Can't anyone else hear that?'

'What the hell are you on about H?'

'I'm afraid I don't hear it.' added Barry.

'Hello! Will someone tell me what the fuck is goin' on?' Shauna asked crossly.

'Don't fear the reaper.' I responded.

'Bloody charming. No need to take that attitude.'

Berni chuckled to herself and Barry leaned back in his armchair and smiled.

'No you idiot. It's the song I can hear and occasionally one of Flint's pearls of wisdom.'

'You've lost the bleedin' plot H.'

I looked around the group, in search of some reassurance.

'No one else can hear the voices of their old Guides then? Not since we left?' Everyone shook their heads.

'It's probably just some old messages that somehow got trapped and delayed as Berni said.' Barry said reassuringly. Now it was my turn to shake my head.

'Flint spoke to me. How do you explain that?'

No-one answered. 'He said that it wasn't like just flicking off a switch, it wasn't something that you could just suddenly stop.'

'And yet Helena, that is exactly what it is. It is merely a computer program, which can of course, be wiped, even from the hard drive.' Barry said carefully.

'You forget that there was also hypnosis used and the oxygen levels were altered.'

'Berni those factors would not affect the computer program…'

'Maybe not directly, but…'

Shauna interrupted. 'What I don't bloody get is why you can only hear one of the Guides. Why can't you hear Dame Judi?'

'Ladies I feel that we may have lost sight of the job in hand. Even if we do, 'fear the reaper' as the song suggests, right now we seem to be trapped.'

'You're right Barry. I only mentioned it as it may have been relevant and…'

I was interrupted by Berni sitting bolt upright and gesturing me to stop speaking.

Shauna crept towards the door. 'I can hear footsteps and voices.'

We all stood together instinctively, each one of us facing the door.

The key turned in the lock and frustratingly, the door opened outwards.

Then we saw them. Andy and Brian. They seemed to tumble into the room and the door was swiftly locked behind them.

'Hell's teeth. Where the 'ell are we?' asked Andy his Welsh accent unmistakable as always. Brian looked a little shaky, he was always a little more reserved. 'Didn't think we'd all be together again so soon.' he said with a half-smile.

After a very welcome group hug, the remaining refreshments were given to the newcomers. Now it was time to share our very limited information. Andy and Brian were as puzzled as everyone else, although Andy had overheard a tiny snippet of conversation that was not for his ears. When he was first accompanied to the BMW it was done rather hurriedly, as Brian needed to be picked up immediately after. Andy was bundled into the back of the waiting car and the familiar tinted black screen between the front and back seats was in place. However, the internal intercom had not been switched off, which meant that anything the driver said, Andy could hear. There was another passenger in the front who had the appearance of an Official, possibly from the Home Office. He wasn't speaking to the driver but did take a call on his mobile. Andy stared out of the window in a dazed silence in order to appear oblivious to the conversation. The driver had a habit of checking on him in his rearview mirror. The Official spoke quickly and seemed agitated.

'What the fuck did you hear then?' Shauna demanded as Andy paused for a slug of coffee.

'All I could make out was the name of the company *XP* and the program *Watcher 22* and then he listed our names. I did hear the words cybersecurity alert and breach of the mainframe.' Andy seemed to hesitate and looked down at his shoes.

'It's OK Andy. Take your time. What is it that's troubling you?'

Shauna raised her eyebrows and tutted at Berni's reassuring approach, muttering obscenities under her breath. Berni shot her a warning glance and Shauna's cheeks flushed slightly as she began nervously fiddling with a red wrist band which had the words 'I'm drug free' stamped on it in large white letters.

'I think that they're going to move us again, and soon.' Andy added. 'The people that are after us. They're dangerous. Turns out they really want this program and they've been trained not to stop until they get it...'

'Bollocks! Who the hell would dare try it? We have the best Armed Forces in the world and our SAS are legendary. There would be nowhere to bleedin' hide if they stole our stuff!'

I'd never realised Shauna was so nationalistic. And I was surprised that she separated the Armed Forces from the Police, whom she still held in some disregard.

Barry was stroking his chin, deep in thought.

'I hate to interrupt Shauna's quite surprisingly patriotic rant, but there's one assumption we all seem to be making, that this is somehow domestic.'

I knew by Shauna's frown that she hadn't understood Barry's words of wisdom. I was signalling for her to wait before speaking, by gently shaking my head.

'What the fuck does that mean? Some flamin' maid or butler has stolen the program and is trying to flog it? This isn't a remake of *Downton Abbey* you know. Sorry Andy, I think you're one crumpet short of a load.'

Shauna chuckled to herself, which was handy as it allowed everyone to smile. Brian gently took Shauna to one side and swiftly put her in the picture.

I could see that Barry had been doing some serious thinking and tempting as it was to lift the mood, now wasn't the time. Shauna began shuffling around, determined to show no interest after her misunderstanding.

'I would like each member of the group to listen carefully, I value everyone's opinion and that includes you Shauna. This is a very dangerous situation and I am not referring to being held by our British captors. It appears that there is an external threat which means that we, well... there is a possibility that we could be taken because of our experience in using the program.'

'Jesus Jones! What are you saying? Do you think it's the Ruskies, the Chinese or some terrorist threat or the Yanks or maybe...'

Andy was rudely interrupted as the key rattled in the lock and the door was flung open and Brown entered the room.

'Kindly gather your belongings. We need to relocate and quickly. We have everything in hand, but time is of the essence. I'm not at liberty to answer any questions at this point. Just follow me!'

We didn't need to be told twice, we all grabbed our coats and bags and silently obeyed. This was not the time to ask for explanations. We headed out of the building and back into the sleek, black BMWs. Silence hung in the air. Berni, Shauna and I were in the first car and the men followed behind in the second car. There was a Police escort with flashing lights, but no sirens. We held hands in the darkness as we headed back into the night, destination unknown.

I am the passenger
Iggy Pop

I smiled to myself. Flint was relentless, I'd give him that. Strangely, I felt reassured that he was there, well somewhere out there. Berni and Shauna were nodding off. It was turning out to be quite a long journey as we were avoiding the motorways and taking the scenic route. It was pitch black and the powerful engines merely purred, as they ate up the miles.

'Engines don't purr dear Helena. Even your metaphors are incompetent. And don't try and ask me anything, as I have been alluded to as a figment of your rather disturbed imagination, I can clearly be of no help. And yes Pink (Dame Judi) is a little too busy just now with some luvvies nonsense, to put in her two pennyworth worth. However, I will say this, Barry is on the right lines and you all need to pay attention. It is not in our interest for anything to go wrong. And lastly that ghastly girl with the dreadful name, Shauna. Is anyone really so stupid? Don't answer, it was rhetorical.' and with that Flint clicked off. I smiled to myself. I'd share an edited version of this conversation with the group later. I could feel my eyelids drooping it had been an extremely long day.

I awoke with a start as the engines slowed and the gaudy city lights began to filter into the darkness.

'We're in London.' Berni announced, stifling a yawn. Shauna opened one eye, before rousing herself. Everyone stretched and changed positions, eager to see our destination. We appeared to be going around the back streets. The dawn light spilled across the sky, as the City began to wake up. Suddenly, we increased in speed and took a sharp left turn, along with the rest of our convoy. We headed down a steep slope into the bowels of a building and stopped abruptly at a barrier manned by some heavily uniformed guards. Credentials were shown and paperwork exchanged. A man with an instrument that resembled a metal detector was kneeling down and checking under the car.

'What the feckin' hell...' Shauna said turning around repeatedly as if trying to make sense of our bizarre situation. Before anyone could respond the barrier was lifted and the convoy moved onwards, continuing to circle downwards. Eventually, the cars slowed as we approached a solid metal, double door. The police escort vehicles peeled off to leave us and the drivers gave them a farewell salute. This was as far as they were allowed to go. Our driver stopped and slid down the electric window, carefully removing one glove. He entered a code into a silver keypad and then pressed his index finger onto a fingerprint scanner. A small black camera made a silent record of our visit, the red flashing light above it marking time. The solid metal door started to slide upwards. I turned around to check that the other BMW was still behind us. As I turned back, we were already moving forward into a well-lit car park. Both cars drove towards a metal grill, which had already started to lift before we got to it. We drove under it and parked. The BMWs now seemed dwarfed amongst the fleet of gleaming, high-performance cars.

There was a clicking sound as the car doors were unlocked by the driver and we all sat awaiting instruction. The intercom flicked on and we were asked to exit the vehicle. We grabbed our handbags and shuffled along the seat, eager to get out of the same door. I checked that our male contingent was present.

'Kindly follow me.' Brown announced politely and headed towards a lift which was situated at the corner of the car park. He pressed some buttons and turned to smile at us reassuringly.

'Won't be long now.' he added.

Brian, Andy and Barry were stood behind us and there was a uniformed policeman behind them, his radio beeping and giving out incomprehensible messages. Brown frowned at him and he hurriedly switched it off. There was probably no proper signal down here, wherever we were.

'Everyone all right?' asked Andy.

'Fuck no …'

'If you could just maintain silence until we debrief it would be much appreciated.' Brown said somewhat sharply. I just glanced over at Shauna and shrugged my shoulders. She bit her lip as Barry frowned at her, willing her to keep quiet. Brian patted her on the shoulder, but she shrugged his hand off in annoyance. A few moments later the doors pinged open and we were directed toward a suite of rooms. Brown handed each of us a large drawstring bag.

'I would ask everyone to leave all your possessions including handbags, wallets, etc. on the table over here.

Then go through to the changing areas and kindly place your clothes into the laundry bags, shower and then dress in the clothing provided. Any clothing you remove will be washed and pressed and it is vital that you follow procedure.'

'Jesus! Is this the way you treat the bloody innocent and is anyone going to 'kindly' tell us where the feck we are?'

This time it was Andy who interceded.

'Steady now Shauna,' he said firmly, before turning to Brown, 'she does have a point though, doesn't she? We are here of our own free will and quite willing to cooperate and...'

Brown interrupted, looking suitably bored before delivering a mechanical response.

'This is beyond my control now. These are not my rules, but those of our hosts. I can tell you that we are now at the headquarters of the British Intelligence Service in Vauxhall. That should indicate just how serious this situation is. Kindly follow the instructions and you will be debriefed by the Chief of Staff from the Joint Intelligence Committee. Your clothes and possessions are being removed in case they have been tampered with and before you ask, no you wouldn't have noticed. When it comes to matters of National Security there are NO exceptions!'

You could have cut the air with a knife, the gravity of the situation suddenly hit home, we all silently followed instructions.

'Thank you. Ladies to the left, Gentlemen to the right. I will be in the meeting with you, just to represent you as clients and also to represent *XP*. Once you are washed and dressed the Guards will accompany you to the meeting room.'

We all looked at each other for reassurance. Barry naturally took the lead, he was always good in a crisis. He nodded his head, signifying his agreement and we went our separate ways.

No one spoke in the changing rooms. The sterile white tiles and doorless cubicles didn't inspire confidence. It reminded me of the rather jaded girl's changing rooms in the gym at High school, impersonal and bleak – at least these were cleaner. Berni hummed mindlessly to herself and I could hear Shauna thrashing around in her cubicle as she attempted to shampoo her long curly mane. We'd put the towels and folded clothes at arm's reach, to avoid any embarrassment, we still had some standards. It felt strange wearing the black jumpsuits with the Velcro fastening as if we couldn't be trusted with a simple zip.

After much huffing, puffing and blow-drying, we were ready. As there were no mirrors, the lack of make-up and hair straighteners had less of an impact. We stood awkwardly together, holding our pump bags, like three dejected gymnasts ready to head for home. Uncannily on cue, the outer door opened and we met up with the male group members. The men were dressed in the same attire, like a weird group from *Prison Break* but with no clear line of escape.

Brown checked each one us carefully, before nodding to himself and leading us down a clinically white, windowless corridor towards yet another lift. We walked in silence, wondering what on earth would happen next. Brown called the lift and we seemed to be shooting upwards extremely quickly. When the lift stopped, the door opened on the opposite side which appeared to be a mirrored wall. Brian turned to us and merely raised his eyebrows.

'Come along. 'Brown said somewhat snappily. More impersonal hospital corridors and finally we were lead through a steel door into a waiting room.

'Take a seat.' he ordered curtly. I didn't like his tone. He was only a businessman not a member of the Secret Service.

Flint then cut in, 'Really! You make such assumptions dear Helena! What have I taught you? If Pink hadn't been shilly-shallying around, you may have learned a little more. Do you always judge people on their first impressions? That's a little shallow, even for you.'

I pursed my lips and shook my head at the impudence of the man or voice or hallucination...

'Charming! The silent treatment is a little childish even for you. I bid you adieu.'

'Wait, Flint...' Ah, that was said aloud and not in my head. This was confirmed by everyone looking at me and Barry frowning as Berni shot me a warning glance. Thankfully Brown had left the room.

'Barry, what the fuck is goin' on? Can they really hold us here? Don't we have rights and how come...'

Shauna didn't complete the sentence as we were summoned by Brown into a room with tinted glass windows, low key lighting and a large glass meeting table with metal framed chairs surrounding it. Brown indicated for us to sit before opening a side door and two men and a woman came into the room. They were smartly dressed and carried clipboards. Shiny security tags with photo ID were laced around their necks. They took their places opposite us.

'It's like the feckin' Apprentice without that Sugar bloke.' Shauna murmured. It was hard to keep a straight face and one of the businessmen seemed to chew on the inside of his cheek as if smothering a smile. The woman in the centre of the two men showed no response and threw Shauna a warning glance before standing up.

'Let us begin.' she said as a large, glass screen slid down from the ceiling at the end of the table. 'And be assured, this is much more serious than the feckin' Apprentice.' she added wryly.

For your eyes only
Sheena Easton

Berni frowned across at me and rubbed her ear discreetly. Could she hear the music I wondered? Then something weird happened. Shauna gave me a bony elbow in the ribs, Brian looked a little startled, Barry frowned and Andy emitted a little snort of amusement. They could hear the song! It wasn't just me anymore that would be subjected to Flint's cynical song choice.

'I'm afraid it will just be you that can hear my dulcet tones, Helena. However, your little group has just been brought into the loop and can hear the music, basically to add to your credibility. We don't want them hauling you off to the asylum. You'll be delighted to know that our cosy little 'thought chats' are still exclusive. Unless some of the other Guides come forward, which is unlikely as it is quite a complicated procedure, hence dear Pink's absence.'

The lady with the clipboard stood up and leaned forward over the desk, eyeing us all as she spoke.

'If you could pay attention. I don't wish to alarm you, but this is a serious situation and lives could be at risk!' she left an awkward pause. 'We realise that you are civilians but this is a matter of national security. This meeting is 'top secret' everything that is said in this room stays in this room. Our role here at MI6 is to obtain and provide information which relates to the actions or intentions of people outside the British Isles and perform tasks relating to these, in the interests of national security. Before you intervene and ask questions – firstly yes this does involve you and secondly yes this is in connection with *XP* and *Watcher 22*. No, you haven't done anything wrong and yes your experiences are extremely valuable to us. At times you may not understand what relevance our questions have, or what right we have to ask them. We ask for your cooperation, but please do not underestimate our legal powers should we be forced to use them.' She stopped for dramatic effect. It worked. 'You may address me as Inspector and my colleagues as Cagney and Lacey, Cagney is the dark-haired one.' There was a glimmer of a smile. The two men seemed to shuffle uncomfortably in their seats, there was clearly no love lost between them. As one of the youngest members of the team, Shauna was unable to disguise her confusion. I could hear Berni quietly explaining that '*Cagney and Lacey*' was a TV detective series in the 1980s which broke the mould, as the detectives were female. She looked nonplussed but was soon brought back into the fold by the Inspector.

'What I am about to tell you is detailed in the Official Secrets Act, which you have all signed. I am obliged to refer you to Section 1, Point 4 regarding disclosure:

'a) Disclosure is damaging if it causes damage to the work of, or of any part of, the security and intelligence services or b) It is of information or a document or other article which is such that its unauthorised disclosure would be likely to cause such damage or which falls within a class or description of information, documents or articles the unauthorised disclosure of which would be likely to have that effect'.'

The Inspector paused. 'What this means is that you can't tell anybody about your experience with the program, as it could put our agents at risk, especially our undercover agents. I think you can all understand the importance of this.' The Inspector then nodded to her counterparts who sprang obediently into action and gave each one of us a handout with various exerts and amendments from the Act. Shauna sighed and started to fold her piece of paper into what seemed to resemble a paper aeroplane.

Barry came to the rescue. 'Coffee, could we trouble you for coffee and sandwiches Inspector. All this new information and such serious discussion require a little break and some light refreshment.'

The Inspector sighed and once again signalled for her minions to meet our demands. The two men exited hurriedly and returned pushing a trolley apiece loaded with prepared sandwiches, cakes and flagons of tea and coffee. Everyone dived in and refuelled. The Inspector tapped the desk impatiently with her pen. Cagney and Lacey looked at our spoils somewhat enviously. The Inspector relented and jerked her head towards the trolley indicating they could help themselves. They didn't need a second invitation. I smiled as Lacey, with his cheek bulging with a ham roll, asked the Inspector if she would like a drink. She huffed impatiently, but then seemed to relent and was given a cup of coffee, black of course.

Everyone stood and stretched after the repast, before retaking their seats and preparing for round two. Spirits had lifted, for the moment at least.

'Let's continue. I realise that I need to explain your involvement. As you may have deduced the *Watcher 22* program has proved to be a great success. We were hoping that we could keep the program under military control with limited access for private enterprise.

However, I want you to understand how serious the situation is both here at home and internationally. Our tech guys are having to contend with computer hackers from groups like 'Anonymous' which some of you may have heard of.'

Barry and Andy nodded at each other, whilst the rest of us looked and shook our heads.

'This is an international network of activist and hacktivist entities. This Team became known for a series of their renowned publicity stunts and distributed denial-of-service attacks on government, religious, and corporate websites. Later targets of Anonymous' hacktivism includes government agencies of the US, Israel, Tunisia, Uganda, and others. I'm sure all of you are aware of WikiLeaks and the cyberattacks that have been targeting government agencies and military agencies. Just to stress the powerful status of this group, Anonymous has targeted some of the most influential leaders in the world including Donald Trump and other high profile leaders and organisations.'

'The Church of Scientology.' Barry added.

The Inspector shot him a disparaging glare. 'Yes amongst others. If I may continue. We also have to contend with *Stuxnet* which is a computer worm. It was designed to attack industrial programmable logic controllers. This computer virus successfully shut down a machine in Iran. Our main concerns are therefore twofold. Firstly, the International threat by hackers to steal the program. I have to inform you that some communications gear and mobile phones were supplied by China, who would be very interested in *Watcher 22*. You all know about the controversy surrounding Huawei.' The Inspector paused to look around the room, everyone even Shauna kept quiet. Berni was overwhelmed but disguised it beautifully.

'Secondly, as the successful survivors of *Watcher 22*, your first-hand experience of the program would be highly desirable to the International community, both domestic and military. This explains your involvement. You were the first group to respond so positively and to escape from the program. Unfortunately, news of your success soon leaked into the global arena which fuelled interest. One country in particular, began to increase surveillance and energetically pursued *XP* employers and people like yourselves. The security was increased and MI6 was drafted in, to control the availability of the program and monitor the clients closely. Within days it became obvious that hackers were targeting *XP* and our finest security techies were drafted in to upgrade firewalls, update security patches and secure ports. Domestic and international hackers have a lot of time on their hands and these IT Gurus are not driven solely by financial rewards, they value their reputations and seek to crack the very highest levels of security. It's a very competitive area, highly lucrative and *Watcher 22* became highly prized both domestically and globally. You can see our predicament. Safeguarding became top of our agenda for both the program and yourselves. In the wrong hands, this program could have the most unspeakable consequences. Our agents out in the field and the Intelligence Service itself could be put at risk, as this program can access the memory better than any truth serum or torture method could ever do. It cannot be altered as it uses flashbacks to the actual event. This would leave our agents wide open if caught. As yet no training exists which could counter this. It taps straight into the memory and we have no way of preventing this or protecting our agents.'

'Could I say somethin'?' Andy asked nervously. The Inspector disguised her irritation at being interrupted.

'Very well.'

'It was voluntary. What I'm meanin' is when we did it, the program, we all signed up. None of us was forced see. Just wanted to say.'

'Yes yes, I take your point ... Andrew is it?' Andy nodded and blushed. 'Our agents in research are working closely with the IT department. We were all hoping that a big part of the program's success is that it can to open your mind and revisit selected memories and...'

'Hang on a minute. I didn't feel like I had much of a bleedin' choice of these 'selected memories' when we were reliving some of my past events.'

'Shauna's right when I had to relive the events surrounding Toby's death, I didn't want to go back and...'

'I think you'll find that when you signed up for *Watcher 22* you agreed to the flashbacks and reruns of any past events. That memory was blocked in order for you to participate. You gave away the element of choice right at the start when you signed up. The research suggests that our agents won't be in a position to refuse or select which memories they will be made to revisit. You can see how dangerous and disastrous this will be if this program gets into the wrong hands. However, intervention has been swift and we do now have you all safely here with us. I feel that this debrief has run its course for today at least. We will finish at this point and reconvene tomorrow. I appreciate that there has been a lot to take in and thank you for your compliance. I would like to stress that you are perfectly safe here and your relatives have been told that you have all been recalled to *XP* to work on some urgent updates to the program. We may consider returning your phones and tablets tomorrow once they have been assessed and cleared, but for now, you will have to bear with us. Cagney and Lacey will escort you to the Leisure Suite and show you all the sleeping arrangements.' and with that, the Inspector gave the two agents a silent nod and left the room.

We seemed to collectively breathe a sigh of relief, as did the two agents. The Inspector was certainly a force to be reckoned with. Berni rounded everyone up and we were lead to a more comfortable venue. It was nice to be away from the glaring lights of the formal meeting room. The Leisure Suite was comprised of comfortable armchairs, large screen TV and a small kitchen. A suite of bedrooms led off from the lounge area. We were suitably contained. Cagney and Lacey bid us farewell and the door clicked shut behind them. We knew it was locked without checking.

'Don't think there's any getting' out of this one.' Andy said glumly.

'Any messages from that bloody *Die Hard* wonder boy of yours?' Shauna asked.

'No. Flint seems to have gone ominously quiet. Do you think it's the Americans or the Ruskies chasing our tail? What do you think Barry?'

Barry leaned back, putting his arms behind his head.

'Neither. This smacks to me of our Chinese friends, they have infiltrated the IT market and I've been reading about the massive conglomerates who are among the world's leading suppliers of mobile phones and other telecommunications equipment. Reports show that the Americans have been concerned for some time about espionage fears as China has been dominating the market. There has been growing concern about cyberattacks traced to China and the US government computer systems do not include any components from Chinese firms because that could pose an espionage risk. China has the means, the opportunity, and the motive to use telecommunications companies for malicious purposes. The world has been buying Chinese products to use in their infrastructure and they have a massive market in telecommunications network gear. I know that they would love to get their hands on this software. China has banned Google. They are astute and well organised and if their computer components are globally installed who's to say that they cannot access whatever they like.'

'Jesus Jones! What the fuck have we got ourselves into!!?'

'It's a good job they came for us when they did. We're the safest we can be, for now at least.'

'It's all beyond me.' Berni said in a resigned voice.

'Me too Berni!' added Shauna

''Let's hit the sack.' Brian said sensibly. 'I'm sure there will be a lot more to come tomorrow.'

'I'm sure there bloody well will.' Andy said tersely. 'Let's turn in.'

We all retired to our sleeping quarters. Men's dorms on one side, women on the other. We decided to leave the adjoining door ajar, as we felt a sense of security in the connection.

'Goodnight John-boy!' shouted Shauna mischievously. And with that, we all shouted our Walton's good-nights before drifting into an exhausted sleep.

China in your hand
T'pau

It was a restless night for everyone. After all, we weren't used to sleeping in such close proximity and we'd had the privacy of our own pods back at *XP*. The occasional snort escaped from the boys' room. After a lot of tossing and turning, we did manage to get some sleep. It must have been about 8.30am when we were collectively roused by a holiday camp style, wake up call. It was obviously someone's idea of a joke. Shauna was in her element.

'Oy. Welshy. Did you set this bleedin' alarm! Hi de bloody Hi!'

Berni and I grinned at each other.

'No I bloody well didn't. What powers do you think I 'ave in here?'

'Ho de ho ho ho.' added Barry in his cut-glass accent.

'I suppose they have to get us up somehow.' I added, desperately trying to ignore Flint's attempts at a relevant musical joke as I could hear *China in your hand* playing in the background. If only China was in our hands, but we seemed to be the underdog in this new world of technology. Typical of us Brits to design a dynamic new program, without paying much attention to its protection. In a time before patents, this must have been rife.

'Good God woman. You're meant to be the optimist in the group...'

Flint was interrupted by Shauna's excited shriek, which could only mean one thing–breakfast.

'You'd think she never been fed before.' Flint added in his clipped tone. 'Helena, I think it only fair to warn you that the threat to you all is very real. No one really knows the true potential of the *Watcher 22* program. As you have guessed, there do seem to be some residual effects, me for example. It is possible that some other members of your motley crew may pick up their Guides' voices at some point. I believe that it is my strength of character and tenacity that's pushed me through and...'

'Balderdash! You always talk nonsense, Flint!' There was no mistaking the rounded vowels of Dame Judi Dench, my other Guide on *Watcher 22*.

'I was unaware that you had the capabilities to enter this new reality. How much assistance you can offer is, of course, questionable.'

'Flint! We need all the help we can get, albeit in my own consciousness.' I tried appealing to their better natures which had always had limited success.

'Farewell for now Helena. I just wanted my presence to be felt, due to the severity of your situation.'

'Yap yap yap. Dammit, I was having a perfectly good time perfecting my music choice and guiding 'dear' Helena...'

'Yes well, we really must dash and let you get on.' And with that, there were some familiar clicking noises and the voices stopped.

'Come on H! Look at this spread. Don't want you ending up schizo by listening to the 'voices in your head'!' yelled Shauna from the dining room. She was as politically correct as ever. Although I had to admit, I was rather hungry. The 'spread' was rather impressive with everything from fresh fruit to all the components of a full English breakfast. It was beautifully presented on silver platters and everyone tucked in with relish. We were interrupted by another pre-recorded message advising us to be ready in thirty minutes. None of us could spot any speakers or an intercom.

'I think they're using some sort of quirky tannoy system to make us feel more at home.'

'I think you're correct in your assumption Andy. It may also be that they are using an outdated system, to avoid using any technology. This way is much safer without needing computers to program it and cannot be traced by a signal.' Barry said thoughtfully.

'It is a blast from the past though. Maybe we'll have to go without from now on, return to the old ways.' Andy added winking at Brian.

'We don't have to scrub ourselves down with carbolic soap in a tin bath in front of the fire as well do we?' Berni said chuckling to herself. Brian laughed and joined in.

'Maybe we could put an LP on the radiogram while we are getting ready!'

'I'd have put my curlers in if I'd known.'

'You are fuckin' jokin' aren't you?' Shauna looked horrified. 'It's bad enough not having my phone, never mind my straighteners and ....Hang on, hang on. You bastards! The bloody telly screen is flickering away in that corner. That's not fuckin' funny!'

Andy was laughing uncontrollably and Brian had a cushion over his mouth. Berni was biting her lip politely and I was covering my mouth to hide the giggles. The hilarity was heightened by the seriousness of the situation.

'Twenty minutes remain before your first debrief.' The message seemed more urgent and broke the laughter as everyone ran towards the showers.

Twenty minutes later we weren't exactly stood by our beds awaiting inspection, but we were all washed and dressed. Some of us were a little damper than others. I suspected it would take a good while for Shauna's long curly mane to dry out. Cagney and Lacey sauntered in, looking past us enviously at the remnants of the breakfast buffet. Cagney elbowed Lacey in the ribs.

'Thank you for being so prompt. The Inspector is waiting for you in the debrief room. Follow me if you would. Cagney led on and Lacey was clearly 'on point'. We were lead in single file back to the same room we were in the day before.

'Take your seats quickly. There's been a development. Oh and good morning by the way.'

The Inspector said somewhat distractedly. She was wearing the same practical navy suit with a different blouse. Her auburn hair was swept off her forehead and scraped into an efficient bun, held in place with plain, black Kirby grips, no bobbles or flouncy scrunchies for an Inspector at MI6.

'Do you ever concentrate?' Flint never knew when to stay OUT of my head.

'Do you have a problem, er, Helena is it? Well, do you?' The Inspector had the look of someone with high blood pressure and a temper to match.

'If we could begin. It is a matter of National Security.' She said somewhat patronisingly.

'There's been some movement on the Dark Web.'

'What the feck does that mean?' Shauna muttered under her breath. The Inspector's honey coloured eyes seemed to glow and her body stiffened as she turned towards Shauna. Barry managed to intercede before the Inspector had a chance to unleash her verbal armoury.

'This might be a good time for a very quick team update. Some of us are less tech-savvy than others. Due to no fault of our own.' Barry added as Shauna rounded on him.

Lacey backed him up. 'Ma'am there was an important call you said you needed to take. Sergeant, I mean Cagney and I have got this and they will all need to have some basic knowledge if they're going to be useful in the operation.'

We all nodded, blinking in agreement. After all none of us worked in IT and we hadn't been brought here because of our computer skills. She paused with a resigned sigh,

'Very well. I will be back after lunch. I will expect you to have grabbed the basics by then.'

Barry discreetly asked Andy and Brian if they wanted to explain the technicalities to the rest of the group. Both had some knowledge, but were happy to let Barry deliver.

'I'm just going to give you some background. Although I'm perfectly happy for anyone to ask questions or contribute, I would ask that you wait until I have finished to prevent it from becoming disjointed.'

Shauna raised her eyebrows and began pulling at some frayed cotton on the cuff of her blouse. Berni nodded and gave her usual reassuring smile and both Brian and Andy looked keen and interested. Anyway, we had no choice and I would rather listen to Barry's explanation than the Inspectors.

'Before we begin Barry, do you think I will need to take notes? It's just that I don't always remember things.' Berni asked with concern.

'It's OK Berni, no worries love. Barry's just giving us some background and there won't be a test at the end.' Andy said and patted her gently on the shoulder.

'Thank you, Andy.' Berni said and settled back into her seat.

'Firstly, it is important that we all understand that our flashy, black mobile phones and our activity on the Internet also serves as the most effective invisible tracking technology that has ever been made available.'

'But Barry who the fuck would be interested in me ordering some cheap Converse trainers or downloading some iTunes?' Shauna said, clearly irritated.

'All he's saying is that our habits and whereabouts can be tracked Shauna, not that we are all tracked, but that we can be.' Brian stated calmly. Shauna shrugged and Berni nodded to show her understanding.

'That is correct Brian, Thank you. You may not be aware that our browsing habits on the Internet, or purchases as Shauna has mentioned, are often auctioned off and information is sold to the highest bidder. Tracking information from mobile phones has been used by governments as part of surveillance. Not everyone realises that this is taking place and that our privacy is not always being protected. Everyone with me so far? Just look at what has happened with Facebook and Wikileaks. Client data has been used without consent and fake news has also been on the site. This free advertising and misuse of our personal information should have been stopped with immediate effect by Facebook.'

'Jason Bourne, that's where I learned about the phone tracking.' I added thoughtfully and Andy and Brian nodded in agreement.

'Due to the concerns about privacy on the Internet, The Onion Router was set up and messages are encapsulated in layers of encryption.'

Shauna was wriggling in her seat, I felt it was only a matter of time before she mentioned onion rings.

'Do you think you could pay attention Helena, rather than focusing on what ditzy girl might be thinking?' Flint added impatiently,

'So just think of your message being positioned in the centre of an onion and all the layers are wrapped around it to protect it see?' Andy added enthusiastically.

'And then all that happens is that the message is sent through a series of network nodes, which are easy to remember because they are called onion routers. The message arrives at its destination and each layer is peeled away, and the sender remains anonymous.'

'I know a film that shows that! I sat up excitedly 'It was a *Die Hard* film with Bruce Willis, you know the one about the hackers and that guy named the erm, the Warlock who works from his basement.'

Andy and Brian nodded, whilst Berni shrugged her shoulders.

'They're all the fuckin' same those *Die Hard* films. Could 'ave been any of them.'

'I quite like them, Shauna. I think it was *Die Hard 4*.' I added.

There was a familiar clicking sound. I felt there may be trouble ahead.

'Yes of course, it was *Die Hard 4*, you imbecile. And I would like to point out that the films are all completely different! Especially the first one which was, after all the best and the most iconic. I am sure that most, if not all, of your motley crew, will remember Hans Gruber.'

'You can hear him can't you?' Shauna asked perceptively.

'Of course, Rickman was famously in the first film, he was a Russian terrorist I think.' Brian said somewhat vaguely.

I don't really know how it happened, but somehow Flint managed to broadcast his angry response to everyone.

'Good God you're all idiots! For your information, Hans Gruber, my character, was an ex-member of a radical West German movement called the Volksfry and the leader of a group of ruthless psychopaths. Basic film history, basic!' Flint clicked off. I shrugged my shoulders and winced apologetically. I was happy to contain Flint's flippant comments in my own mind, after all, I had selected him as my Guide. But I didn't want his acerbic wit affecting any of my comrades.

Berni looked thoughtful, Brian frowned a little as he had been targeted and Andy pursed his lips in annoyance. Shauna shook her black mane in an attempt to remove him from her mind.

'No point in getting wound up chaps. We know from the past how volatile Flint can be. I am a little surprised that he can jump uninvited into all of our heads, but we have neither the time nor the inclination to solve this right now. I feel that it is vital that I mention the 'dark web' to you at this point.'

'What the fuck is that all about Barry! What have we got ourselves into?'

'Shauna just listen to him, they'll be back soon.'

'In about five minutes actually.' Berni said firmly. It was reassuring to know that she could still tap into some of her powers, even in these bleak circumstances.

' The 'dark web' is just part of the World Wide Web which is NOT indexed by search engines and uses anonymity tools like the Onion to hide the user's IP address. Now then who do you think could benefit from using the 'dark web' Shauna?'

'This I can answer. Feckin' druggies and paedos!

Andy paused for a split second, trying not to display his disdain at the tabloid terms used so enthusiastically by Shauna.

'That's exactly the right answer Shauna!' Andy added giving her a high five.

Shauna grinned.

'But what has that to do with us?' Berni asked thoughtfully.

'You simply need to be aware of it from the anonymity point of view. Our program could be hacked and easily be auctioned on the dark web to the highest bidder.' Barry folded his hands in his lap to signify that his speech was over. Everyone stretched and yawned as they tried to absorb all the information.

Cagney and Lacey congratulated Barry enthusiastically, but the mood soon changed as the door slammed and the Inspector began her speech which would see the beginning of the twists and turns in all our futures.

Do you know where you're going to?
Diana Ross

Chapter

'Now your 'lesson' is over, we need to address the latest Intel. *Watcher 22* has been hacked and *XP* has suspended it's services. This is where you come into play.' The Inspector was very direct.

'What can we do? Surely you're gonna need your top people on this, not a mixed group of amateurs like us.'

I flinched as Andy finished his sentence and the Inspector rounded on him. Her once pale cheeks, now piqued with scarlet blotches of anger. Berni shrank back in her seat and even Shauna plucked at her bottom lip in readiness for the onslaught.

It never came. Instead, the Inspector gave Andy such a look of contempt that a rice pudding would have given up its skin voluntarily.

'No more interruptions.' the Inspector said in a very measured tone. 'Clearly, you would be of little use in detecting the hackers or tracking their whereabouts. We do have our own crack team of skilled professionals for that very purpose. I do, however, find myself in rather a quandary when considering how best to utilise this particular group's very mixed skill set.' she paused. 'I have decided that Cagney should accompany Team Beta back to *XP*, that is Shauna, Berni and Helena.

Andy, Barry and Brian are Team Alpha and will stay here at HQ.'

Now it was Berni's turn to interrupt, 'Forgive me Inspector, but I would have thought that our main strength would be to stick together as a group, after all, that is how we escaped *Watcher 22.*' she said, in an equally measured tone.

'I don't recall asking your opinion.' the Inspector said somewhat snappily. 'However, I can tell you that *XP* has requested the assistance of those named because a number of clients appear to be ... shall we say trapped in the program and you may or may not be able to guide them. Meanwhile, the male contingent will assist our team with the knowledge and the experience they have gleaned from participating in *Watcher 22.* My decision is final. This is not a team game or an episode of *The Crystal Maze.* And just to be clear I am not *asking* you. These are direct orders. Our national security is at risk, we need to track and retrieve *Watcher 22* and urgently recall and protect *XP*'s other clients before they can be compromised.'

'Just to remind you, Inspector we are also *Watcher 22*'s other clients. Who's going to watch our backs and stop us from being compromised? No offence Cagney, I'm sure you're bloody good, but if this is as big a deal as you're making it out to be, we won't need more guards?'

Everyone nodded in agreement.

'Of course Helena,' the Inspector said impatiently, rolling her eyes in annoyance, 'if I had been allowed to finish, I would have told you about the security that I have already put in place. Cagney will accompany Team Beta along with our Security Ops mobile team. Team

Alpha will remain here, which is of course perfectly secure. We break for lunch now for half an hour, before you go your separate ways. That will be all.' The Inspector turned on her heels and marched herself out of the room, the door was once again locked behind her.

'Jesus Christ! Do we even get fuckin' asked? I want to help the country and those poor sods stuck in the program, but when do we get our lives back?' Shauna stood up and walked over to the door, kicking it half-heartedly. Lacey saw her and looked irritated and ready to move in. Andy immediately moved in, whilst Barry distracted him with a bogus security question. Cagney was walking towards Shauna, fiddling somewhat nervously with the clip on his sidearm. Andy got there first.

'Shauna, I need you to come over here with me. Helena wants to ask you something. Right now.' Andy glared over at me, as he marched her away from the door and towards me.

Shauna shrugged off his arm. Her lips were set in a determined line. I'd seen this once before at *XP* when she'd been made to return to a particularly unpleasant scene from her past. She was stubborn all right.

'Yes erm, Shauna. I need to tell you about the case I was working on with Berni before we came here. She was a survivor of domestic violence. Anyway, she could be one of the ones, erm one of those stuck in the program, needing our help.' My voice was jerky but my eyes pleaded with her to behave. 'We need to be together, to help her and any others.' I said, eager to persuade her.

'It could have been us Shauna.' Berni added quietly. 'It could easily have been one of us stuck in the program.'

'Well, it bloody well wasn't! I want to go home, now! Fuck this! They can't make us do it. And why can't I have my phone back, my tablet, my stuff, basically my life!!'

Our attempts at calming Shauna were not going well. I felt sure that the Inspector could insist on using some Official Secrets Act legislation to make us stay, but that would only serve to exacerbate the tension in this increasingly volatile situation and Shauna could blow at any moment.

Barry was staring over at us, desperate for things to improve as Lacey was gaining interest. Shauna kicked the base of the table, beginning to enjoy the physical release of her frustration. She appeared quite set on a path of destruction, her eyes flashed in anger as she turned towards both Cagney and Lacey. And then it happened. We all heard it and I knew that for the first time Flint had targeted everyone in the room, possibly a desperate measure. And the song was loud, loud enough to stop everyone in their tracks including Shauna. The aptly selected song, '*All About You*' by Mcfly could be heard by everyone in the room. Cagney and Lacey held their heads in shock, signalling to each other, confirming that they both heard the same thing. Shauna sat down despondently, ever so slightly embarrassed that her behaviour was so publicly targeted. I had a feeling I knew what was coming, but I didn't realise how universal it would be.

'Children, children. You are pathetic! I question how useful any of you are going to be. I wouldn't have picked a single one of you, and before you ask dear Helena that does include you. This is MI6 asking for your assistance, not to be an usherette at the cinema, but to help with something so important that it could affect our national security! Quite honestly I am astounded. There are real lives at stake here. You need to step up or get out!' A familiar crackle and Flint had gone.

Although my fellow inmates were surprised, that was nothing compared to the shock on Cagney and Lacey's faces.

'How does he do that? It was Alan Rickman right? Did you all hear him?' Cagney asked anxiously.

'Flamin' hell! Helena when does your bleedin' Guide give up. Ours all went long since. And how did he do that?'

'He is right.' Barry said thoughtfully. ' On this occasion Flint is right. We are just going to have to comply. This is deadly serious and there is more than just us at stake here.'

'You're right Barry, 'Brian chipped in. 'and as it's so important I think that I should swap with Shauna. I was a Social Worker. I've worked with cases of domestic violence and I know very little about cybercrime.'

'Me neither Brian.' Shauna interrupted.

'But you're more up to date with your social networking than I am and you have good IT skills.' Brian paused, 'Unless of course, you don't want to change groups.'

'That does make perfect sense Shauna and each team may benefit from some input from the opposite sex.' Barry said sensibly.

'Steady on their boyo, it's a bit early for that banter.' Andy smiled and winked at Barry.

'I simply meant there would a better balance in the team, you randy old goat.' Barry winked back. God knows the mood needed lightening. Shauna looked down at her boots, then across at Berni and I.

'I'll do it. Just remember I'm not one of those Handmaidens from that mini-series. And no man-handling Brian.' Shauna added smiling at last.

'Shauna, don't take all the fun out of it. A ménage à trois doesn't always have to be a bad thing!'

What the hell is a manager twa...'

'Whoa!.' Barry's timely interruption prevented Shauna from voicing her own unique translation. 'Here comes our delicious repast now. I'm glad that we have come to such an amicable arrangement.'

'Can't you buggers speak proper English?'

'It's almost painful not to comment.' Flint burst into my head. I checked around, pleased that he returned to an audience of one, me. I willed him to leave. No more distractions, this was serious.

'Just a word of advice.' Lacey leaned over the sandwiches. 'I would ask rather than tell when it comes to the Inspector.'

'He's right.' mumbled Cagney through his sausage roll. And right on cue, in walked the Inspector.

'Who's right and why?' the Inspector said abruptly.

'If I may explain Inspector.' Barry said, charm oozing from him. He expertly corralled the Inspector into a quiet corner, after effortlessly lifting a glass of chilled orange juice from the table and handing it to her as he spoke. Barry's charm was working its magic. I glanced over at one point and there was just the tiniest flicker of a smile on those clamped, mulberry lips. The Inspector replaced her now empty glass onto the table, nodded her approval at Barry and faced the rest of the group.

'I understand the situation and if you are all in agreement,' she paused while we nodded,

'then we will proceed. Say your goodbyes. The cars are waiting.'

She turned abruptly and left the room. We didn't have any belongings to pack, as we didn't have any belongings, no bags or phones to worry about forgetting. Everyone hugged and shook hands. It felt strange to be leaving, but there was a sense that the real work was just about to begin.

It was strange being back at *XP*. It felt as though we had been away for weeks instead of just a couple of days. True to the Inspector's word, we had been accompanied on our journey by Cagney and Security Ops mobile, which consisted of 6 men and 2 women with earphones and bulging jackets. I suspected that they were armed. However, as eye contact and conversation were equally avoided, it was likely we would never know. The journey had been long and uneventful. Brian proved a cheerful travel buddy and Berni was her usual laid-back self. The security team secured the building, whilst the remaining officers spoke seriously into their collars or cuffs, exchanging messages. Berni patted my hand reassuringly and there was a refreshing air of calmness around Brian. It was a change from Shauna's somewhat volatile nature, fond of her as I am.

After about twenty minutes, we were given the green light to enter the building. Good old Brown was waiting faithfully at the door for us. It was nice to see a familiar face. He guided us to one of the offices and seemed very pleased to see us all. We were soon seated and suitably caffeinated, ready to begin the briefing. Before Brown began, Berni raised her hand.

'Good afternoon Brown, may I ask when we will be permitted to contact our loved ones and nearest and dearest again. I realise that there is a security issue, but now we are back at *XP*, I was hoping that we could speak to our relatives or partners, if that's possible of course.'

Brown sighed before responding.

'I understand your request. Messages have been given to your loved ones. No one here is permitted to use mobile phones, emails or text messages. Even handwritten letters are too risky. I hope you can understand the seriousness of the situation. All forms of technology that can be tapped or hacked into-are a 'no go'. So in answer to your question, no you cannot speak to your relatives. In an emergency, we can contact them using the local Police force. We cannot risk your conversations and indeed voices being traced and tracked back to *XP*. It's too dangerous. Now if we could get on.'

Berni looked down at her shoes. I know she missed her husband and the chatter of her grandchildren. I was, of course, missing Charlie, but we had no choice. I wasn't aware of Brian's domestic circumstances, but he too looked disappointed.

'Team Beta will be monitored and Cagney will stay with you at all times. Everyone assisting your team has been put in place to protect you, not to spy on you. The Inspector has briefed me this morning. I understand that you know about the problems we have been encountering here at *XP*. I'm pleased to tell Berni and Helena that Joanna has been safely discharged from the program following your assistance.' Berni and I were both relieved. Such a troubled woman with a burdened past. 'However, as you now know the *Watcher 22* program has been hacked and we had to close the program down very quickly. Luckily we had started to withdraw most of our clients, due to advanced warnings we received from MI6. We got almost all of them out in time...' again Brown paused.

'Almost all ...?' Brian seemed to wince as he asked.

'Yes, it was terribly unfortunate. We did manage to disconnect eight clients, without too much disruption and hardly any side effects.'

'Yes Brown. We of all people are aware of the side effects, but I don't think that's what you are referring to here.' persisted Brian, determined to push Brown.

'You're quite right Brian. We are very concerned about two of our clients who we couldn't safely pull out of the program. As we found with Joanna, it is too dangerous to just flick a switch or pull the client out, as it may cause serious physical and emotional problems. Both Helena and Brian have experienced the retrieval process first hand when things begin to get out of control or vital signs are affected. Our experts can advise at this stage, but they do not have the experience to simply jump into the flashback, analyse the situation and assist. It's complex and needs very careful planning which is why we chose ex-clients for assistance.' Brown paused again and took a swig of what had to be cold coffee.

'There here are two clients we have been unable to retrieve and one of them is 'locked in.''

'What the hell does that mean?' Brian asked, looking over at us both.

'It means that the clients are frozen in the memory. It's the best we could do. Actually, it was all we could do. We simply paused the scene and well, they are just stuck there in a kind of freeze-frame. Their bodies are of course still in the pods, breathing and existing normally. It's a bit like being in a coma only with your brain being artificially held in a kind of stasis. We're not sure if the clients are dreaming or if their thoughts are simply on hold. It's an unknown situation and it needs an urgent resolution. It's a temporary measure in a desperate situation.' Brown paused. 'Anyway, we are so glad that you were released back to us. The Inspector wanted to keep you all to herself over there, it almost took an Injunction to get you three back here.'

'May we know the names of these poor souls?'

'Of course. Firstly we have Jonah, aged 39. His case is critical and the one that we will begin working on first. I will impart his background shortly. Before that I need to mention the other client, Amelia, her needs are not as urgent. She isn't locked in, but we are struggling to bring her back. She appears to be stuck in a semi-dream status. Her thought patterns are active, but she seems to drift between the two worlds. Although in the short term this isn't serious or totally unexpected, it needs resolving.'

'Amelia sounds like a very young name Brown. Please don't tell me this is a child.'

Brown lowered his head and took a deep breath. 'Our focus is bringing back Jonah right now or he may never return. You are very perceptive Helena, Amelia is our youngest client. Many of us were apprehensive about enrolling her in the program.' Brown shook his head.

'I cannot go into detail right now. Amelia is stable and Jonah is not. We must press on and focus on his retrieval before we lose him.' Cagney was shuffling his feet, clearly uncomfortable. It must have been a lot of information for him to take in. After all, we were more *au fait* with this strange world.

'I can sense that Jonah is very distressed. Let's press on.' Berni said anxiously.

'You are correct. Let me précis the case study for you. Jonah came to us with recurrent nightmares and acute anxiety. He was unable to move forward and felt that by revisiting his past, he may be able to resolve some of his issues and put them to rest. He has been a fireman for fifteen years and had encountered some horrific scenes. However, there was one particular case that haunted him, one that he was unable to move on from, one which was affecting his ability to cope on a daily basis. He had been through many forms of counselling, but with little success. In Plenni, he was reserved, reluctant and reticent, His social interaction had been severely affected after the incident. This put an uncomfortable distance between him and his team. Your particular group was unusual, as you managed to create a bond very quickly, possibly because you feared for your very existence. Jonah had no such fears as he had given up on his future, unable to reconcile his past. He did not fear for his own life, which meant that he found Plenni awkward and unnecessary. He did not bond with his group. This left him with little respite from his own situation. And before you ask, he had tried medication and other forms of alternative therapy without success.'

'Do we know the details of the incident that has affected Jonah so severely leading to his withdrawal?' I asked cautiously.

'Yes. As you know, before you are allowed on the *Watcher 22* program, you have to agree to full disclosure of confidential information. We cross-referenced Jonah's statement with his employer before we agreed to accept him on the program. We run a professional and accountable service and we screen very thoroughly. The report regarding this particular incident outlined the tragedy that had led Jonah to breaking point. One evening Jonah was on duty with Blue Shift, when they were called out to a fire in a large country house. The fire started in one of the bedrooms on the west wing, possibly due to faulty electrical wiring. The fire was raging when the fire engines arrived at the location and there were problems connecting to the mains supply, as the house was in the heart of the countryside. They had to pump water from the swimming pool situated at the back of the house. Jonah was one of the first firemen in the building. He made steady progress and the fire seemed to be coming under control. His team had managed to rescue two children from their beds in the west wing and together with their Nanny, they were safely carried out of the house. Once outside, even in a breathless condition, the Nanny kept shouting the name of another child, Matilda. The Nanny was Polish and although her English was good, she was very distressed. The shock of the fire combined with smoke inhalation meant that communication was difficult. The message got back through to Jonah that there may be another child in the building and that the children had been playing hide and seek.

The fire in the main staircase seemed to be under control, but no chances were being taken and Jonah and his team worked diligently checking the numerous bedrooms. Apparently, the children's parents were working abroad and their Nanny was in charge, along with a small team of staff who helped to run the household. Jonah followed procedure and continued to check each room. Then they got the message to evacuate. Jonah tried to get more information. The messages were crackly and delayed. There was an echo after each word. But the word 'evacuate' came through loud and clear. The smoke was thick and acrid and visibility was poor. Jonah's colleague tapped him on the shoulder once more and signalled to evacuate. But Jonah knew that the East wing had not been checked. The ground floor had been a priority for the other team, as they feared a gas explosion. Jonah signalled for them to check the other wing. However, the staircase was now ablaze and as it was the only escape route, there was little choice but to evacuate. Jonah's colleagues made their way to the top of the staircase and began to descend. Instinct pulled Jonah towards the East wing and its suite of five bedrooms. He managed to bang back the doors of the first two adjacent rooms, each ablaze. He knew he couldn't progress much further down the corridor due to the intensity of the heat. But Jonah couldn't pull himself away, not until he had checked every room. His colleague gave a tug on his breathing tube and pointed towards the staircase. Jonah nodded and indicated that his colleague should go ahead. Just two more doors, opposite each other. He knew he wouldn't make it to the door at the far end which was facing him. Again he successfully banged open the doors on his left and right and both rooms were ablaze. Just as he was about to make his way back, he managed to grab the handle of the door which was facing him. It was locked. He banged on it, before losing his grip as the smoke overwhelmed him. There was no choice now. He had to get out and fast. Jonah crawled down the passageway on all fours, towards the start of the staircase. He pulled himself up on the newel post. The East wing was thick with smoke and flames licked the open doorways. He glanced back one final time. He wished he hadn't. The door of the locked room now appeared to be open and in the doorway he thought he saw a small girl in a pink dressing gown, Matilda.'

'Oh lord No!' said Berni, clearly distressed. I wiped away a tear and Brian bit his lip, close to tears himself.

'Jonah had no choice. He knew he couldn't get to her. His colleague dragged him down the staircase and they got just outside the front door when the explosion blew them back onto the gravel driveway. Jonah was unconscious, as his colleague dragged him back behind the fire engine.

'Good God! And did he see a small girl, was there a child, Matilda left in the house?' asked Brian.

'Yes, I'm afraid there was. The Nanny confirmed there were three children. But the experts and fire investigators told Jonah that he had probably hallucinated her image due to lack of oxygen and also that he could not have saved her. Jonah broke his collar bone and right arm and suffered from smoke inhalation, He made a full recovery physically, but not emotionally. He is racked with guilt that he should have saved the child and that's why he can't move forward with his life.'

'And now he's stuck in a flashback, reliving God knows what. All because of some damn hacker!' Berni said sadly.

'It's the saddest story. He must have seen her. How would he have known about the colour of her dressing gown?' I asked quietly.

'Here at *XP*, we can't change the outcome of events, as you well know Helena. The best we can do is watch and relive them just once and hope that we can find some peace.' Brown paused. 'We did wonder if *Watcher 22* was right for him, but he had tried all the other options. The room fell silent.

'We will break for refreshments now. After lunch we will work out who's going in and the best way to bring Jonah back.'

'Tactless Flint! And in such bloody awful taste!'
I said, looking around to see if anyone else had
heard. Luckily no one had. I knew my friends well enough
to know there would have been a reaction by now.

'Poor dear Helena. Has your sentimental side got a
hold of you?'

'No just my human side Flint.'

'In hindsight ....it was perhaps a poor choice.'

'You think so?'

A crackle of static as both the music and Flint clicked
off, which was a great relief.

Lunch was merely picked at, no one felt like eating, not
even Cagney who could always be relied upon to enjoy
his food. It was hurriedly cleared away and the room
made ready for our deliberations. We all sat around the
large, glass table and notebooks and pencils were put
out before us. A glass screen came up through the
middle of the table. Brown entered the room and used a
remote device to upload an image of Jonah in his pod.
He was clad in his white suit and visor and attached to a
breathing tube. The camera zoomed in on his face and
we could see his closed eyes through the visor. We all

noted that his eyes were moving from side to side in REM. The poor devil was obviously stuck in one of his revisited scenes. Time was of the essence and we all knew it.

'Jonah was on his third flashback when we had to disconnect the program and pull our clients out. He had coped quite easily with his first two re-visits. They were straightforward enough, one from his childhood and one from his adolescence. He only really wanted to return to the fire scene, to watch himself and his so-called 'failure'. Our team managed to persuade him that he would need time to adjust to the program before doing so. As you all know it can be a traumatic process, not only reliving the scene, but watching yourself from the outside. Of course, it had to be that damned fire scene he got stuck in.'

'What can we do Brown? How can we help Jonah?' Berni asked, desperate to hurry along with Jonah's rescue.

'We need to send you in to assess his condition and accompany him back to the present. Berni and Helena have experienced this process when they brought Joanna back. However, under the circumstances, we feel that Brian and Helena should go. There will undoubtedly be a lot of smoke and confusion and three strangers arriving in the flashback may be overwhelming. We will need your calming and supportive skills here Berni to assist Jonah when he is coming out of his unconscious state. Berni nodded. She looked somewhat relieved.

'I think that's the best use of our skills Brown.'

'Good. We need to move quickly. I will take Berni down to the monitoring bay to assist the nurses and be on standby, in case Jonah comes back too quickly. The nurses can take care of the medical side of things, but you will be very helpful in reassuring him as you know how it feels. We want to do our very best for Jonah.'

Without further ado, Berni was whisked away and we were led to an empty pod. Shivers ran down my spine, it took me right back to my own experience at *XP*. Brian looked a little unsure, but we knew that Jonah needed help. For some reason, we held hands which we squeezed tightly, before starting the process. The room contained two white leather chairs placed side by side, instead of a solitary bed. I was so relieved that Brian and I would be in the same room. We made ourselves comfortable and Brown gave us each a suit and a visor which was attached to a large white cylinder and this, in turn, was wired into a computer. We dressed hurriedly, familiar with the attire. Brown was organising the cross patch into Jonah's flashback. As soon as he attached the cables, the screen flickered into life and the crackling sound of static began. It felt familiar, but it was a messy transfer, which took longer than normal. Eventually, we were inserted into Jonah's flashback. It must have been a difficult process and seemed to take longer than I remembered. Both of us were disoriented on arrival and blinking to get the scene into focus.

'It's the smoke remember!' Brian shouted across to me. 'The fire! We must be at the bottom of the stairs in the country house.'

'You're right!' I shouted back. 'Maybe they couldn't transport us directly beside Jonah, due to the ferocity of the fire.'

'Remember Jonah is wearing his protective, fire fighting uniform and he also has oxygen tanks. The staircase swirled with smoke, but we could just make out the fork at the top of the stairs which lead to the West and East wings. It was noisy and chaotic. Firemen were hastily dragging hoses through the swirling smoke, accompanied by the sound of crashing timber as panels fell from ceilings and the house creaked in pain.

'We've got to act quickly and find both Jonahs.' Brian shouted across at me. We cautiously mounted the staircase, taking care not to tread on the hoses or get in the way of any of the Firemen. We were unsure as to our own physicality, but we weren't taking any risks. '*The Matrix*' had taught me that much. We turned right and came across the older version of Jonah, he was stood stock still, staring at the very door he knew was locked. His face was expressionless as chaos and smoke swirled around him. He seemed as if in a trance and there was no response when we spoke to him. He just stared listlessly into space. Suddenly, his younger self bounded past us, desperately searching for the missing child. We tried in vain to block the visiting Jonah's view.

'It's time to go back now Jonah.' Brian said firmly. 'Come on mate there's nothing for you here! You know the story. There's nothing to be done!'

Suddenly a message from Berni burst into our heads. 'Brian, Helena! His vitals are dropping. Get back here now! Just make the connection and bring him around so we can bring him back!' Berni sounded desperate. But it was easier said than done with young Jonah cavorting around, slamming back doors and crossing our paths on many occasions. Then something surprising happened. Brian blocked his view and I looked straight into Jonah's eyes to try and force a connection, but his pale blue eyes seemed fixed and glazed. And then it happened, just as young Jonah was being dragged past me by a fellow fireman. I was frozen to the spot by what I saw. It was the girl. The girl in the pink dressing gown. I saw her reflected in Jonahs' eyes. Tears streamed down his face. Then suddenly he blinked and that door had closed and the girl had gone. We knew we couldn't change the past and we also knew that the floor of the bedroom had collapsed and she had died instantly. But now was not the time for explanations. I shouted to Brian. We urgently needed to get Jonah back. The release of tears seemed to have brought him around a little, enabling him to walk with us towards the head of the staircase, Brian gave the instructions to take all three of us back.

It was a great relief to be back in the pod with Brian. We both took a few moments to come around. Then we carefully disconnected ourselves and removed the suit and visors. Something made us hug one another. Perhaps it was relief or just memories of our time in Plenni (replenishments) with the old group, which now seemed like a lifetime ago. Cagney escorted us to Jonah's pod which was crammed with nurses and doctors. Berni managed to extricate herself from the chaos and came straight over to us.

'He's back. Thank goodness. It was really frightening. We all thought we would lose him. You made the connection just in time. It makes you realise just how dangerous *Watcher 22* actually is and how close we all came to not coming back.' Berni shook her head reflectively.

'Well, Jonah's back now and in recovery. We all did well and Jonah is safe. But we couldn't save the girl, Matilda.'

'That wasn't your objective and was never a possibility due the confines of the program. It was tough watching those scenes, but our priority was to get Jonah back. Good work Team Beta. Now let's get some shut-eye as tomorrow we start work on Amelia's case. Let's hope your counterparts are just as successful back at HQ.' Brown said wistfully, before nodding goodnight to the Team and retiring to bed.

'Why did Helena have to leave bleedin' Rickman behind with us?' Shauna asked loudly. 'Can everyone hear that God awful music?' Nods were traded around the room.

'Sod off Flint! Your precious Helena has buggered off.' The music faded away slowly.

'If we could all get to the table before the Inspector comes in, it would make my life a whole lot easier.' Lacey said firmly. He was well aware that he had his hands full with the characters in this group. The decision-making process had been a little basic, a coin was tossed to determine which team they got and Cagney's smile had said it all when he got Team Beta and headed off to *XP*.

'I'm not sure Helena had any choice in the matter. Rickman appears to be omnipresent.' Barry said knowingly.

Shauna shrugged her shoulders. 'Not my idea of a bleedin' present or whatever the hell that means!'

'He's just saying a big word to show off, all Barry means is that Flint is everywhere at the same time. No big deal.' Andy explained.

'Should've just said that. Tosser.'

'That's quite enough of that!' The Inspector said as she entered the room and approached the table. She looked stressed and short of a good many nights' sleep.

'I don't have time to listen to your juvenile banter. There have been some developments and some of *my own* team have been put at risk. If you could just apply yourselves for a moment I would be grateful. You know that *Watcher 22* has been hacked, altered and possibly copied by foreign powers. This puts us all in jeopardy, but at immediate risk are agents in the field. If they get intercepted, their past training in keeping state secrets will be useless against this program. As you all know there is nowhere to hide in *Watcher 22* and memories cannot be altered. This is a very powerful weapon and espionage training will never be the same again. The Americans are panicking as well and don't even ask which countries would benefit the most. The list merely starts with China, Russia, Korea, not forgetting the jihadists. We have recalled as many agents as we can, but there are some sleepers.' The Inspector looked across at Shauna and then continued. 'Agents who are on foreign soil who have not been activated yet and some undercover agents who are unable to withdraw easily. You don't need to know all the details and it's above your clearance level anyway. What you can do to help, is to work with my team, using your own experience of *Watcher 22* which will help us to work out its capabilities. I'm assigning one of our Ops agents to Team Alpha. All I want you to do today is to answer the list of questions put to you. Nothing more. It's a fact-gathering process before we begin to look at the technology. I think you should all know that we have the highest political clearance and the ear of the Prime

Minister. On that note, I leave you with Lacey and Agent K who will be along in five minutes. Don't let me down.' The Inspector gave the order and hastily left the room.

Shauna looked across to Andy. 'Jesus Jones! This is bleedin' serious. I hope we can help in some way.'

'No worries Shauna. We can only do our best.' Andy added stoically.

'I feel confident that if we answer the questions accurately we will contribute in some way.' Barry said firmly. Agent K entered the room. Lacey nodded an acknowledgement as everyone braced themselves. Agent K was clearly a hardened professional. Late 30's, well suited and booted with a severe military haircut. An air of calm efficiency seemed to enter the room alongside him. His face was pockmarked and his intense blue eyes made everyone pay attention.

'Good morning. I'm Agent K. I'm here to collect data. Save your opinions and theories for another briefing. I'm only interested in facts.' he then placed a very small digital Dictaphone on the table and pulled out a Tablet from which he read the questions. Again Shauna looked to Andy for reassurance, he winked across at her and Barry gave her a comforting nod.

'In the first instance do you think *XP* screened its applicants effectively?'

Barry responded swiftly. 'We can only comment on our own experience of the screening process. However, I think I can speak for us all when I say that we replied to an advertisement in a newspaper and then made a written application, before attending an interview and a medical examination.' Everyone nodded in agreement.

'Were you aware of any applicants who were not accepted on the program?'

Shauna shifted uneasily on her seat. Andy inclined his head, indicating that she should speak. Agent K immediately picked up on it.

'You must share all your experiences and information, however insignificant you may think it may be. Withholding information is classed as a criminal offence. Lives are at risk and even the smallest detail may be of vital importance.' His eyes bore into Shauna's eyes, which made her push herself back into her seat. Andy could tell that Shauna had frozen, threats did not work well with her.

'One moment K.' Andy interceded. He turned to Shauna. 'It's OK now,' he patted her hand, 'just tell him whatever you know.'

Shauna took a deep breath. 'It was Kirsty that showed me the ad in the local rag. She said we could go together. But she never showed up at the feckin' bus stop so I just thought she'd bailed. Probably nothing.'

'Last name, Kirsty's last name.' Agent K said impatiently.

'Tipton. 'Shauna smiled. 'We used to call her PG, you know PG Tips.' Agent K just stared straight at Shauna, before he bulldozed on.

'Address?'

'Dunno, we worked together. Local girl.'

'Thank you.' Agent K tapped away at his tablet and continued.

'Anyone else?'

'At the interview, there was an elderly lady in the waiting room, sat beside me. I didn't take much notice of her. I was called in before her see and ...'

'Jot a description down, all details and I'll cross-check it with the records.'

Agent K then looked across at Barry.

'I saw the advert in The Times, sent in an application form and was called to an Interview. I didn't speak to anyone about it as I was unsure what it entailed or indeed if it was genuine. When I arrived at *XP* there was no one else in the waiting room, but I did see someone come out of the Interview room. A rather smart woman, late forties, beige raincoat. Quite ordinary really, there was one thing that I do remember, silly really.' Barry paused. Agent K tapped his foot impatiently. 'She had a mauve handbag, a very expensive handbag that didn't seem to match with her attire. I don't notice such things except my ex-wife had always wanted one and I was a little taken aback at the price tag. She was wearing practical brown brogues, a beige coat and her hair was scraped back very efficiently into a bun. She wasn't wearing any make-up, not even a hint of lipstick. All the trappings of a hard- working life, which is why the expensive handbag stood out.'

By this time Shauna had her hand in the air and was looking agitated.

'I saw her too. On the stairs on the way out! I thought the same. How come she had a bleedin' Burberry handbag and it was such a weird colour?'

' I saw her too! In the coffee lounge after the medical. What does it mean?' Andy asked excitedly.

'Probably nothing. But one thing is certain, there are no such things as coincidences. Lacey go and find a sketch artist and quick about it.'

Lacey hurriedly left.

'I want each one of you to spend time with the sketch artist. You'll be taken to separate rooms to prevent any further conferring. This could be important so it takes priority. Thank you for your co-operation so far.'

Lacey hurriedly entered the room, almost dragging a bewildered policewoman alongside him. Agent K nodded in approval and left before the sketching process began.

'I don't know how the hell you put up with Flint Helena! He's relentless.' Brian said forlornly.

'I must admit even I am astounded by his persistence.' Berni said shaking her head.

'Yes, he is rather an acquired taste.' I admitted. 'I'm just glad that you can hear him and it's not just me. I do so like to share.' Cagney handed out glasses of orange juice. We had been told that today we would be working on Amelia's case and everyone was tense, as this involved a youngster. The door clicked shut and Brown entered the room. He looked somewhat deflated and browbeaten.

'I don't have much time, Team Alpha has made some progress and we will need to transport you back to MI6 immediately after...well once we've finished here. Brown sat down and the files spilled across the table in front of him. For a split second his mask seemed to drop and his face revealed the weariness he so obviously felt.

'Are you all right Brown?' Berni asked gently. 'Could I just say this, the baby will be fine.'

Brown was astounded. 'How did you...we only found out a few days ago and after last time, we agreed that we wouldn't tell anyone!' There was a respectful silence in the room. 'Seriously Berni. How did you know? If you've left the building or got hold of a phone or...'

'Brown it's me you're talking to. Not Houdini or Derren Brown. Of course I haven't left the building. I just happen to pick up messages sometimes and this one came through.'

'She's done it before Brown. Don't get freaked out about it.' Brian said reassuringly.

'It's just Berni's psychic way and one of the things that helped us to escape from our pods.'

Brown looked hesitant. 'I have to report even the slightest breach in security.' he said solemnly.

'Check your blessed CCTV Brown. We've not been out of the building or made a receiver out of an old hanger and some sticky back plastic!' I said, trying to lift the mood. Brown shook his head as if trying to shake off a ridiculous idea. He then turned to Berni.' Psychic? Really?'

'Really.' Berni nodded. 'It will be fine this time.' Brown glazed over for a moment as he tried to absorb the information. 'No. You shouldn't tell her.' Berni said looking straight at him.'

'But how did you know I was going to say that?' Berni raised her eyebrows, sighed and said, 'The message was for you Brown. Your wife will only be happy when the little one is in her arms, you know that.' Brown nodded in agreement, before straightening his tie and organising his files. He coughed abruptly.

'Anyway, back to business, Jonah is making a good recovery and after a full debrief will be returning home. Great work Team Beta. He's very grateful to you all and has at last found some inner peace. His words.' Brown said somewhat abruptly. 'However, we may not be so lucky with the next case. It's reached a critical stage now, so we don't have a lot of time. I will give you the background and then we must act quickly.' Everyone nodded in agreement.

'When Amelia came to us she was too young to be accepted into the program. The rules are very clear and strictly adhered to. However, her condition began to deteriorate and an exception was made. She was desperate to try the program and we had parental consent. The doctors and specialists had tried their best with medication and alternative therapies, but she made little progress. We accepted her on the program once she was off of all medication and feeling reasonably stable.'

Everyone nodded their understanding. 'Could I just ask how old she is now?'

'Yes Berni that I can tell you, she's just turned 16.'

There was a shaking of heads. She was so very young.

'What you need to understand is that Amelia needed hope, almost as much as she needed help. *XP* consulted with her doctors, who confirmed that her problem was not a physical one, but her issues were causing physical symptoms.'

'Can you reveal these issues Brown?' Berni asked quietly.

'Yes. Although we are bound by the confines of confidentiality, under extreme circumstances we are permitted to reveal what is 'deemed necessary' in order to resolve a critical situation. Amelia came to us as she was haunted by nightmares. Nightmares that she could never properly remember. She began to lose weight and became emotionally disturbed after long bouts of wakefulness and her sleep pattern was erratic. The professionals and specialists agreed that this was not a physical problem. She had counselling and regression therapy, but she didn't improve. Her parents were desperate and constantly questioning themselves about what could have happened to their beautiful daughter to have made her so distressed and so unhappy,' Brown paused. 'Amelia is indeed a beautiful young girl, in need of our help.' again he paused. 'Anyway, her history was taken and preparations were made. Her Guides were chosen with great care...'

Brian interrupted, 'May we ask who she chose? In case it's relevant.'

'Erm. Yes, I suppose that's OK. She chose Emma Watson and Justin Bieber.'

'Ah yes. That makes sense. Don't worry Berni we'll explain who they are later.' Brian said reassuringly. Berni nodded slowly.

'What was it Brown, that caused this young girl's trauma?' she asked.

'We didn't know until the flashbacks began. The first few were routine, childhood mischief and such like. She sailed through those and got used to the process, just as you all did. Due to Amelia's age, we shortened the sessions and monitored them closely. Everything seemed to be going well and she was settling nicely into a very carefully selected group in Plenni. She seemed relieved to be here, to be trying to improve things. I think it was the fourth flashback when her vitals went sky high. She was revisiting a Brownie meeting. Amelia and a friend were in the kitchen cleaning up and when they were ready to leave. The lock on the door jammed. Panic set in, even though there were other people around. The

Brownie hut itself was close to home. That was our first clue. Amelia became hysterical. She totally overreacted and the feeling of being trapped caused initial panic followed by hysteria.'

'Were you in communication with Amelia's parents at this point?' I asked.

'Yes. On a daily basis. We felt that we should push onto the next flashback and then assess the situation. We had consulted with the medical team and they felt that we were close to discovering what was traumatising Amelia. She had even started to join in more at Plenni, so we felt reasonably confident that she was progressing. The next scene was at her Uncle's house, where she often liked to play and was comfortable in his company. Even before Amelia entered the house her blood pressure was rising and heartbeat increasing. She was sweating and close to having a panic attack. But we had discussed this before she revisited the scene and Amelia herself insisted that unless it was life-threatening, she wanted to remain in the flashback and face whatever it was that was ruining her life. We stabilised her and then the program was hacked. In her case it stalled and we were able to freeze the program, similar to putting a film on pause. That worked perfectly while the techies were frantically trying to get everyone back. But yesterday the program began to reboot due to the hackers' intrusion. We've paused it now but we don't know for how long and we can't leave her stuck between the two worlds. Due to the unusual circumstances and the fact that we're so close to finding a solution, we wanted Berni and Helena to jump in and bring her back.'

We both nodded. 'It may be very disturbing, we don't know if this case involves abuse, sexual or physical or psychological, The Uncle is now deceased and although the parents have absolutely no concern about his behaviour, something very dreadful must have happened in that house. Something so bad, that Amelia has suppressed it deep within her subconscious and let it be. We are unable to give you any clues, but we have selected females to return to Amelia, in case there has been any abuse. Here at *XP*, we have always refused to work with abuse cases until the program has been proven. This case was the exception and it would have to be this poor girl who was caught in *Watcher 22*. All our clients are equally important, but you can understand the sensitivity surrounding this particular case.'

'I think we should all go.' Brian suddenly blurted out.

'I agree.' stated Berni quite firmly. 'There's something very dark here and we may all react differently. Brian is trained in dealing with serious domestic cases and he may respond more swiftly than Helena and I.'

Brown frowned and began tapping his finger on the desk. It contravened his instructions. Berni looked straight at him.

'We don't know what we're going to find. I can't stress enough how much we may all be needed in getting this poor girl out.'

Brown hit the desk with resolve.

'All right then. But we must act immediately. I will go to the Director for clearance. Please accompany Cagney to the pods to prepare. I'll meet you down there.'

Brown left and we were moved to a pod close to Amelia's. We knew the routine and we were all suited up and connected to the program in record time. Cagney held his earpiece and then nodded as the agreement to proceed came through. Within seconds we were transported to the scene, to the Uncle's house. It took a little time to take in what was happening. The connection was weak and there was a soft white haze in the room, which made things seem quite surreal as if things couldn't be surreal enough. As I was getting my bearings I looked through the window and saw the terrified face of a young Amelia. She was frozen to the spot. Her eyes showed her terror and her mouth stifled a silent scream.

(Team Alpha – MI6 HQ)
The first time ever I saw your face
Roberta Flack

Chapter

Flint was obviously still around. Shauna, Andy and Barry shared a knowing look and couldn't resist a smile. Agent K had stressed the importance of getting a portrait of the unknown woman who had mysteriously appeared, either before or after each of their interviews. The door slammed as Lacey escorted the sketch artist into the room.

'I'm Rachel.' announced a short, tidy, bubbly woman in her early thirties. Her blonde hair was scooped back into a ponytail, which bobbed around almost as energetically as she did. 'I have been briefed and advised that on separate occasions you have all seen the same perp erm person.' she corrected herself and half-smiled. 'We don't yet know how significant this may be, but we do know that there is no such thing as coincidence, not in our line of work anyway.' she paused.

'Before we begin I'd like to explain a little about the exciting new program that we now use. It's called EvoFIT and has a much higher success rate than anything we've ever used before. In the past, identikits have worked by asking witnesses to remember key features such as the nose and eyes in isolation, but

9 5

research indicates that unconsciously we remember faces as a whole, rather than features in isolation.'

Shauna was not famous for her tact and diplomacy. She yawned, just a tad too loudly. Miss Ponytail was clearly not amused.

'I'm sorry if I'm boring you. After all, it's only a matter of life and death that may be riding on this. If you could manage to concentrate or let's put it this way if you are able to concentrate then now is the time to do it.' Rachel said curtly. Andy knew only too well that this response could easily be interpreted as fighting talk by Shauna. He quickly leaned over and whispered in her ear. Shauna kicked out at the chair beside her. Andy flashed Barry a look which meant that someone needed to intervene.

'It is genuinely fascinating stuff Rachel. Could I make a suggestion? It's been rather a while since we've been near a watering hole. I think coffee and sandwiches would be beneficial for all, yourself included of course.' Rachel half squinted her eyes at Shauna, who was staring at the floor. Andy looked over at Rachel and nodded his head in acquiescence.

'Yes. Alright, I suppose it is past lunchtime. Lacey took the hint and within minutes the refreshments were wheeled in, much to everyone's relief. Even Shauna relented and the atmosphere in the room became more relaxed. Miss Ponytail rammed her sandwiches down in super quick style and was fiddling with her clipboard before the last Kipling French Fancy had been devoured. Barry gave her the nod and gave Shauna a stern glare before Rachel continued.

'As I was saying a man called Hancock, who was a chemist by trade, combined his knowledge with computer science. He described the brain as a chemical computer.

It has been known for a long time that there is a problem building faces by bits and Photo-FIT left us with a jigsaw, as there were never enough features.'

'Actually, that's bloody interestin'. Pardon my Welsh.' Andy smiled, begin to warm to little Miss Ponytail.

Barry nodded in agreement and even Shauna looked less bored.

'The first step is to choose from one of sixty databases covering gender, race and age. The faces are devoid of hair, ears and other 'external' details that might be a distraction from the core features of the face. So it's simple, just choose the ideal width or length of a face – known as the 'facial aspect'. Once this has been highlighted we move on to determining the facial 'shape'. Next, we move on to focus on the 'texture' of the assailant's face, which involves skin tone, darkness or lightness of eyes and eyebrows, for example. All the composites are in grey scale as, surprisingly, all the research so far indicates that the addition of colour to EvoFIT offers no statistical improvement in identification. Are you all with me so far?'

Everyone nodded. Even Shauna. It was more interesting than they had thought.

'You will be guided through this by me. Depending on your choices the faces 'evolve' through a complex set of algorithms, which allow the faces and features that you select to transfer across to the next generation of faces that confront you on screen. It is an amazing program to work with.'

'Is the success rate much higher?' Andy asked.

'Yes it is, the suspect identification rate is about 60 percent.'

'I used to love Funny Fits when I was a kid.' Shauna suddenly announced.

Miss Ponytail was quick to encourage her. 'Good Shauna. That was how it used to be done. But it wasn't as good as this program. Just a few last things. A series of 'holistic tools' focus on the fine detail, tinkering with face width, considered age, pleasantness, health, honesty, maleness, femaleness and how threatening they look. We then go on to the tone of the eyebrows, irises, eye bags and laughter lines. EvoFIT uses a 'slider' on the screen to alter the face with surprising simplicity and subtlety. With women, for instance, the clearest sign of ageing can be witnessed in the disappearance of the youthful pouting lips.'

'Bloody great, so looking forward to that.'

Barry shot Shauna a look. 'Do continue Rachel.' he said in his silkiest voice.

'Finally, we move on to the 'external features' such as the hairstyle and how the hair is brushed. The finishing touches can be completed thanks to a 'shape tool', which imposes a grid pattern on the subject's face and allows the eyes and hairline to be altered. Voilà! C'est fini!'

'Wow, that is bloody amazing! That's real progress that is. Nice to hear of computers being used for something useful instead of stupid bloody video games.' Andy said excitedly.

'I think I get it. You just guide us through different screens and we build up a more erm... overall view instead of the way Funny Fits does it, in sections.'

'Shauna I am impressed. Thank you for paying such close attention. I wanted to explain this new program to you as may be asked to use it many times.' she paused. Lacey discreetly tapped on his watch. 'Ah we must begin, they are rather desperate for these images.'

'May one ask who the powers that be, think this woman is or from whence she hails.'

'Can't you talk in bleedin' English?' Shauna asked with a smile.

'You know better than that Barry. Even if I knew, which I don't, I couldn't possibly tell you. She may just be an employee or an interested party. Now we really must get on. I'll begin with Shauna if that's all right, as you seem very interested.'

This was a good tactic, despite being fully aware of the backhanded compliment, Shauna was happy to take it just the same.

Miss Ponytail and Shauna left the room and Barry and Andy sighed with relief.

'You both did well there with Shauna.' Lacey said nodding his head. 'She's a lively one.'

'She certainly is.' Barry said in agreement.

'We need to get her, this woman. We need to identify her and locate her. Things are getting serious. More serious than I can say. Team Beta are working hard, but it's been no picnic, *Watcher 22* has been seriously compromised.' Lacey said, volunteering the information unprompted for a change.

'You've heard from them? The others?'

'Keep it to yourselves. Just a few bits I pick up on my travels. They need to get a move on though as really we need them back here at HQ.'

'When do you think that may be...?'

Lacey never got to answer the question as Miss Ponytail and Shauna bounced back into the room.

'She did an amazing job. So brilliant in fact, that we already have a direct match. Honestly Shauna, for such an erratic brain your observation and recall of image are very impressive!!'

Shauna lit up like a Christmas tree, blushing as she looked down at her shoes.

'As we have a direct match, the suspect is being traced as we speak. All I need to do is do a line up of thirty images on the computer and ask each of you to identify the image which is most like her.'

Without further ado, the line up was shown to both Barry and Andy separately and it was of no surprise that they both identified the same woman from Shauna's composite.

'That's fantastic! Thanks everyone. You did a grand job. Especially you Shauna.'

The door slammed as Agent K walked in.

'You can leave now Rachel.' he said somewhat curtly. 'I hear that you've done well. Let's hope that it's in time. You may have your evening meal and then I need you to examine some footage taken while your group were at the last Plenni, before you er, well before you escaped.'

It was faint, but I could hear it. This was a low blow even for Flint. Thankfully the music faded away. I shrugged myself to get my focus back. I had arrived in the Uncle's kitchen and Berni and Brian were outside. To my right, the 16-year-old Amelia is staring at her younger self through the window. Her face expressionless, but we can hear the shrill screams of young Amelia, as she batters on the door desperately trying to get in. I look round at her Uncle, who is in a drug-induced sleep. His hand has now loosened its grip on the new tub of blood pressure tablets. Thank God, the Uncle's innocence remains intact. Relief flooded through me.

'How simply lovely for you dear Helena.' Flint chipped in, for once just at the right time.

'There is just the small case of rescuing a child if you could drag yourself away from your cosy moment.' On this occasion Flint was right. I had secured the inside of the house, now I could turn my attention to the outside.

The window looked out upon a small garden and I could see Berni was now stood next to the terrified young Amelia. Brian is standing between them on one side and a huge Alsatian dog on the other. It wasn't barking, just staring at Amelia and the ice cream, which innocently dripped raspberry sauce down her hand. It had set her in its sights. A powerful beast, almost as big as the 7-year-old. The young girl had long since stopped banging on the solid door, the rusty old latch had a habit of dropping down when the door was slammed. Young Amelia knew that she couldn't get back into the safety of the kitchen and turned to face her fate. Brian signalled to Berni.

'Can you get that bloody door open?' he said through his teeth. The dog had started to snarl.

'We can't touch the door. You know that Brian. Even if we wanted to, we have no physical presence! All I can do is reach out and connect with Helena and see if she can harness the power that we had last time in Plenni. Brian, you must stand in front of Amelia whilst I do this. She cannot see you of course, but she can sense your protection and so can the dog.'

The teenage Amelia and I were watching in stunned silence from the window. I went to grab Amelia's hand. She quickly turned and moved her hand away.

'No! You'll mess up the program! We're not allowed to touch or I could get stuck here in this repressed memory. Please, find a way to help me. A way to get that 'little me' into this house!!! Please, Helena!'

'She's right.' Berni's voice boomed into my head. 'Helena you need to try and lift the latch. I know you can't touch it. Just join me and concentrate as we did in Plenni.' I was shocked to hear Berni's voice in my head, but these were strange times and she is a psychic. The dog still hadn't moved, but the growling grew more and more intense. Outside Brian stood between the young

Amelia and the dog. Berni faced the window and closed her eyes, willing me to visualise the door. Inside the house, I closed my eyes and felt the connection with Berni almost immediately. I had to clear my mind and focus on seeing the door, which was difficult in these circumstances. After a few seconds, I managed to see the door in my mind's eye and I concentrated on lifting the latch. After a few seconds, the latch began to rattle. I was worried that the dog would hear it and pounce on the terrified Amelia, which would have meant that our intervention had made things worse. I lost concentration, only to be berated by Berni.

'Helena! For goodness' sake. Would you please concentrate.' I bit my lip and forced the image of the latch into my mind. It worked. I could see it! I focused as hard as I could. Imagining it lifting. I could hear the static crackling in my head but persevered. Suddenly, the latch began squeaking as it slowly lifted. There was a click and a flurry of action as the young Amelia fell in backwards through the door. I could see that she had thrown the ice cream onto the grass and the dog took the bait and wolfed it down, before turning to chase its young prey. In the doorway, the little girl crawled forward and slammed the door shut. She leaned her small panting body against the solid wooden door, as the dog scratched furiously desperate to gain entry. The sound of the door slamming roused Amelia's Uncle. Through her sobs, she managed to explain what had happened. A tear rolled down the cheek of the 16-year-old girl as she watched her Uncle comfort his young niece and carry her over to the rocking chair, He wrapped her in a tartan blanket before returning to the door and bolting it. He looked out through the window, but the dog had gone.

We all stood together knowing we would be returning to the pod. The older Amelia sobbed quietly.

'I remember. I remember it all.' she whispered. 'That's how I got the scar on my arm. I didn't get through the door, I know I didn't. That bastard dog bit me and I screamed so loud that Uncle woke up and managed to drag me in and kicked that brutish dog. I had to have stitches. See?'

Amelia pulled back the sleeve of her sweatshirt, then seeing nothing checked her other arm.

'Oh my God! They're gone. The stitches, the scar it's gone!!! But we're not allowed to change things! She ran over to the rocking chair and looked for the scar on her seven-year-old arm. It wasn't there.

Brian looked over at Berni and shook his head.

'Shit! What will happen Berni? We've changed it, we've altered the past. We've changed it!!'

'Yes, we have.' Berni said quietly. 'I don't know, but I do know that we made the right decision. We had to act, we couldn't stand by and watch this little girl being attacked.'

'We're not stuck here, are we? Forever? Just stuck here in my Uncle's kitchen?'

'Don't panic Amelia. You are safe and sound and we are all together. I'm sure we'll be recalled soon. They're probably just working out how to get all four of us back together.'

'Don't leave me here on my own! I want to go back now!' Amelia began to panic. She was after all only 16 years old.

There was a familiar crackling of static in the air, then suddenly Berni and Brian disappeared.

Wow! I'd never seen anyone go back to *XP* before. This was the first time I'd seen *Watcher 22* from this perspective and it was surreal. To watch as people disappear right in front of you was at the very least unnerving, at best quite thrilling.

Amelia was now clearly distressed. 'You'll go next! I know it! You'll go and I'll just be left here...'

I didn't hear the end of the sentence as the static crackled and within seconds I was back in the pod. Brian and Berni hastily helped me out of the suit.

'Where is she?' I asked as we looked into the pod where Amelia's body was still attached to the mainframe.

'They need to bring her back now! She was terrified. Someone needs to...'

The door slammed and Brown bounced into the room.

'As if I haven't got enough fucking problems!! What in God's name were you thinking! You know the rules. You can't change the past! We didn't think it possible, but even so you broke the rules! From day one at *XP*, it was made always perfectly clear that you are observers ONLY! The past cannot be changed.'

'Well, it has been.' Berni said slowly. 'We had no choice Brown. Don't tell me you wouldn't have done the same thing, all we need to do now is to get her back. Right now!'

'It's not that easy. This is unknown territory. They're working on it. But this has never happened before and we don't even know if it's possible. Viewing past events is not the same as changing them. The program was not designed to cope with changes. All the parameters have moved. Do you understand the kind of implications this may have? This interactivity could set a precedent beyond anything we could ever have imagined!'

'Could that be seen as a good thing?' Brian asked cautiously.

Brown turned towards him. 'Not if it destroys the program and leaves one of our clients stuck in her own past, you idiot!' Brown slammed his fist against the table.

'Just bring her back. That's all you were asked to do and …'

The sound of a siren interrupted Brown's tirade.

'Brilliant! Now we have to evacuate. I didn't think things could get any worse. Follow me!'

'But what about Amelia?' I asked. I was terrified that I already knew the answer.

'That's no longer any of your concern. Let's go!'

Brown flung open the door and pushed us all hurriedly into the corridor. It was chaos. Blue flashing lights and emergency sirens shrieked angrily. People were running down the corridors tightly grasping their clipboards, some were pushing machines and others were pushing beds from the pods. I looked for Amelia, but the beds were all empty.

'You have to go back to HQ now. There's no choice. It's too dangerous here for you after what you've done. We cannot begin to imagine what the implications of your actions might be, we'll have to abort and rescue what we can.' Brown paused. 'I know that you did what you felt you had to. I do understand. But the system wasn't designed for this. Do you understand that by rescuing Amelia you have changed history! It's mind-blowing, there is no precedent for this, history could be rewritten. You need to go and we need to decamp. I will let you know about Amelia. Our guys will do their best. Now go!' and with that Brown turned tail and disappeared into the melee.

It was unbelievable, everything was happening so quickly. Cagney gave us our coats and escorted us out of the building. Reality us all as we stepped out into the cold night air. The shiny, black BMW screeched to a halt. This time it had two Police escorts and a lot of security. We were ushered into the car and driven away into the darkness, all of us unsure about what would happen next.

The evening meal was served swiftly albeit amidst a strained silence. Although everyone felt a sense of relief at having identified the woman they had seen at their interviews, still there was a sense of unease.

'Wonder how Helena's getting on,' Shauna said before yawning. 'and Berni and Brian of course.'

'I wish we could go outside, just to get some fresh air.' Andy said, stretching his legs out, before jumping up and proceeding to jog on the spot.

'I think you'll find old chap, that there's not much fresh air to be had in central London.'

Barry said sadly.

'Not like the valleys!' Shauna said in a dreadful Welsh accent.

I didn't know you could do a Scottish accent Shauna.' Andy said smiling. 'Good job.' Even Lacey was sporting a grin, that was until the door was wrenched open by Agent K.

'The Inspector has instructed me to press on. We are going to a different room. Give you a change of air and environment.'

Andy winked at his colleagues. They'd always suspected that their conversations were monitored day and night. Agent K hurriedly escorted the group into a small private viewing room.

'There's fresh orange juice or lemonade if you need a quick pick me up.' Agent K pointed to a table with some jugs of juice and glasses. 'Hurry along and take your seats.' he added impatiently.

'No popcorn then?' Shauna said, grinning. Agent K gave her a stony look. Everyone got a drink and took a seat. It was a small room with six large half-moon shaped seats all facing a viewing screen. They were suitably covered in red velvet, the only sign of comfort in the clinical, white room. Agent K took centre stage. 'This evening we will be viewing your last Plenni (replenishment session) which was filmed on your last night at *XP* when you escaped. We have limited footage due to the corruption of the *Watcher 22* program. The Inspector was hoping that you would be able to fill in the blanks and explain how things played out. I need to know...' Agent K was interrupted and held his earpiece. He was obviously getting a message. 'Shit. Sit tight, I need to go down to the Base Room. Lacey keep your eye on them and don't touch any of the equipment or there'll be hell to pay.' snapped Agent K before departing.

'What the flippin' hell is goin' on now?' Andy asked, directing his question at Lacey.

'Obviously, I don't know. He outranks me. I'm just security. A glorified bouncer.'

'No you're not Lacey. We know you know things. Any chance of a shot of vodka in this orange, just to brighten things up?'

'Shauna! You're incorrigible.'

'I might be if I knew what the fuck that meant.' Shauna smiled at Barry.

'Bit tactless that. What with Barry being on the wagon an' all.' Andy said, trying to wind Shauna up. Before she had a chance to rise to the bait, Lacey put his hand in the air to stop the conversation. He too was getting a message. 'Jesus.' He muttered under his breath.

'OK, that's fuckin' it! What the hell is happening? Is it about our friends Lacey? Please just tell us!'

'Erm... can't comment at this stage. K will brief you. Those are my orders. So don't ask me anything else.' Lacey then began murmuring into his microphone sleeve and turned his back on the group.

'What do you think it is Barry?' Shauna asked quietly, her lack of expletives indicating how serious the situation was.

Barry frowned. 'I feel it might involve the other half of our group. They want to screen our last Plenni with some urgency. However, they have chosen to delay which means it must be pretty damned bad. What's your take on this Andy?'

'Am thinking along the same lines as you Barry. There's been some breach or cock-up at *XP*, we know that the program is unstable. I just hope our friends are OK. Seems as though we're living in a dangerous world, I never thought things would get this serious.'

'Who would have thought that just by answering that bloody advert we would have leapfrogged into this bleedin' nightmare? I'd feel so much better if we had the old team back together again. It's a bit lonely being the only female in the dorms. I just didn't see this coming, Berni might have though!' Shauna said smiling.

'Berni might have what?' a voice came from the back of the viewing room. 'Have I caught you talking about me, young Shauna?' Shauna jumped to her feet excitedly.

'You're back Berni! Thank God. Have you got Helena and Bri with you?'

'You mean us?' Helena and Brian popped their heads around the door together.

Shauna was unable to contain herself and bounded towards them like a young pup. Even Andy and Barry seemed relieved and were up off their seats to welcome their friends.

Following a group hug, that Shauna had insisted upon, the newcomers got themselves a drink. Team Beta wasted no time in putting Team Alpha in the picture.

'So that's where we stand. The Jonah situation was resolved as best we could and we rescued young Amelia from the dog, but not from the life situation. We were removed before we could check and we don't know if she got back safely. I'm so worried about her. 'There was another tiny glitch.' Berni explained.

'A tiny glitch?' Agent K had made his appearance. 'Some glitch!!' he said again. Berni looked directly at Agent K.

'I don't believe we've been introduced.'

'I know who *you* all are.' he snapped back at her.

'Then I'm at a disadvantage. Manners are cheap.' Berni said curtly.

Shauna stifled a giggle and I bit my lip to prevent myself from smiling. The man just stared back at her in stony silence.

'I don't have the time for idle chit chat. I'm Agent K. Have you told Team Alpha what you did?'

'We were just about to when you made your entrance.'

'Ah.' he paused. 'Go ahead then. I'll grab a drink.'

Berni half-smiled, before continuing.

'Where was I before I was so rudely interrupted? Ah yes, deciding on young Amelia's fate.

I'm afraid that we had to make a split second call to prevent Amelia from being mauled by a rather large brute of a dog. We simply couldn't stand back and do nothing.'

'Like you were supposed to. Your brief was to return her, not to change anything, or mess with anything. It interferes with the space-time continuum.'

'Am I to take it that if you had been there, which you weren't, you would have stood back and done nothing? You can honestly say that in our shoes, you would not have tried anything to help that child. Seriously?' Berni paused.

Agent K turned his head away from her.

'Kindly remember that we had no physical presence. It was an emergency we had to try anything we could.' Berni said in a measured tone.

'What the hell did you do?' Shauna asked, clearly intrigued. Berni looked across at me to take the lead.

'We used the same technique that the group used to escape Plenni. Brian blocked the eye contact between the dog and Amelia. Berni and I concentrated on lifting the latch. Somehow we succeeded and Amelia got away from the dog unscathed.'

'It was over in a split second. It was were brilliant. Bloody amazing. That's some power you've got there. You could feel the air fizzing with electricity!' Brian added excitedly.

'Just one thing you've omitted. Just one very important thing. *The* most important thing! Can any of you remember that 'other' thing?' Agent K asked, his frustration almost tangible.

'Ah. Well yes, there was one other thing. We did change things, just a tad. The actual rescue was one thing, but we did change something else.' I looked over at Brian. Agent K was standing to attention with his lips pursed in annoyance, his hands on his hips.

'Yes. Well, there was the small matter of the scar.' he said pointedly.

There was a gasp from Andy.

'Oh shit. You really have changed something.' Shauna said animatedly.

'Yes! They *really* have!'

'Because we managed to get Amelia back into the safety of the house that meant that she wasn't ravaged by the dog. The scar on the arm of both the young and the old Amelia disappeared.'

Another round of gasps and a whistle signifying disbelief.

'I see. Wow! That is mind-blowing. The implications are beyond comprehension. How can that have happened?' Barry asked. Everyone was stunned. The power and potential of the *Watcher 22* program had just reached a new level.

'Now can you see the seriousness of Team Beta's actions? Not only have they disrupted the space/time continuum, but also Amelia (the elder) is still there and the program is corrupt. Good work Team Beta. I bet Team Alpha are all delighted to have you back.' Agent K could not disguise his fury.

The door slammed, breaking the silence and heralding the arrival of the Inspector.

'I have news. K, you can leave us. Everyone be seated and prepare yourselves to be working through the night.' The Inspector glared at us all.

'You will all be paying the price for Team Beta's humanity.'

No one said a word as the pencils and clipboards were handed out.

'Let's begin.'

(Team Alpha & Team Beta – MI6 HQ)
If I could turn back time
Cher

18

'If you could pay attention! What's wrong with you all? Can you hear something that I can't?'

'Quite possibly Inspector.' I said in an annoyance. Flint just didn't know when to stop.

'What is it? What the hell's going on here?'

'Inspector, it is simply a kind of echo from the program. One of the Guides, Alan Rickman, selects inappropriate songs to illustrate our situation. Or should I say how he sees our situation.' Barry paused. Andy picked up the gauntlet,

'At first, it was only Helena that could hear him, he was her Guide see. But now we all bloody well can.'

Andy glanced around the room for acknowledgement. Everyone nodded. The Inspector looked stunned. 'Why can't I hear this music?'

'Maybe it's because you haven't been through the program.' Brian said thoughtfully.

'Anyway Inspector, the songs he chooses are normally tactless and somewhat insensitive.' Andy explained.

'And can I ask how long this has been going on for?' the Inspector glared at the group.

'We didn't mention it because it didn't seem important, Flint has always done it and...'

'Did I ask for your opinion Helena? I will ask again. How long this has been going on for?'

'I suppose that we all started to hear Flint after we met up at Helena's Wizard of Oz reunion party.' Berni said slowly and deliberately. The Inspector just shrugged her shoulders.

'Please don't explain about the party, just tell me when it was.'

'March 27th. Just a few days ago, although it doesn't seem like that now.'

'And before that, who could hear Flint?'

'Only Helena. We never heard each other's Guides speak when we were in the program.'

'More may come of this, but right now we need to urgently review your last Plenni. We're hoping that you may remember something or be able to give us some clues to help solve the Amelia case. As you know Amelia is trapped in the past. It's almost as though the precise moment that you changed has been frozen or put on hold. There is not that much footage left from your escape from Plenni. But we've patched together the bits that we do have. Whilst I am pleased to have the whole group here, I would have preferred it to have been under different circumstances. But it is what it is. Please make notes and write any questions down. I feel that you will benefit from watching this turn of events from the position of a third party, which should give you all a better perspective. Is everyone clear about what they have to do? Just watch and write down ANYTHING that pops into your head. We will have a debrief once it's finished. Cagney, please begin playing the film and Lacey grab the lights. Oh and Barry I'm aware that you had left *XP* by this time, to be made into biscuits to feed the human race or so your team members thought!' The Inspector paused, disguising a smile. 'One too many Sci-Fi films I feel, I think that particular one was called *Soylent Green*. I'm sure that Barry is aware that Andy's farewell party from *XP* had a *Rocky Horror* Show theme. I would be interested in any comments you can make as you watch this for the very first time.'

The familiar crackling and fizzing began. A picture flickered onto the screen and Cagney paused the image, while he adjusted the focus. The film restarted and we all recognised ourselves at our old Plenni, even though we were all dressed up in our *Rocky Horror* costumes. Barry gasped in amazement.

'I have heard a great deal about this performance, I must say that I am impressed.'

The large screen showed the whole Team dressed in their costumes. Andy was dressed impressively as Dr. Frank-N-Furter, Brian was Brad, Helena played Janet, Berni looked amazing as Little Nell and Shauna was dressed as the saucy Magenta. The rain even fell on the characters as they sang *There's a light*. The Inspector seemed a little captivated by the performance, 'That's quite a remarkable transformation. Who would have thought that Andy would make such an amazing Frank-N-Furter? Not that I've watched that film many times.' she added with a half-smile. We all linked arms in our seats. It was a happy memory, even in this weird and strained environment. We all hummed along, unable to resist. Cagney threw Lacey a rare smile and the mood in the room lifted, albeit for a short time. Everyone joined in with the final line.

"There's a light, light in the darkness of everybody's life"

Then the screen flickered and moved onto the next scene. The group had changed back into the Plenni uniform of jeans and t-shirts and Andy was scrubbing away at his make-up. The group was sat around the table and Andy and Shauna were sharing the story of Barry's departure. I looked over at Barry whose lips were pursed together as his eyes glistened with tears. It had been such an emotional experience. Watching it with hindsight was easy, but seeing our faces was a poignant reminder about the uncertainty surrounding our future. Andy could have been going to his death, for all we knew. Now we all understood about the *Watcher 22* program, but back then we had no idea.

The next scene showed Brian edging nearer to a plug socket as he pretended to tie his laces. Andy had blocked the view of the camera by leaning against my chair. Brian coughed twice and Berni nodded and tapped the table three times. We watched the women hold hands to make a connection, as they began to will the bolt on the door to move. Brian was waiting to cut the power. The screen crackled, just as it had at the time. Andy gave Brian the nod as the metal bolt shot back across the door.

Brian thrust the silver foil stick into the plug socket and all the lights and screens went off. It was pitch black. In the background, you could hear whispering.

'Just to explain, we were all holding hands and moving towards the door. We had no idea what the hell we would find!'

'I think we stood in a semi-circle, arm in arm. It was a united front, a team effort.' I added nodding.

The picture changed angle and there was the tiniest flicker of light from the screen behind us, which for a second, cast a strange shadow of five figures onto the facing wall. Brian brought down the door handle and again the camera angle changed to show a long dark corridor, with a pinprick of light in the distance. The next shot showed five figures jogging together towards the light. The screen then changed to a new set of shots that must have been taken by a camera set above the doorway. It showed Brian pushing open the wooden door and a shaft of light streaming in from the gap.

'You all know the rest. You successfully escaped and found the operations room at *XP* where the *Watcher 22* program was monitored 24 hours a day...'

'May I interrupt Inspector? 'Barry paused, his timing as ever was impeccable. 'I understand the seriousness of the situation, but would it be at all possible for me to just see the operations room? You see I didn't escape with this motley crew, I simply awoke in my bed in the recovery room, was debriefed and then driven home. Judging by the poor quality of this film and I would guess our limited access to it, could I possibly see a few more minutes?'

The Inspector looked uncertain and chewed the inside of her cheek. She checked her watch looked over at Cagney and Lacey, who nodded their assurance together. It was with some reluctance that the Inspector allowed us to see the last moments of our escape.

The screen burst back into life and the camera was now above the Base Room which resembled something out of *Mission Impossible*. Under each of our names was a hologram, a computer screen and a mini sound wave monitor. Every client had their own computer programmer and counsellor. Weirdly, on each side of the TV screen was a holographic image of each of our Guides. We each honed in on our own monitors as we weren't the only clients at *XP*. They were quite easy to locate as the 5 screens were all black and the sound waves were flat. The techie support team was frantically trying to restart the program. We had obviously managed to send *Watcher 22* down, either through cutting the power or through telepathy. But the other screens seemed to be flickering with life, so perhaps it was a combination of both. Either way, it was a big deal and something that the Inspector would be looking to draw on to assist with our present dilemma.

Amazingly, the screen then changed to show 'real-time' feed of the Team. It was strange to see everyone becoming self-conscious, realising that the camera was filming them. They realised that they were still in crisis mode and suddenly felt a little embarrassed that they were still holding hands. It seemed a little childish now under the harsh glare of the electric lights. The chain was then broken as everyone broke hands.

Back in the room, Shauna gave a pretend cough. She had clearly remembered what had happened next.

'You get the idea Barry? Inspector let's get this bleedin' case sorted. Time to move on.'

Shauna said insistently.

'What's the rush Shauna? There are only a few more minutes of footage left. We'll see it through now.' Shauna kicked her chair back from the table and her eyes flashed dangerously. I'd seen this scenario before and Shauna's temper was a force to be reckoned with.

Fortunately, the picture quality was poor and the sound muffled. The image of Shauna flirting with her programmer whilst dressed as Magenta from the *Rocky Horror Show* will remain as a memory that did not need to be relived. The screen went black and Shauna sighed and the fight went out of her eyes.

'I want each one of you to focus now. Think about the scene, when you sent *Watcher 22* down. The telepathy that you used, how it felt and how you think it worked. We may have to rely solely on your experience to rescue Amelia and bring her back. No discussion. Just write your own take on that scene down. You will begin now.'

The Inspector collected the clipboards after about twenty minutes. We were given refreshments and the freedom to move around and stretch our legs. Hopefully, we would now be allowed to leave or at least have a visit home to see our families.

'You're an idiot.' Flint chipped into my thoughts.

'Do you have to do that?' I asked him, feeling irritated by the intrusion.

'I think I need to say it again. You are an idiot. Does your feeble mind really believe that you would qualify for visitation rights? When you are assisting the most *secret* of secret services? Your naivety, dear Helena, never ceases to amaze me!'

'Get lost, Flint! If I want to have an irrational thought in the privacy of my own head, then I can do so!! Just buzz off. I'm sure the Inspector would love a visit from you. If you're brave enough of course.'

'Your childish tactics serve neither to tempt nor intimidate me. You are transparent, if I chose to, I could easily penetrate the psyche of the Inspector. However, rules restrict us from entering the minds of those who have not been through the program.'

'If that's the case then answer me this...' Flint sighed.

'If you don't mind, could I finish?' I asked, mirroring his rudeness.

'Yes yes, if you must!'

I had prepared my question carefully. 'If it's true that you can't pop into the minds of those who have not been through the *Watcher 22* program, then how come Cagney and Lacey can hear your delightful musical selections?'

'You don't listen dear Helena, do you? I did not say that I *couldn't* barge into their heads just that as Guides, we are not permitted to. Music is quite different. The attention is in the detail! I thought at the very least I'd taught you that...'

'What's going on?' The Inspector interrupted the frantic dialogue with Flint. Shit, I didn't want to explain. I had heard Flint click off as soon as the Inspector began talking.

'Just reminiscing, you know about *Rocky Horror* and all that shenanigans.' I didn't even sound convincing to myself.

'I see. Then can I assume that you are not hearing the dulcet tones of Mr. Rickman?'

A siren sounded, just in the nick of time. I could hear Flint chuckling somewhere in the distance.

'Everyone move!' Cagney herded us to the doorway and down a staircase.

'Room 12 Lacey! Get them down there!'

'Yes, Ma'am.'

The Inspector let her formal address slip, an indication of the seriousness of the situation. We were hurriedly marched down sterile white corridors and marched into room 12. Lacey locked the door behind us and we were instructed to sit. The room was decked out with rows of high tech computers and appeared to be more of a research IT room than an emergency bunker.

The Inspector entered the room accompanied by two men.

'Meet Bill and Ben.' We all nodded acknowledgement.

'We have to act now, to save Amelia. At the moment the program has stalled, a bit like pausing a video. Bill and Ben can get into the program, but we need Berni, Helena and Brian to return to the scene. This is a little awkward, but Berni we need you to focus on keeping young Amelia either asleep or distracted while we engage with the older Amelia and bring her back home. It is of vital importance that Shauna, Barry and Andy assist Bill and Ben with the timing of the restart and watch the screens to warn of any impending danger.'

Bill and Ben had already accessed the program and we had a very blurry image of the kitchen, where both Amelias appeared to be standing appearing almost statuesque.

'You three go down to the pods and get suited up and quickly, please. We have minutes before *Watcher 22* crashes and Amelia is the last client that we have to get out.'

We left. We ran down the corridor with Lacey by our side. Once we reached the pods we knew the drill and got ourselves changed and hooked up.

This time the fizzing and flashing lasted a little longer and when we arrived in the kitchen the light was almost sepia. The air was still and cloying and I sensed the imbalance, a feeling of almost sinister anticipation. Berni looked visibly shaken but knew we had to act quickly. She shook her head from side to side to rouse herself, before bending over young Amelia. The light flickered. Brian and I approached the older Amelia who was leaning with her back against the door and staring straight ahead. Brian clicked his fingers in front of her eyes. Nothing. We called her name and made loud noises. Still she stared straight ahead.

'It's no good Berni, we can't rouse her!' I called over as the lights continued to flicker. 'We need you here now!'

'I think you're right. Brian come and watch over the youngster.'

Brian and Berni swapped places.

'There's no choice now Helena. Hold my left hand and reach your right hand out toward her. I'll do the same on the other side. We can't physically touch her, this is as near as we can get. Close your eyes and focus on Amelia. We need to wake her up!'

I followed Berni's instructions and the light faded even more. Brian and young Amelia were merely dark shadows in the corner.

Amelia's eyes began to flicker, but her body remained stationary.

'I think it's working. Keep going!!' Brian shouted over.

Berni squeezed my hand.

'One last effort. Concentrate hard.'

Suddenly both Amelias gasped simultaneously. Both slumped forward, the light fizzed with an electrical charge and then the world went black.

I came around very slowly. Feeling the familiar discomfort of the pod and its encumbrances.

'Awake at last! Good grief woman. Everyone else is up an about! Even Berni.'

'Ah Flint, how I've missed your early morning ramblings. Could I just have a moment…?'

'Of course, if you feel happy lying there relaxing while one of your team is locked in.'

'What!! Of course I don't. Is it Berni? Flint, no time to be a knob, just tell me!'

'What a lovely turn of phrase.'

'Flint, now!'

I struggled to get dressed as Flint explained that Berni may have overexerted herself and hadn't returned to *XP*. Her body had, but she hadn't regained consciousness. Brian was OK and Amelia was now in debrief. No one knew what the long term effects would be. If the *Watcher 22* program could change the past and history could be changed then the possibilities were unfathomable.

'They want to shut it down.' Flint added in a sombre tone.

'Maybe it's just as well.' I added hastily whilst putting on my trainers.

'Sometimes you can be very insensitive Helena, for one so allegedly wise. You do realise that if the program is pulled I go with it! I don't exist outside the program.'

'Whoops! Shit! Sorry Flint!' I'd genuinely overlooked Flint's dependency on the program.

'I thought you existed in my head. You know after some sort of glitch in the program.' I said while frantically trying to tie my laces.

'You're an imbecile Helena. I simply despair! You're not a schizophrenic. You're not hearing voices. I am a product of the program and while it transmits, I exist. However, you are correct about there being a glitch in the program. I was able to use the server to make contact with you and anyone on the database. That will all be taken from me now. No morning tunes to make you smile or helpful reprimands to assist you. I fear the worst Helena. This may be our last conversation.'

'It was never a conversation Flint! That would involve two people discussing things by choice. Whereas you just jump into my head unannounced, then state your business, take the mickey out of me then leave. Hardly a two-way process!'

'Dear dear! That's a little harsh. I kept you sane and made you smile. But if that's how you feel I'll say adieu.'

'Oh Flint please don't leave, not now. Stay! Stay and help me with Berni… Flint!'

I could hear a very faint chuckle. What a swine! Still, I had no time to pander to his tantrum. Berni needed me. Brian burst into my pod without knocking.

'Helena! Thank God you're awake! It's Berni. Her vitals are slowing and we can't bring her round. We need to get down there now. The others are already there.'

My heart was pounding. Had this last revisit been one too far. After all, we had been disconnected from *Watcher 22* for over a year now. We hadn't been prepped or suitably monitored, before gallivanting in and out of time zones and other people's lives. It had been very stressful and Berni was always one of the first to offer her assistance.

Lacey was waiting outside the door. His hand to his earpiece.

'Follow me! We need to hurry!' Without further ado, Brian and I ran with Lacey as fast as we could to the recovery room. Was it too late? The others stood outside under the flashing red light as resuscitation took place and the nurses and doctors fought to save Berni. The red flat line on the monitor signified just how desperate the situation was. We all held hands, at first just for comfort, but then a strange flow of energy seemed to run through my body. I looked around at everyone else. Their eyes were fixed in a stare. No words had been spoken, but we all knew we had harnessed something very special. Whether or not we could risk using it on Berni was a call that would have to be made.

'If you're going to do it, do it now!' Flint almost shouted as the music began to fade. We had made a circuit by joining hands and forming a circle.

'Berni said we could tap into the unconscious mind using our combined force, maybe we can use this to give Berni a jolt, a kind of jump-start...'

'No more talking! You need to act *now!*' I could tell that everyone had heard Flint's voice.

'I think we should just visualise her face and will her to wake up...'

'Then in the name of all that's holy do it NOW!' There was an edge of panic in Flint's voice. We all closed our eyes, held each other's hands tightly and focused on the image of our dear Berni. The lights in the corridor flickered.

'Try harder, all of you!' We seemed to take a collective deep breath and willed our friend to awaken. There was a popping sound as the strip lights went off and we were cloaked in darkness. I could feel Shauna's hand sweating in mine. Barry clutched my hand extremely tightly under the dark cloak of silence.

'Hold still everyone. Do not break the circle. Just breathe and focus.' Barry said calmly. It seemed like we had stood there for hours. 'Keep still Brian! Remain focused, everyone.'

Suddenly, the strip lights flicked back on and there was a flurry of activity. We all blinked and tried to adapt to the garish glare. Still we remained connected, still willing our friend to come back to us. Andy stood on his tiptoes trying to see the monitor in the recovery room. He was swiftly admonished by Barry. I felt that time was slipping away from us. Shauna looked at me, her eyes glistening with tears. I bit my lip and held on tightly.

'Keep breathing! Keep focusing! This is Berni. Our Berni.' Brian blurted out, his voice choking with emotion.

The door of the recovery room opened slowly. I could hardly bear to look at the doctor's face. 'Berni is stable.' he said in a measured tone of voice. She did actually die, her heart stopped and then something happened, something that none of us can explain, nor do we want to.' he added, looking tired, but relieved. 'Her body just seemed to restart and fortunately so did her heart. Her condition is critical but stable. I can say no more at this time and would ask that you leave now and let us monitor her. You will be informed about her progress.' The doctor then turned on his heels and returned to the room.

'Can we drop hands now?' Shauna asked timidly.

'Yes, I think we can. If everyone agrees.'

We all nodded and gently unclasped our hands.

'Follow me, if you please.' Lacey said quietly. 'The Inspector would like to speak to you all.'

We walked quite slowly to the Briefing Room. There was an overriding feeling of exhaustion, tinged with relief. Lacey led the way, but even he slowed his pace. I walked alongside Shauna.

'What the fuck is that?' she stopped dead and turned to look at me.

'What now?' I said with some irritation. Then Brian stopped, followed swiftly by Barry and Andy. Lacey had not noticed and ambled on slowly.

'What?' I asked impatiently.

'Can't you hear it? It is *your* crazy bastard of a Guide after all!' Shauna said somewhat accusingly.

'Is it Flint? What the hell is he up to now?'

'I think it's Johnny Mathis. I think Flint is sending you a message.' Barry said quietly.

'Then why can't I hear it? For God's sake…'

'He's preparing you, Helena. He's getting us to tell you, cowardly effing bastard.' Shauna said animatedly.

'Tell me what? What can you hear?' And then I heard it and I knew what was going to happen.

Guess it's over, call it a day
Sorry that it had to end this way
No reason to pretend
We knew it had to end someday

'Flint!! Talk to me. Don't just fade away! At least say goodbye you cowardly swine!' I shouted getting the unwelcome attention of Lacey.

'Quieten down there? Move along. We've had enough weird stuff for one day!'

Everyone picked up the pace. Barry turned around and gave me a wink as the music faded.

'Johnny bloody Mathis.' Shauna muttered under her breath. 'Saddo.'

'I think they're going to switch *Watcher 22* off.'

'Good riddance. It's too bloody dangerous now Helena.'

'I realise that Shauna, but what you don't understand is that if they switch *Watcher 22* off – they switch Flint off as well.'

She stopped for a moment and nodded her understanding.

'I get it. Hence the song.'

'Hence the song, the very last song.' I said with just a slight waver in my voice.

'Still, Johnny bloody Mathis! She said thumping me on the arm and trying to lighten the mood.

'Yeah, well even Flint has a soft side.'

The Inspector was propping the door open as we approached and seemed both frazzled and impatient.

'Everyone in and take your seats. Hurry up, please. There's coffee and some cakes on the table. Tuck in whilst I debrief and quickly explain our plan of action. We silently obeyed. The Inspector explained that we had successfully extracted Amelia and that she was alive and well. She also outlined how seriously ill Berni was but, with time, she should make a full recovery. The Inspector then read out some legal blurb that we had all heard before, but due to the Official Secrets Act, she had to repeat it all again. I felt my mind beginning to wander. Amelia's scar had disappeared. The past had been changed and the implications were unimaginable. In the wrong hands, this program could change history, change lives, change our very existence. My heart began to pound and I felt a little faint. Cagney noticed and signalled to the Inspector. The air con fans hummed into action and I was given a glass of icy cold water. Barry looked over at me with a frown and I nodded in reassurance. The Inspector continued to recite some dates and legal claptrap. Then Shauna interrupted as only she could.

'I need a slash.' she blurted out, quite loudly. 'Before we agree to do anything else or discuss some new plan or code or whatever the fuck we have to do. I need a slash!' Shauna said somewhat edgily. The Inspector stopped speaking and simply glared at her.

'Actually, Shauna is right, on this occasion.' Barry said calmly. 'Our best friend nearly died. I think we could be permitted a ten-minute comfort break.' The Inspector looked at her watch, sighed and agreed.

'Come with me.' Shauna whispered in my ear.

'But I'm OK, I don't need…'

'Yes, you do.' she said grabbing my arm and guiding me to the toilets. Once we were safely through the door, I asked her what she was playing at.

'It's your last chance. You were right and Flint knew it. They *are* going to switch it off, *Watcher 22*. Don't you see it's your last chance to say goodbye to Flint, you dickhead!' She was right. And the window of opportunity was closing. I struggled to start speaking, distracted by the time pressure and the sound of Shauna relieving herself.

'Flint! Can you hear me? I just want to say, er just to say goodbye. It's been …Shauna, I can't think of the words!!' I panicked.

'He knows Helena. Not that I understand what you see in that sarky bastard, but each to their own.' Shauna shouted from her cubicle.

Cagney began knocking on the door.

'Time ladies, if you please.'

'OK here goes. Farewell Flint, it's been an experience, thank you for keeping me sane.' I gulped and took a deep breath and we went back into the room.

Just in the distance and only very faintly, could I hear Flint's last song and a tear fell down my cheek. I looked around, but no one else could hear it. It was just for me.

When you're weary, feeling small
When tears are in your eyes,
I will dry them all
I'm on your side
When times get rough
And friends just can't be found
Like a bridge over troubled water
I will lay me down

I bit my lip and tried not to cry. Flint had been my flawed Jiminy Cricket of conscience, for the very last time.

The music faded. I closed my eyes trying to compose myself and bowed my head.

'You think you can get rid of me that easily.' Flint whispered in my head. 'In the words of that stupid lump Arni Schwarzenegger - I'll be back dear Helena, I will be back.'

(Teams Alpha & Team Beta – MI6 HQ)

We returned to the Briefing Room. The Inspector looked flustered and kept putting her hand to her ear and shaking her head in irritation. She was much aggrieved by the messages she was receiving. Cagney and Lacey looked tense as they stood to attention, mirroring each other like two upper-class bouncers. Shauna shot me a desperate glance and even Andy bit his lip apprehensively. Brian just kept pacing the room like an expectant father, in direct contrast to Barry who sat quietly, his eyes flickering in anticipation.

'Right. The latest Intel has led to a rather drastic decision.' The Inspector said starchily. '*Watcher 22* has proved to be a very dangerous program. We now have evidence that it has the potential to change lives and events and maybe even history. In the wrong hands, this could be disastrous and could destabilise not only the present and the past but also the future. If it fell into the wrong hands, the effects are unimaginable. Computers here at MI6 and the CIA have been successfully hacked. We are unable to take the chance that we can protect our servers and keep the program safe. Obviously, *Watcher 22* has been deleted and the hard drives have been wiped, but these hackers are experts and we simply cannot take the risk. If they can infiltrate the Pentagon, then they are more than capable of gaining access to our entire security program and of course *Watcher 22*.' she paused. 'In the future, research will continue. And before you ask, *yes* we do still need you – probably more than ever! After the cock-up with Edward Snowden and his revelations about *Tempora*, rumours of elections being hacked and then there are the Rainbow Tables with their ability to crack passwords, we have never been under such a threat. Therefore, following an overnight emergency session, the Government has decided, that we have now run out of choices.

Lacey then opened a briefcase and handed the Inspector a black, leather-bound book. The golden crest of the coat of arms caught the light, as she opened it. She flicked through the pages impatiently, then cleared her throat. 'I am duty-bound to read you this, so pay attention!' The Inspector glared at us all, her gaze finally resting on Shauna, who responded by pursing her lips and looking at her feet. 'There are five levels of threat to the security of the United Kingdom. The level is set by the Joint Terrorism Analysis Centre and the Security Service (MI5). Threat levels don't have an expiry date. They can change at any time, as the information becomes available to security agents. There are five levels of threat as outlined by the Government regarding terrorism and national emergencies:

- Low - an attack is unlikely
- Moderate - an attack is possible but not likely
- Substantial - an attack is a strong possibility
- Severe - an attack is highly likely
- Critical - an attack is expected imminently

(www.gov.uk/terrorism-national-emergency)

Right now, we have increased the level to severe. We are in 'lockdown' here at MI6, due to the serious nature of events. I now have to announce that we are in a position where we have no choice. We will have to hit the Kill Switch.'

A gasp went around the room. Whatever it meant, it sounded serious.

'And will someone explain what the fuck that is?' Shauna demanded loudly, her eyes wild with agitation. 'Are you going to kill us all?' The Inspector sighed. She looked exhausted.

'May I?' Barry asked politely.

'Please do.' she raised her hands in agreement, before taking a seat and gratefully sipping her coffee.

'The Internet kill switch is a countermeasure against cybercrime...'

'Bloody hell Barry! In simple laywoman's terms, if that's possible.' Shauna interrupted rudely.

'Basically, it means that the Internet will be switched off.'

'A shut off mechanism will be activated for all Internet traffic. To protect it from hackers and the like...' Andy added helpfully. Barry shot him a look that would splinter wood and then continued.

'In this instance, I would imagine that by switching the Internet off, we will be protected from unspecified assailants. This is the only way to be certain that national security is not breached. They will have to ensure that *Watcher 22* remains safely within the confines of MI6. Will that suffice?'

'Hang on a fuckin' minute! Are you saying we can't use computers, no Wi-Fi, no Google, no email, no Instagram, no internet shopping or banking, no

Facebook – what about mobile phones, no Netflix? No bleedin' way!' Shauna said quite tersely.

'That really is the least of our worries Shauna.' Brian said wearily.

'I would think that we will all be returning to landlines as far as phones go. Cell phones would probably still function as voice devices, but their data capabilities would be inhibited or killed.' The Inspector nodded her agreement towards Lacey as Shauna crossed her arms in a sulk.

'Please understand that this will have global implications and the impact will be felt far beyond the Stock Market, this will affect all businesses particularly those that rely on online ordering such as e Bay and Amazon. We will all have to revert to using the methods that we had before. No more email, social networking sites or Smart-phones. We will return to a reliance on the Post Office to deliver letters once again.'

'What the fuck! You've gotta be joking me right?' Shauna looked around at us, searching for some sort of solidarity.

'Hell, that's gonna be tough! Everyone will have to make a lot of changes. But the pace of life will slow down a bit…'

'Bollocks!' Shauna shouted interrupting poor Andy. 'It'll be like going back to the Middle Ages!!'

'Actually Shauna, I remember a time when we didn't have all this technology and somehow we survived.' Barry said in a measured tone.

'Yeah, but you were all bored to death! Like we're gonna be now. How are we supposed to keep in touch with our friends and keep up to date with things? I just don't get why we can't have our phones at least!'

Shauna looked close to tears, she was the one who had struggled the most when we had first arrived and had all our possessions taken.

'Come on Shauna, we'll survive. No one will have them, not just us, isn't that right Inspector?' Brian asked calmly.

'Yes that's correct and I think that you're missing the point here! Not only are the lives of our agents in the field at risk, but also the security we take for granted in our past, present and even the future. Don't you understand? We may already be too late and the very foundations of everyday life that we rely on, our memories and plans could be corrupted if *Watcher 22* gets into the wrong hands! There could be a run on the pound and all financial institutions and banks will have to introduce emergency security measures. Debit and credit cards will not work and from here on in will merely serve as a means to withdraw cash from the pop-up banks that will have to be put in place. There may be issues with the National grid and food supplies will be affected as will the supply of medicines. So forgive me if you're a little inconvenienced by not being able to play the latest version of *Call of Duty or Whats-app* your friends. Not being able to access *Facebook* or book online train tickets, pales into pathetic insignificance when you understand the bigger picture here! Get a grip! I expect you all to work with our teams now and put your selfish inconveniences to one side.' she paused and looked squarely at each one of us. 'Make no mistake, what is happening here is deadly serious and on the scale of a terrorist attack. We will need everyone to work together to ensure that we have a future to look forward to.'

The Inspector then threw the black leather book onto the glass table, handed a sheet of instructions to Lacey and slammed the door as she left the room. There was a stunned silence.

'Holy shite! I didn't realise, I mean, I didn't get it. Fuck. Now I do. I had no idea. This is massive...'

'It is massive. Brian interrupted. 'I thought we'd been through the worst after escaping the program, who could have guessed that this was going to happen.'

'I think we're in for the long haul. 'Barry said quietly.

'I don't think we'll be going home for some time, that's for sure.'

'We need Berni back, Lacey could you find out how she's doing please?'

'Will do Helena. In the meantime, Cagney will bring in some food before we make a start on Operation Offline. There's a lot to do and we're all going to have to put some hours in.'

'I don't know what else we can bleedin' say. They know everything we know for fuck's sake!'

Lacey left the room to check on Berni.

'That's where you're wrong Shauna. 'Cagney said quietly. 'In fact, you couldn't be more wrong.'

It had been a late night. Cagney and Lacey had had the dubious task of getting us up to speed with everything. There were a lot of technical jargon, legal rules and regulations to plough through. We followed it all as best we could, whilst still reeling with the shocking news about implementing the 'kill switch.'

The next morning we had an unexpected visitor.

'Wake up sleepy head.' said a familiar voice. 'Good grief! Have you all been hitting the sherry since I've been away?' Berni asked chirpily.

'Who drinks fuckin' sherry in this day and age?' Shauna said blearily as we tried to rouse ourselves.

'You've obviously missed me. Don't worry I can tell. But if you're too tired to wheel me in for breakfast...'

'Berni is that you? Shauna, Berni's back!! It's great to have you back, we've been so worried Berni! But hang on a minute, why are you in a wheelchair?'

'Wheelchair! Berni? What the Fuck?' Shauna suddenly came around.

'Oh, this old thing? It's just to cover them, for Insurance, Health and Safety and all that shenanigans.'

'Are you're OK Berni. How are you feeling?'

'Shit we nearly lost you! And...'

'Shauna. Enough of that for now, let's just celebrate having our dear Berni back.'

'I'm only here for a couple of hours, then bed rest in the afternoons. I had to argue with the High Command to get that.' Berni said crossly.

'Was it Inspector Gadget?'

'Shauna, be careful.' I said, smiling to myself.

'Yes she was there, but there were other people, all in uniform, military types that we rarely see here.'

'Did you hear about the fuckin' killer switch'?'

'Yes I did and I'm not sorry as the threat to our national security worries me more.' she was interrupted by Cagney banging on the door.

'Time ladies, please! Shower and sh... erm, powder your noses or whatever you get up to in there. Chop chop! Twenty minutes to the briefing.'

We performed our ablutions and arrived on time, if not a little damp. Berni's return had lifted all our spirits and everyone welcomed her back to the Team. Just before we began, Berni leaned over to me,

'I don't hear him, Flint I mean, I don't hear him any more, has he gone?' she whispered.

'Yes, I think he has.' I said sadly. 'They were going to flick the kill switch in the early hours. His last song was *Bridge over Troubled Waters*.'

'That's rather sentimental for Flint. Are you sure it was him?'

'Either that or some other sadistic sod has infiltrated my headspace, but then who knows in this place?' The door slammed and we all knew it hailed the Inspector's entrance. We braced ourselves for the next challenge.

'I would like to read you this formal statement that I have received from upstairs.' the Inspector nodded her head upwards. 'All over the world, intentional internet shutdowns and deliberate slowdowns are becoming more and more common. Both China and America are rumoured to have developed a kill switch. We are now under the threat of a cyberattack, due to the newly discovered potential of *Watcher22*. In the short term, planes can fly without the internet, and trains and buses will continue to run. Longer outages will make it hard for businesses to operate. We can now confirm that at zero two hundred hours we implemented the kill switch and the Internet is now officially switched off. We are unsure at this stage of the timescale but we can assure you that it will last into the foreseeable future. In place of emails and mobile phones, we will be using landlines and written directives, for now at least. The Post Office has been on full alert for some time now, due to the expected increase in letter volume. The Phone companies have also working day and night to avert panic and reactivate landlines and install public telephone boxes. All military reserves have been called up to assist with the implementation of the new infrastructure. This will be a massive adjustment for everyone. The banking sector and stock market are also working flat out to meet customer demand as internet banking and online trading no longer exist.' the Inspector paused. 'Are there any questions?'

'Yes. Inspector, if I may, should one have savings or stocks and shares, hypothetically speaking of course – would they be secure?'

'Yes, Barry. The banks have assured us that all bank accounts and stock and shares are protected. Internet banking is not available, but each customer's account is quite safe.'

'Shame really.' Shauna said quietly.

'What!' the Inspector turned on Shauna.

'Could have wiped off some of my debts and that bastard student loan!'

Sensing impending aggravation, Berni patted Shauna's hand and took control.

'Before we watch the Prime Minister's speech, could you outline our involvement? I have to return to the ward shortly?'

'Yes, of course, Berni.' her interruption had the desired effect and diffused the situation.

'Very briefly then. You will all be remaining with us. One of our agents has set up a meeting with the creator of *Watcher 22*, we'll call him Gavin. This is no mean feat, as we have been holding him in protective custody and he is just a tad uncooperative. He has, however, agreed to talk, but only if he gets to meet you, the users of his program. Things happened so quickly, he never really had a chance to get any feedback. Of course, we care little for his damaged feelings, we simply need to extract as much information as we can.'

'That's charming that is, are we just bait then? Just being dangled in front of him and held here to please you, so you can get information from some program designer is that it?'

This was an unlikely outburst for Andy, he must have had some past issues on his mind.

Cagney and Lacey braced themselves, expecting the worst. The Inspector rounded on Andy.

'Well Andy, you are for once absolutely right. We are using you, all of you! That's what we do!! We always have and we always will, whatever it takes to get what we need. You're not being subjected to waterboarding or being given electric shock therapy. Get a grip and suck it up! That's what's needed and that's what you'll do!' The Inspector glared at us all, her cheeks now adorned with those familiar fiery red spots of fury. She squinted over at Shauna, daring her to speak. But even Shauna knew when to keep quiet and that time had come.

Lacey broke the silence, muttering something about bringing in the television and some new connections due to the effect on digital TV. Cagney was only too happy to join him and they left the room together.

'Watch and learn! You will be notified once the meeting with Gavin has been set up. It will be within the next 24 hours, so be prepared.' she paused. Then a complete change of tone as she addressed Berni. 'Would you like to return to your room Berni?'

'I would like to stay, with my friends if that's alright and watch the speech. It helps to watch these things as a Team, I'm sure you understand.'

'Yes, of course.' she said quietly and left the room as Cagney and Lacey wheeled in the large TV on legs which had an aerial balanced precariously on the top.

'Good grief! The last time I saw a TV like this was when I was a schoolgirl and the Americans landed on the moon! I was 7 years old at the time, so you can tell how long ago that was!' I added laughing.

'Good God, that's bloody frightening. It looks like something from *Day of the Triffids!* No flat screen and 3D then.' Andy said light-heartedly.

'Everything has reverted to the old ways. They're even using the old cables and guess what?'

'OK, what?' Brian gave in first.

'Brace yourselves....'

'Oh no. It's not black and white is it?' Shauna jumped in.

'No, nothing that bad.' Cagney winked at Lacey who was connecting some wires at the back of the TV.

'Maybe there's no sound!' Berni said joining in.

'Nope. Any more guesses?'

'Subtitles maybe or snow on the screen?'

'No Barry. Well, hopefully neither, though there are no guarantees. Andy? Last chance saloon.'

'Well, I was thinkin' maybe it's not about the picture or the sound, maybe it's more to do with choice. Could it be that there are only 3 channels like there were back in the day?'

'Bingo! We have ourselves a winner!'

Just as Shauna was about to explode with fury, the serious tones of the Prime Minister invaded the air space and all fell silent. The picture flickered, which added to the heightened tension. Suddenly, it had all become real.

(Team Alpha & Team Beta – MI6 HQ)

The Prime Minister's speech was long and quite dull. The PM did manage to keep a modicum of sincerity, but the pained expression on her face suggested more deep-rooted problems. Issues with our European friends and our 'special relationship' with America were of great concern to the politicians. The Queen and the royal family were 'sympathetic' to the problems that everyone would face, but we were reminded that the security and safety of our nation were paramount. After all, we had survived two world wars, how bad could it be. In essence, the Prime Minister recapped the information that the Inspector had already imparted. She did add, that there would also be some 'serious problems' with travelling. Planes and trains relied upon the Cloud for their timetabling and airspace planning. There could be mass disruption. Life without both the internet and social media would revert to the way it had been before. Letters, landlines and telegrams would replace emails and Smart Phones. Online shopping would no longer exist and local shops and supermarkets would now be called upon to fill this void. Photographs would now have to be printed as hard copy and become hand-held commodities once again. Banks would now reopen and pop-up banks would be available as online banking was no longer an option. Life would resume at a slower pace. The Prime Minister stressed that the safety of the country came first and once the threat had been eliminated then the internet would be restored.

'Bollocks.' Shauna stated predictably. 'Nowt there we didn't already know.'

'I'm quite glad we're in here.' Brian said quietly. 'We've already had time to get used to this weird existence and adapt to losing all those things already.'

'That really is a splendid way of looking at things Brian. You're absolutely right. In a way, we're ahead of the game.'

'It's still bollocks. Everything's changing and we're still stuck in this shit-hole.'

'But just think Shauna, it's affecting everything! Trains, planes, banks, the food supply, the Stock Exchange…'

'And of course, no Instagram or Facebook. I'd rather be in my own place. I'd just like to fuck off home.'

'Well you can't, she won't let you. No chance. You heard what she said, the Inspector?' Andy added, whilst wheeling Berni toward the door and handing her over to Lacey.

'Toodle pip everyone. I need my beauty sleep. They hook me up to a drip at night. I don't know what's in it, but I sleep like a baby.'

'Really?' Shauna became interested for all the wrong reasons. 'I wonder what…'

'Shauna! In the name of all that's holy!'

'I'm fuckin' jokin' Andy! Loosen up a bit.'

'Nite Berni. Sleep well.' I intervened, reminding them that Berni was the important one here.

'I'll be back in the morning to meet Gavin. Rather a strange chap I expect, we may have to be a little bit careful...' Berni said thoughtfully as she was being pushed through the doorway.

'Right you lot. A bit of homework before you retire to bed. There will be a late supper at nine o'clock and then you will turn in for the night.' Cagney said firmly.

'Steady on there Cagney. We are volunteers after all.' Barry said in a measured tone.

'Yeah, what about our bleedin' human rights! The lack of *our* freedom and *our* speech. No contact allowed with the outside world. We can't talk to family or friends! Surely there's some law against this continuous imprisonment and questioning and while we're at it...'

'Oh Come on Shauna, less of the dramatics.'

'Hang on there a minute Cagney, she's got a point there has Shauna.' Everyone nodded in silent agreement with Andy.

'To be fair, we have complied willingly up to now. Maybe we just need a little TLC.' Cagney's normally pleasant expression turned to blue thunder, I already regretted opening my mouth.

'TLC! This is a matter of National Security, for God's sake! There is more at stake here than your freedom to call home and 'chat' with friends. We are hoping that somewhere in your collective memories are the keys to unlocking the glitch in *Watcher 22*. We're not here to pamper you, this isn't a spa! As it happens you have been staying in our best suite of rooms and great consideration has been taken to accommodate your needs and support your welfare!'

Cagney went quiet as he shook his head in despair. We all glanced at each other and grimaced uncomfortably, like small children in the classroom.

'Shit. Sorry, Cagney. We just lose our fuckin'
perspective locked up in here.' Everyone muttered their
apologies sheepishly.

'All right, All right. Enough. There is just one point
I would like to make perfectly clear. By law, we can hold
you for 14 days under the Terrorism Act without having
to answer to anyone. However...' he paused, putting his
flat palms up at shoulder height to calm us. 'in your
situation that is unnecessary as we are detaining you
under house arrest – partly for your own safety. You are
a valuable commodity to our enemies, they will know,
just as we do, that your experiences are crucial to
understanding the program. Make no mistake, this is
the safest place for each and every one of you right now.
There is, of course, low key surveillance on your homes
and closest family members. However, it is so chaotic
out there with communication, travel and network links
seriously affected, tracking anybody would be nigh on
impossible. The roads are gridlocked due to the
cancellation of trains and as Internet banking no longer
works the queues in the banks are unprecedented. BT
are frantically installing land-lines and the demand for
house phones has rocketed. The world as you knew it
no longer exists. It's almost as though we have travelled
back to the 1960s.' he paused.

'That's before I was born.' Shauna said quietly.

'And me.' Brian added.

'We were just infants,' Barry added tactfully.

Cagney seemed spent. 'Me too. There was one thing
which I wanted to mention, as it was so strange.'
Cagney paused. 'On my way into work yesterday. I was
following an open back transit van which had a very
unusual cargo.'

'Rhinoceroses! On the way to Noah's Ark as the world's gone mad?' Shauna asked gleefully.

Cagney shot her a telling look.

'Please tell us, Cagney. We're not all crazy.' I asked gently.

'OK then. The cargo was unexpected; eight brand new, shiny, red phone boxes. Can you believe it?'

'Why would you need those? We just used to use them as...'

'Yes Brian, we are all aware of what they were used for back in the day. Hopefully, that will change in the present circumstances and people will use them for making phone calls instead of as public toilets or a place to meet young ladies. They will be vital for emergencies.'

'It's like going back to the war years! We'll all be digging for victory and raising chickens next!'

'The situation is certainly critical Andy, there's no denying it. We're dependent on road transport for food deliveries. There is a curfew on the roads at night so that the lorries can use the motorways and get their deliveries through to the supermarkets. Due to the lack of trains, everyone is having to use their cars. Fuel is also restricted due to the sharp increase in demand. The priority is to keep the country safe and to keep people working. That way we can feed everyone and keep the power on.' Cagney was interrupted as his watch made a sharp beeping sound. It was an alarm reminder, now there weren't any mobile phones to use.

'Right you lot. You've distracted me enough. Please help me out now and sit down and take a notebook and pencil each. This is what we have to use for now, for security reasons.'

We all took a seat after grabbing a bottle of water each from the side table.

'Names on the front please and just so you understand, the books may be seen by anyone, so use them appropriately. No good bringing the Chief down to show him something and finding a giant cock drawn inside the front cover.' he said glaring at Shauna who smiled straight back at him.

'The notebooks are provided for you to record events and ideas on an individual basis. Due to the unknown capacity of *Watcher 22*, we need to analyse some of the last visits carefully. Each one of you will have a different version of the same event. It is vitally important for us to gather as much information as we can from each of you. It may be that the tiniest detail that one of you remembers that is crucial in helping us to understand the way the program works.'

'We'll do our best.' I reassured him as he looked quite stressed.

'Please hurry along, before supper arrives. I put my neck on the line having that last conversation.'

'And we thank you and will do our utmost to complete our accounts of the events as requested.' Barry said fairly.

'Fair dos. We'll all do our bit. 'Andy adding reassuringly.

'It was really interesting to hear about the outside world. Thank you Cagney,' I said carefully.

'Jesus Jones! He's not the bleedin' Messiah!' Shauna blurted out loudly. The group rounded on her. 'But to be fair Cagney you showed that you're human and we do need to know what's goin' on so if you need a blow...'

'Shauna. Enough!'

'Oh dear, Barry. That was a little premature.' Shauna laughed impishly. 'I was going to say if Cagney needed a blow by blow account of events, I'm your girl!'

Cagney hid his smile with his hand, as the rest of us concealed our laughter, Even Barry admitted defeat and gave a little snort before returning to his notebook. The air had been cleared and Shauna had thoroughly enjoyed being centre stage once again.

(Team Alpha & Team Beta – MI6 HQ)

Berni woke us gently. She was the nicest alarm clock anyone could wish for. I was already awake and wondering how things were back at home and how Charlie was getting along and more to the point how many times he'd eaten tinned soup or had a chippy tea. My daughters have long since grown up and moved away from home. They are no longer as dependent on me as they once were and would understand the situation I found myself in. I missed chatting to them, their enthusiasm for life is infectious. Shauna delivered one of her famous yawn/snores on queue and Berni and I laughed. A sure-fire way to awaken her.

'Would you two just feck off! Just leave me alone to wake up. What's the soddin' time?'

'It's better that you don't know.' Berni said quietly. 'Apparently, there have been some 'serious developments' and we're making an early start.'

Lacey banged on the door. 'Ten minutes ladies please, chop-chop.'

'The situation is now so serious that instructions have come down from on high.'

'Well, unless you mean from God, they can just... '

'Yes, we know. They can just feck off.' Berni said laughing. 'It may interest you to know that Cagney said he has easy access to jugs of cold water with ice cubes, should it be deemed necessary. I would be happy to administer them as would Helena.'

'Ugh. Really Berni. You must be...' Shauna was interrupted by more banging on the door.

'Five minutes ladies!'

After much protesting, we were finally all seated around the table, some with damper hair than others. Shauna yawned loudly, with no attempt to disguise it. Even Brian looked sleepy-eyed and weary. A nurse came in and took Berni's wheelchair back to sickbay.

'Erm, hang about there nurse. 'Andy said loudly. 'How's Berni meant to get back to her bed?'

The nurse half turned her head, 'I'm just following instructions.' she stated flatly. Berni winked at Andy and smiled one of her half excited smiles.

'I think that Bernadette knows a little more than we do, about what we can expect.'

Before Berni could respond the door clicked shut and the Inspector bounded in. She seemed less harassed and eager to share her news.

'Right everyone, listen up. There have been some developments and I can, at last, give you some good news. As you all worked so hard last night, the powers that be have decided you can have a two-night pass.' she paused for effect, looking around for some recognition or maybe even some thanks.

'A pass? What like a night club pass?' Shauna asked carefully.

'I think the Inspector is telling us that we can go home.'

'Thank you, Barry. That's correct. But just for two nights. And before you say it Andy, we know that you have the furthest to travel and we can't exactly conjure up a Jump Jet to whizz you back to Cardiff. Although this is only a two-night pass, it is actually a 3-day release. Hence the early start. I'd make the best of it if I were you. It may be a while until we let you go again. The techie guys are working on the program, High Command is working on strategies to keep all our agents secure and the country is creaking slowly back into action. You all deserve a break and we don't want to hold you for any longer than necessary. You will have to sign the documentation to agree to return and you *really* must return. Each one of you is a key player in cracking this thing wide open. I have trusted you all and am personally vouching for your reliability and loyalty. I fully expect each one of you to do the right thing. Should one of you fail to return, then the others will suffer the consequences. Do I make myself crystal clear?'

We all nodded.

'Why is everyone looking at me?' Shauna said, her cheeks beginning to glow in annoyance.

'I wouldn't let the team down if that's what your soddin' well thinking.' Andy winked at her and Barry patted her reassuringly on the shoulder.

'Of course, not Shauna. No one in this group would ever jeopardise national security or their team members, especially considering what we've already been through.' Barry said somewhat ironically considering the choices he will have to face.

'No Sir.' Brian said saluting uncharacteristically. Someone was excited about going home.

'Anyone wishing to stay here would be more than welcome.' A quizzical frown of disbelief seemed to pass from person to person.

'Are you insane?' I asked, wearing the aforementioned frown. 'Really? Do you think that our lives are so dull, that we'd prefer to forgo all our freedom and be locked up at night like criminals?'

The Inspector winced a little.

'You must think we're fuckin' saddos if …'

'Shauna.' Barry said firmly. 'I think we should focus on the fact that we *are* being given a pass home, which I have no doubt was a hard-fought struggle.' he stared at Shauna, willing her to be quiet.

'That's right.' I picked up the reins. 'Thank you, Inspector. As we don't have any belongings to pack, we are ready when you are.' The door once again clicked open. Lacey went over and held it open and the Inspector waved us through and we were escorted out. There was an air of eager anticipation at the thought of returning to our loved ones.

'I wonder what we'll find when we go out there?' Andy asked hesitantly.

'I know what you mean Andy. It's only been a matter of days, but the world has changed. Last time, when we came out of *XP*, we had changed. Now it will be the other way around.'

'I agree with you Helena. This has been an unprecedented turn of events. I suspect that we are in for quite a surprise.'

'Bet the teenagers are pissed off! Most of them had mobile phones given them in their cots.' Andy said smiling.

'Well, at least we'll have videos to watch and the old style, dial phones back. I rather liked those…'

'No internet. No buying online or downloads or social media..'

'What! No friggin' Facebook? No email, no texts. How the bloody hell are we supposed to communicate?'

'Well, you can write letters and make phone calls and there will probably be a few channels working on the TV – if the TV works at all.' I said quietly.

'Wait a feckin' minute! That won't work! It's all too bleedin' slow. We're used to instant messaging...'

'Shauna, we all survived perfectly well before the internet. Life may seem just a little slower, a bit less intense than you are used to. Who knows, you may even get to like it. ' Barry said slowly, flashing one of his rare smiles at her. 'And there are things such as shops.'

'Bollocks! I'll hate it. You all know I'll hate it! I don't know how we're meant to get in touch with anyone, sort out when to meet up and find out what's going on.'

'You simply arrange to meet your friends and then go to the cinema or pub or whatever you decide and then before you leave, you plan the next get together. Everyone knows that they have to turn up or telephone to cancel. '

Shauna stared at Berni. The whole idea seemed to paralyse her and as we entered the glass lift she continued to shake her head.'

'You'll get used to it Shauna. We all will. Anyway, it's not like there's a choice.'

'I'm glad we're going out there now.' Brian said thoughtfully. 'We need to reconnect and see how our world is changing. Otherwise, we would struggle to cope when we are eventually released.'

'You're makin' it sound like we're prisoners, out on a bleedin' weekend pass.'

'In a way, you are right Shauna. It may serve you well to remember that, while you are 'visiting' your home.'

'Look, we just need to make the most of it and enjoy our new found freedom – even if it is only for a few days. I'm just glad that Berni is well enough to go home.'

Berni smiled and patted my arm.

'Will you go out dancing Shauna, tripping the light fantastic?' Berni said almost wistfully. Barry gave Shauna the patriarchal stare and Andy nodded over at her to join in and play along.

'Oh er yes Berni. I'll be sure to get my dancing shoes on and boogie on down.' Shauna said somewhat woodenly.

'How lovely.' Berni said smiling. And then the weirdest thing happened. The light flickered in the lift and it seemed to slow down as if everything was in slow motion. Then I heard it, the music. The strains of '*Yes Sir I can boogie*.' by Baccara filled the lift and I could tell that everyone could hear it, even Cagney and Lacey. It was over in a moment and the world returned to normal. Shauna nudged my elbow.

'Someone's back!' she said knowingly. Andy just smiled at me and Barry shook his head in despair. Brian gave way to a concealed chuckle as he came out of the lift. We made our way toward the sliding glass doors. The black BMW's were waiting for us and we were hurriedly bundled into the cars. Shauna and Berni accompanied me, Barry and Brian went together and Andy had been provided with his own car. I looked out of the back window at the massive glass building and at Cagney and Lacey who were still outside. I started laughing uncontrollably.

'What the feck?' Shauna said and then followed my gaze. She elbowed Berni, who carefully manoeuvred herself so she could see. And then came the icing on the cake. Flint had surpassed himself. The speakers in the armrests came to life again. Cagney and Lacey could obviously hear Flint's music and were boogying together. Even the cars slowed down as we passed and the driver chuckled to himself. It was hilarious and gave us all a much-needed boost at the start of the long journey home.

I awoke in a state of confusion. It had been a long journey home as the traffic had been congested due to the challenges with public transport. Charlie and I had stayed up until the early hours of the morning, catching up on all the latest news. It was great to be back and Charlie had missed me. But the combination of suddenly being at home and Flint being reinstated had thrown me out of kilter. I should probably report Flint's resurrection to someone, but Cagney and Lacey had both been party to it and so far today I hadn't had the pleasure of hearing any of Flint's cryptic comments. The faint smell of coffee and toast prompted me to shower and go downstairs.

'Have you seen the 'new' phone?' Charlie asked me, as he indicated toward it with his head. And there it was, on the glass coffee table. A black Bakelite phone complete with a dial, which I immediately had to get my hands on.

'Wow!' I said, as waves of nostalgia coursed through me. I picked up the receiver to hear the familiar buzz of the dialling tone. I held down the two switch hooks so that I could use the dial without actually making a call. It felt both familiar and weird, at the same time. The curly black wire, the phone's umbilicus, which I automatically hook around my fingers without even thinking. This symbolised the start of the new restrictions. A mobile phone it certainly wasn't and I had a whole host of memories about trying to have a private conversation, whilst my family watched TV. Phones were definitely not mobile back in the day and if they were situated in the front room then it became more of a family phone call than a private one. Across the country, it had surely been the cause of many, many rows. If you moved even a few feet, then you took the phone along with you and even then you could only go as far as the phone wire would stretch. I could imagine the horror felt by many teenagers who had been brought up with the freedom to take a call anywhere they liked, away from the prying ears of anxious parents. I picked up the receiver again, testing its weight, it felt huge and cumbersome. And then I remembered that you could prop the receiver to your ear with your shoulder and free up both hands. But it was the dial that I played with the most. I could visualise Shauna's disgust as she struggled with the slow and clunky old phones from the past. It made me laugh out loud.

'Something amusing you Helena?' Charlie asked while bringing in the coffee.

'I'm just imagining the look on Shauna's face when she's faced with this old beast.' I said, placing the phone back on the coffee table.

'Well, we're lucky to have one. They are standard issue, but they soon ran out.'

'I see and only available in black?'

'Yep. Some people managed to get the old recondi-tioned models in a variety of colours, but this is one of the new lines which the government had the foresight to churn out en masse.'

'Quite an operation, as you say.'

'Especially with the transport problems we've been having. Trains are offering a limited local service now that a basic timetable has been agreed upon. There's no internet or email and mobile banks have had to be introduced, but they soon run out of cash. As you'd expect there are food and petrol shortages. We're not quite at the rationing stage, but we have been warned that it hasn't been ruled out. At least the power is still on, for now at least. These are desperate times. The infrastructure has taken a battering and the government is on high alert due to the terrorist threat and the massive fall out from hitting the kill switch. Few planes can fly and the roads are only open during the day and are chock-a-block as you probably noticed. There is a curfew at night on all roads and motorways to ensure that the lorries can transport food. You will have been given special permits to travel here and back. It's improving, but there are still many shortages.'

'Wow, it sounds like everything has changed so quickly! Do we have TV?'

'There is a limited service. To be honest there has been so much to do and everything takes so much longer, that I have only really been watching the news when I can. One good thing though...' Charlie smiles and paused for effect.

'Yes?'

'Well, football matches are no longer available on TV. The government decided that it wasn't really a necessity...'

'Which it isn't.'

'And so the tickets have been set with fixed prices by the Government, depending on which league the team is in.'

'That is amazing. Some of the foreign owners and Sport's channels must have lost millions!'

'Shame!!!' we both said together.

'Well, that's one benefit then, for footy fans at least.'

'But what about the food shortages and petrol restrictions, how are they affecting the elderly and the sick?'

'It was awful at first. As you can imagine there was mass panic and the strongest and richest pushed forward. But then it was odd how it happened, I can't remember exactly when it happened…' Charlie paused, deep in thought. 'Anyway. People started pulling together, actually talking to each other. Checking on neighbours, sharing news and advice and generally becoming more caring about other people and the community.'

'That's just so unexpected. And in such a short space of time.'

'To be honest I think that some of it was caused by boredom in the first instance…'

'Charlie! That's not a very nice thing to say.'

'Hear me out, Helena. I said in the first instance. When all the phones went off, the TV went down and the Internet was effectively switched off, everyone seemed to go into a state of shock. I think they were just stunned. We had all got so used to instant messaging, social media, online banking and shopping, vast choices of entertainment and music to choose from. We were our own Directors of TV and communication, controllers of so many things that have now been removed altogether.'

'I expect that the young ones, who were born with everything quite literally at their fingertips, felt it the hardest.'

'Initially, there were some protests, I wouldn't call them riots. I think it was a knee jerk reaction to what happened. They knew it wouldn't change anything but just wanted to have a voice of some kind. After all, the technology that they've relied so heavily on was taken without warning.'

'I suppose we're quite lucky, being able to remember life before the internet and the slower pace. We had more trouble adapting the other way around, having to speed up and trying to keep up as things changed so quickly.'

'Well not only are the brakes on, but we're now going in reverse.'

'You're right. Has there been any word about switching it all back on?'

'You probably know more than I do on that one.' Charlie said swigging his coffee, eyeing me closely.

'You must be joking. We knew it was going off and why, but no more than that. I don't think they'll be able to resolve all the issues and make things safe very quickly. There seems to be an awful lot to sort out. Serious things, way beyond my pay grade.'

'Aw well. It was worth asking. And while we're at it, how long will you be home for exactly?'

'Didn't they tell you?'

'No.' Charlie scoffed. 'We commoners are not privy to such details.'

'Charlie, we're only there because of...'

'You can say it. Because of *Watcher 22*. I do remember. It was in the newspaper for God's sake, hardly top secret.'

'You don't need to be like that about it. It's not as if I have any choice in the matter.'

Charlie shrugged and was about to speak when the doorbell rang.

'That will be the postie.'

'Really?'

'Yeah. There are four or five deliveries a day now and if there's anything larger than the normal letter the postie rings the bell.'

'Wow! I like it.'

'Helena! You need to come and sign for this.'

'For me? Really?' I said excitedly moving past Charlie to the open door. Sure enough, there was a postie in full uniform proffering a pen and indicating where to sign.

'Is this a telegram? I asked, now genuinely excited. The postie nodded and half-smiled as if I was challenged in some way. He tipped his cap and I closed the door.

'Wow! A telegram!! I've not had one since I moved down to Bristol and Jamie sent me one when I'd found a flat to rent in 1982.' I paused before shaking away the memory.

'They brought back Telegrams so that urgent messages could be sent, as we now have to rely on letters and phone calls to communicate.' Charlie added, obviously enjoying his advisory role. I suddenly felt a wave of sympathy for him as he'd got the shitty end of the stick. Adapting to the changes and uncertainties on his own. I was in a strange place, but I had the team to lean on and we all helped each other.

'I'm sorry I wasn't here Charlie. I really am. I *have* missed you and it's been bloody awful not being able to contact you...' but before I could finish. Charlie looked into my eyes with a hard glare.

'Well, you seem to be doing alright at being contacted now. You've only been back for one night and like everything else, even this is for you.'

I hadn't expected it to be like this, perhaps I had been a little naive. I sighed deeply. My eyes glanced down at the telegram and somehow I wasn't surprised by the name of the sender.

I smiled for the briefest moment. Flint was definitely stepping up his game. I felt it was only a matter of time before the running commentary returned. There was a faint crackle, suggesting he was getting closer to making verbal contact. Charlie banged around in the kitchen, his irritation being taken out on the dishes.

'Who's it from then?' he asked somewhat brusquely.

'I think it's from Shauna.' I shouted back. 'I'm just so surprised it got here so quickly!'

'Yep. The Post Office and the Sorting Office have taken on a lot of staff and volunteers. They're working pretty much around the clock to cope with demand. Also, public phone boxes have been reinstated to ensure that everyone has access to a phone line in their local area. This has meant a lot of work as many people used mobile phones and stopped having landline connections. The Military Reserves have been called upon to assist with the installation and also to protect the transportation of food and medical supplies. The police have been focusing on riot control and unrest in the communities and have also called upon the community support officers and the Neighbourhood Watch Network. It may seem calm here in the burbs but don't be fooled, there is no area of society unaffected and as we well know where money and finance are concerned, things can get ugly. The Benefits Agency has had to revert to the old system of sending out cheques as has the department of state pensions. Hence the importance of the post, as once received the cheques have to be cashed somewhere. As a high percentage of banks and Post Offices have closed, pop-up banks have been introduced, but the queues are very long. Banks have asked newly retired staff to return and help out. God knows how the Stock Exchange is coping, but we are assured in the nightly Government bulletin, that a contingency plan is in place We think there may be power cuts soon, just like those we had in the 1970s, but there's been no confirmation so far.'

'The pace of life has slowed, as we thought it would have to. No one knew this was going to happen and none of us had a choice. It just shows how changes in technology have affected so many aspects of everyday life. It's almost as if everything was going too fast and now the world needs to slow back down again. It's hard enough for us oldies to, adapt, but the youngsters who have never known anything else must be really stunned and maybe a little lost.'

'Yeah, the grown-ups are coping quite well, as are the older generation. We all have to adapt and change and now it's the turn of the younger generation. Anyway, why should the spotlight always be on them? They have done the least to deserve it, as they have had the least experience of life. The balance had swung too much in their favour and everything revolves around them. It's about bloody time that *we* have some input and the older generation commanded a little more respect. That's what I think anyway.' Charlie said heatedly.

'You've clearly had the time to give this some proper thought.' I said slowly. 'I tend to agree with you. I know the young are enthusiastic and full of life, but the attention they received is unjustified, the balance has swung too much their way. Maybe now some of the social pressure will be removed and they can just concentrate on being kids and playing out.'

'It's the boredom that's getting to them. They're just not used to it.'

'Boredom's good for you. We didn't even think about being bored! Too busy making our own fun, including keeping away from adults. Perhaps the youngsters will learn to play as groups once again and not rely on parents or the computer to provide their entertainment. Boredom pushes you to dig deep and motivates you to invent your own games and adventures.'

'It is a period of adjustment I guess. After all, a lot of young people don't remember a world without phones, home computers, Netflix and online streaming etc.'

'Born with a mobile phone in hand and ready to text on arrival.' I said laughing.

Charlie grunted his approval.

'It is damned inconvenient though. Everything takes so long and the curfew at night is very restrictive.' Charlie paused. 'Is all this really necessary? I mean switching the internet off. Was there no alternative?' Charlie asked, turning around from the sink to pose his question.

'No. As far as I know, there was no choice. The only explanation we were given was that we needed to protect national security and our agents in the field at all costs.'

Charlie muttered his agreement as he continued to slam the mugs onto the drainer. I took this opportunity to open the Telegram and I was right, it was from Shauna. She was feeling a little lost and unhappy. The way she'd coped with life before had involved a strong dependency on a support network, where contact was instant and reliable. This was no longer available, certainly not instantly. The new restrictions had thrown everything into turmoil and as our group has been out of the picture, we had not had the chance to adapt. Shauna was finding the change very challenging and felt that her support network had collapsed while we were away at MI6. We hadn't had the time or the opportunity to consider how hitting the kill switch would affect our everyday life. We had been too busy trying to help the Inspector and there was little choice in the matter.

Eventually, Charlie sat with me at the kitchen table and I told him the basics. We had been given a brief in the car on the way home, listing explicitly what we could and could not say. I followed it to the letter. I wasn't going to risk breaking the Official Secrets Act or putting any of our agents at risk. I then explained Shauna's feelings of despair and isolation.

'What are you saying Helena? We get a two-night pass and God knows how long it will be until I hear from you or see you again! You have just spent every waking minute with that group of yours, doing God knows what and then when you do finally descend on me, I don't get you to myself? Is that it?' Charlie moved towards the door, ready to do a bolt as he always did after he became angry. It was a good tactic and prevented things from getting out of hand.

'Actually, you've jumped the gun.' I said glaring at him. 'If you had waited I would have told you. Shauna is going back to HQ. She feels uncomfortable in this new world and needs time to adjust. Cagney and Lacey have cleared it with the Inspector and there's plenty she can do until we return.'

'Good.' Charlie said snappily. I sidled over to him, putting my arms around his waist and rubbing his back. The tension seemed to leave his body.

'Okay okay. I get it. Just one thing though, Cagney and Lacey? What the hell is that about? I hope they're not using Mary Beth and Christine's names in vain. Do they look like them, is that it?'

I laughed to myself. 'Not exactly Charlie. They're men. It's just to protect their identity. I don't think they had much choice in the matter.'

I manoeuvred Charlie into the front room and things began to feel a little more normal. We worked out our finances. I had been assured that I was being remunerated whilst I worked for the Government. Charlie was reassured, but obviously, we couldn't check the accounts as there wasn't any internet banking. We ploughed through the paperwork and then walked over to my parents' house. The outside world looked the same. There were noticeably more children playing out on the streets than there had been before. There seemed a little more outdoor activity and more people were out walking, very few cars passed us.

'Even for me it's quite strange not having a mobile phone in my bag, and I didn't use it that often. I can imagine it feels quite isolating for youngsters. Charlie pulled me back from the kerb as a group of young cyclists whizzed by, some riding with no hands and whooping with delight. Their enthusiasm was infectious and Charlie and I laughed at their antics. We took a short cut over the fields and it was lovely to see the multicoloured kites darting along the skyline.

'Is there anything else you've noticed?' Charlie asked smiling. I stopped for a moment. Of course, it was very quiet. People were saving petrol for emergency journeys and work, so the roads were practically clear.

'Fewer cars? More red phone boxes? More posties out delivering mail?'

'That's obvious.' he said in his mocking tone. 'I suppose you want a clue?' I nodded reluctantly and pursed my mouth in annoyance. I didn't like help. Charlie tipped back his head and looked toward the sky.

'Oh my God"!' I cried out. 'Of course. There aren't any planes!!' We didn't live under a flight path, but we were only eight miles from the airport and used to the regular drone of the planes overhead and the white streams of jet wash that criss-crossed the sky. Now the sky was perfectly blue and unblemished. But it was the lack of engine noise from either car or plane which made the most difference. The only time that I had encountered this before was when volcanic ash had been ejected during the 2010 eruptions of Eyjafjallajökull in Iceland. The ash could damage aircraft engines and the controlled airspace of many European countries was closed, resulting in the largest air traffic shutdown since World War II. There had once been a very bad winter when frozen snow and ice meant that cars were frozen onto their drives and roads were deserted. I loved it then and I love it now. Despite all the inconvenience, I felt a sense of freedom and excitement. I was sure that the novelty would soon wear off and I hadn't had to live with these changes as yet.

On arrival at my parent's bungalow, I could tell that life went on pretty much as it had before. Although my parents could both use computers and mum was a dab hand at texting, they still did the crossword, listened to music and could occupy themselves quite easily. Dad enjoyed his evening pint and took mum out twice a week and mum enjoyed her classes and keep fit. They had balance in their lives and the new restrictions were simply accepted and life carried on as normal. There was no panic and no drama, just adaptation and a sense of calm. They had lived quite comfortably without technology and had great coping skills which they'd learned in less affluent times.

I received a warm welcome and tea and biscuits. It was reassuring to be somewhere so untouched by the changes. Mum and I discussed how we missed contact with my girls, who had long since fled the nest. Skype, texts and emails had been a brilliant way of keeping in touch. Charlie and Dad discussed the football and the availability of match tickets now that the games were no longer televised. It was a lovely afternoon. After hugs and kisses, Charlie and I set off on our journey home as the light began to fade. It was quite eerie not having to watch the road for cars or have the peace interrupted by an Emirates jet slicing across the sky. This was a new world and I wanted to experience more of it before I had to return, before they switched it all back on.

Life was ticking along at a much slower pace and I liked it. However, the transport issues and curfew were slightly less appealing. It was always easier to cope with these kinds of changes if you didn't have to hold down a job. I knew that my time at home was limited and I was determined to make the most of it. Charlie and I made a meal together and sat down at the table waiting to watch the six o'clock news on the BBC. There was no longer a dedicated news channel. It was yet another blast from the past and the news was shown daily at 6 o'clock and 9 o'clock – but at least it wasn't in black and white! It was noticeable that world issues, which once dominated the News programmes, now took a back seat. The emphasis was on domestic stories and reports that were important to everyone here at home and benefited both viewers and citizens alike. Any news of great international importance was included, but announced towards the end of the programme and not in such depth. The lack of live feed and recent photographs to illustrate the news stories was very noticeable and meant that the camera stayed focused on the news reporter. Occasionally some old, archived footage was retrieved. The lack of flickering images meant that you had to concentrate more and it somehow seemed more intense and serious. It reminded me of how bored I had been as a child when my parents watched the news after tea and then proceeded to sleep through most of it. As an adult, watching a similarly stilted program, I could now understand and yawned accordingly.

The main stories focused on political unrest and widespread criticism about the kill switch being used here at home. The end of the programme focused on the after-effects of flicking the kill switch and the impact it was having on the economy. The infrastructure had taken a battering. It was too early to accurately gauge the impact that all this was having on the Exchange Rate and Stock Market as the market was volatile. The screen then flickered and the picture changed to a pre-recorded report, showing the queues of people waiting outside banks and building societies. The reporter was reassuring everyone that although customers may have to wait a 'little longer' for service, all types of accounts including mortgages, savings, credit cards and loans were safe and intact.

'Bank balances are perfectly safe and won't be wiped out.' A bank representative in a traditional navy pinstripe suit assured us. He went on to inform us that High-Frequency Trading continued, due to the fact they were not reliant on internet lines but secure, physically unique lines. It all sounded complicated, but we at least our bank accounts were secure and had not been breached, which was a great relief. Finally, there was a report from one of those social behaviour analysts who wore a concerned look and an ill-fitting cardigan. The analyst looked quite weary but seemed determined to get her point across. She made some interesting observations, pointing out that people can be addicted to the 'gifts' of the internet and its' 'constant stimulus input'. She pointed out that when the internet was removed, addicts just switched to another addiction, such as sex or gambling, which are both available offline. The report then switched to the problems faced by people who were now being forced to 'withdraw' from Facebook and Instagram and how they needed to find other ways of discovering self-worth. I could sense Charlie's irritation. He had never opened a Facebook account and was not interested in social media. He only used the internet for online banking, researching travel and booking holidays.

'Don't know what all the bloody fuss is about!' he said impatiently. He would normally have switched over to a sports channel by now, but that was no longer an option. 'It'll do them good, having to talk to each other and make their own fun. We had to do it and we survived!'

I raised my eyebrows and looked at Charlie with my 'show some compassion face.'

'I suppose they just need to get used to it. It's been a shock for everyone, if you've never known any different it must be hard to adapt.'

'They just need to get on with it. Simple as! Too spoilt, the lot of them. Well, they'll just have to get on with it now and there's no need for this crappy psychobabble. Next thing you know, we'll all be in therapy.'

'I suppose that some people will cope better than others.'

The analyst continued, pointing out that the Net was meant to have made us all more sociable, but the reverse has happened. It has provided 'automated acquaintanceship' and 'tool sets for real-time self-invention.'

'What the fu...'

'I think she means that no one audits Facebook or My Space so basically you can just invent yourself as no one will check if you're telling the truth or not.'

'Right. Well, we all saw that one coming.' he said nodding his head. The analyst then told us that our capacity for intimacy and human interaction had 'atrophied.'

'Wow! That's a bit strong. I mean not all of us are glued to computers and phones all day!' I said defensively.

'She's bang on the money. Let's just hear her final comment.'

She summed up by telling us that we would have to rebuild social cooperation using the time 'released' by not going on the Internet, to spend with family and friends.

'That's bloody obvious! They should all have been doing that in the first place. Too soft that's the problem. This will toughen them up a bit and make them look for other ways of entertaining themselves.'

'I agree with you on that point. I think interaction has been massively affected by the rise of social media. Young people have been isolated in their bedrooms, playing games on their own or talking to God knows who online.' I shuddered at the thought.

The TV again caught my eye as a rather famous film critic was having the time of his life. The critic was one of Charlie's favourites, despite his upper class twang and strange hairstyle. Marc, yes that is his name, was outlining the fall of celebrity status and couldn't look more delighted about it. He spoke about 'machine-made fame' and 'centripetal attention structures' that bottle celebrity. We both nodded in agreement, we had spoken about this particular topic many times. No one minds if someone has a talent and is adored and followed in appreciation of that talent. But to create celebrity through TV exposure and manipulation may distort the talent pool and creates somewhat hollow stars. The counter-argument focused on magazines which had existed before the rise of the internet. Marc pointed out that magazines have to be purchased which ensures pre-selection. However, TV and the internet are not filtered by price in the same way and their audience is enormous.

'He's right.' Charlie said firmly.

'I agree. I wonder what will happen if the internet remains switched off for a long period. Do you think the 'glamour models' and reality TV presenters will start going on tour and filling the arenas?'

'Nope. You would have to have a real talent to fill an arena. More like a five minute slot introducing a football game or a big concert perhaps. Or switching on the Blackpool lights or opening supermarkets. Nothing more than that. If it goes on for longer the 'celebrity' may become obsolete and people won't know who they are.'

'I think you're right and I don't think it will take people too long to forget them either.'

'At least there are some positives to come out of this situation.'

Charlie went to switch the TV off and was muttering about going to the pub and meeting some friends before we 'atrophied.' I laughed and nodded in agreement. I was going to make the best of this newfound freedom away from MI6 and all that shenanigans.

'We need to sharpen up our tool-sets for some 'real-time self-invention'. I added. Charlie threw a cushion at me and went to get his coat. I heard him muttering something that sounded like 'load of bollocks' to himself and secretly I agreed, but for now I kept it to myself.

I drifted back to consciousness, wondering what on earth Flint was up to. Charlie was already up and at it. My fuzzy head was the product of quite a few drinks in the local pub. It had been a welcome night out and it was lovely to enjoy the familiarity of home and be back in my own bed. I stretched out and enjoyed the luxury of not having to get up. I began to wonder how everyone else was doing, especially Shauna. I stopped myself as I was determined to enjoy my time with Charlie, no one knew when we would be able to come home again.

'Rise and shine sleepy head.' Charlie said, throwing a damp towel at my head.

'Lovely.' I muttered before delicately making my way to the bathroom.

'Coffee and croissants?' he asked.

'Of course my dear.' I answered before diving into the hot blast of the shower.

I realised just how much I had missed Charlie and the comforts of home. I blow-dried my hair, did my make-up and made my way carefully down the stairs. My head throbbing slightly after a night on the booze. We ate breakfast in the conservatory, the weather was cold but clear and the occasional shaft of sunlight lit up the room. I felt at peace and just wanted to stay here, where I belonged.

'Are you phoning the girls today?' Charlie asked whilst brushing flakes of croissant from his chin.

'Yep. I thought I'd phone them this morning or what's left of it.'

'Well make sure you do, I mean phone this morning, as it's almost dinnertime now. We're going out at 4 o'clock.'

'Are we? And where might we be going?'

'To the pictures, you're always saying we don't go enough. And now they have way more screenings per day, due to shite TV. I managed to get us tickets, as a surprise.' Charlie looked across at me. 'What's up? Don't you want to go?' he asked, looking hurt.

'No. NO, of course I do! I always do. It's just....' I paused not wanting to ruin Charlie's surprise. 'I love the pictures! It's a brilliant surprise. Just one thing, what day is it?'

'The 26th.' Charlie said whilst gathering the dishes together, before his assault on them in the sink.

'Yeah, but what day is it?' I asked casually.

''Oh er, well it's Saturday. I managed to swap my days off as you were coming home.' Charlie normally worked on a Saturday and had a day off during the week. He worked in the relentless world of retail and he worked extremely hard.

'Why, does it matter?'

'No. no not at all, I was just wondering.' There was no way I was going to spoil this treat by mentioning Flint's choice of song. How the hell did he know that we would be spending '*Saturday night at the movies*'? After all, I didn't even know until just now, so he couldn't have got it from me. Again I heard a very faint crackle in my head and knew that Flint was never very far away. I couldn't understand how he could have known before I did!

'Earth to Helena!' Charlie said, breaking into my thoughts.

'Yep. Oh sorry, I was just letting the caffeine fight off the blur of the Bacardi. It's been a long time since I've had a real drink.' I said, smiling my reassurance. Charlie eyed me suspiciously.

'Well, if that's all it is.' he said, seeming somewhat unconvinced.

'Of course. Those croissants were divine and the coffee' Charlie tilted his head to one side, he could be very perceptive when he chose to be. I must focus on the here and now. Surely that had been one of the biggest lessons I'd learned from what had happened.

'I'm just going to get dressed. 'I told Charlie and escaped before he could ask any more questions. It was lovely to be able to select my own clothes and until now I hadn't realised how much I'd missed having that choice.

Finally, I was ready and started looking around for my phone and then it dawned on me. No one could use their mobiles, it was the first time this had affected me. I was going to phone Sammy from the bedroom and then it suddenly dawned on me that the word 'mobile' no longer existed when referring to the phone. I was now the one who had to be mobile and go to the phone. Charlie was reading the paper which had now become much thicker and glossier, as publishers took advantage of their newfound popularity. I dialled Sammy's number, then I realised I was phoning her mobile number. She didn't have a landline. We used text messages and WhatsApp to keep in touch. I replaced the receiver, I would have to write to her instead. And then it dawned on me. I couldn't Skype Ellie either, she was now working as a teacher in Vietnam. Not only that, but I couldn't text or WhatsApp. I had no way of getting in touch with her as she didn't have a landline. I had posted letters to Thailand and Dubai when my daughter worked away before and the letters took a very long time to get there. Dammit. I felt a jolt as I realised how much I had taken for granted being able to contact my daughters pretty much whenever and wherever I liked. Suddenly my girls seemed a million miles away. Technology had kept me connected to them both and I had never given it a second thought, until now. Reality hit home and now I was getting a taste of what the youngsters must be feeling. It felt quite isolating and made the world seem like a much bigger place.

'You forgot didn't you, that you can't just get hold of the girls? I must admit, I did at first too.'

'It makes them seem so far away now I can't speak to them.'

I had only been an onlooker so far, but now I was being to understand something about the after-effects and it hit me like a freight train and where it hurts. I have been naive, I am much more reliant on technology than I care to believe. And now I can't speak to my girls!

'We'll just have to find another way.' Charlie said, trying to reassure me. 'The postal service is much better than it used to be. We can buy some special airmail letters from the local newsagents and I'm sure Sammy will get a landline, but in the meantime, you can write to them both.'

'I suppose so.' I said and sighed. 'It's not the same as hearing their voices though or seeing them on Skype.'

'I know. But everyone's in the same boat now and letters do get there quite quickly, so it's not so bad. Why don't you write to Sammy and when we go out you can post that letter and then buy the special airmail paper and envelopes you need to write to Ellie which we can post tomorrow.' Charlie said as he patted me on the shoulder.

'Good plan. It's just a shock realising just how much I had taken the instant contact and messaging for granted. It only really dawned on me how big a deal this was, now that I was back at home and trying to pick up the threads of my normal life.

I wrote my letter to Sammy, being very careful to keep it light and not reveal any of the latest news. I wasn't allowed to mention anything about the last few days or what we had been working on. But I needed to establish contact and gave her our landline number. I felt sure that she would be getting a landline soon. It reminded me of days gone by when Jamie had been away on tour with the Navy and we wrote to each other every day. I enjoyed the process, but I missed being able to chat and hear all the news. My thoughts were broken by Charlie shouting up the stairs asking me to get ready as we had to go. I quickly brushed my hair, treated myself to a spray of my favourite Estée Lauder perfume and applied a thin layer of pink lipstick.

The film was brilliant, ironically a new Sci-Fi film with some spectacular special effects. I loved it and Charlie, who is quite the film buff, was also impressed. He'd been right, the cinemas had taken full advantage of the lack of downloads and TV channels. There were queues reminiscent of our childhood when every screen was booked up. I was so grateful to Charlie for booking our tickets, especially as this now had to be done through the booking office instead of online. It dawned on me that in this new world everything took longer and involved more planning and greater thought. Was this a bad thing? Would it mean that we would once again look forward to things and attach more value to them? It was early days, and I could see both sides of the coin. Perhaps putting more effort into communication and planning activities in advance would bring a greater sense of anticipation in the long run. There was no doubt that the transition would be painful, especially for the youngsters who had known nothing but instant contact through text and email. We drove past one of the newly erected phone boxes, which was painted in the traditional red. The queue snaked down the street and I noticed people in the queue were talking to each other. Probably enjoying the novelty, which I knew would soon wear thin once the rain and the dark nights came along. This all seemed so familiar and made me feel like a teenager again.

It had been a lovely evening. Charlie pulled up onto the drive and switched off the engine and turned to me and smiled. But before he could say anything Lacey opened his car door and Cagney opened mine.

'Where were you?' Cagney asked, looking stressed.

'We went to the cinema, is that alright?' Charlie answered, clearly annoyed.

'No, not really. Time to go.' Lacey said curtly.

'Hang on a minute, I have another night left and there are things I want to do.' I said, feeling my temper starting to rise.

'I'm sorry, you are mistaken if you think you have a choice?' Lacey said tartly. 'National security overrides your social life. Now grab your bag and let's go. We'll meet you in the car. You have ten minutes to say your goodbyes.'

Charlie opened the front door and stood looking somewhat forlornly at me.

'It's not my fault. I don't want to go.' I said as a sob escaped from my throat.

'I know, I know.' he said grabbing me and holding me close to him. I stroked his hair and kissed his face.

'I'll miss you.' I whispered in his ear.

'I'll miss you too.' he whispered back.

(Team Alpha & Team Beta – MI6 HQ)
Never can say goodbye
The Communards

Flint was starting to irritate me now. I was feeling really angry at having my home visit cut short and my privacy invaded. His sarky ditties didn't exactly help. Eventually, I dozed off in the BMW as it glided silently through the night. I needed to make a mental change from the peaceful luxury of home life to the unpredictable demands of MI6. After a very brief and restless sleep, I awoke and tried to brace myself for what would come. I reached for my bag, thinking I would text Charlie for some words of comfort. And then I remembered that I couldn't and yet again it made me feel isolated. Somehow the mobile phone seemed to make you feel connected and close to your loved ones. It provided a much needed link, a feeling of belonging. Help and support were always on hand and you could share your problems or get advice immediately. I think that is what I am missing, the instant response and feeling of closeness which we have all taken for granted. It had been harder to adjust as there had been no warning, no preparation time. The alterations in TV programming, online banking and the lack of internet were a bind but on a personal level, it was the emails and text messages that I missed the most.

We passed through various security checks and the bright lights seemed more intrusive somehow. I decided to keep my eyes firmly closed in avoidance. I knew only too well that this would be the last bit of peace and quiet that I would get for a long time. Being in the car alone was disturbing enough, but not having the use of the mobile just heightened the feeling of loneliness. We came to a sudden stop and the car door was opened for me. I forced my eyes open and squinted into the garish lights of the concrete car park. Cagney inclined his head, indicating for me to move. I reluctantly dragged myself out of the shiny black car and took a deep breath. Back we go on the merry-go-round and yet again I can hear music, ever so faintly, but I know that it's Flint and the unmistakable jingle of the Wurlitzer playing carousel music. I shake my head, trying to shake Flint off like an irritating wasp. Logic played no part here as I knew that Flint lurked somewhere deep within my psyche and no amount of head shaking would remove him. The music stopped and we entered the lift which whizzed efficiently up to the appropriate floor. Cagney remained silent which I valued greatly. The doors opened and I was greeted by an anxious and very chatty Shauna. Cagney stayed in the lift, no doubt collecting the rest of the team. I realised that I was the first one back, besides Shauna, of course, who had not had any company for a while. She filled me in on the snippets of information that she had gleaned. Mostly chit chat and nervous babble, but I could tell she was pleased to see me. It transpired that there was indeed some sort of emergency as a hacker had attempted to access the program. We entered the briefing room and grabbed some coffee.

At intermediate periods, the pinging of the lift marked the return of all the group members over the next hour or so. Andy was the last to return, as Wales was still not blessed with as many motorways. We were fed, watered and given a limited time to catch up before the Inspector marched in with a very stern face and a clear directive to follow. Despite it being a protracted meeting, we could all tell that we weren't being told everything. The Inspector stressed yet again how important our input would be. This was very serious and even though the kill switch had been used and successfully prevented more hacking and corruption, some of the damage had already been done. Our involvement was made crystal clear. If MI6 knew about the program's potential to alter history, then others who had successfully hacked into the program may also know or would do very soon. This was scary news and the possibilities were mind-blowing. The Inspector assured us that if radical changes to the past had been made, then things would have already started to change. We now had a brief window of time available and we had been summoned to test the limits of the program and try to work out, from the inside, how to shut it down for good. There are two tasks we will be involved in, but for now, we are told to focus on the first. The Inspector tells us that we will thankfully remain as one group, but we must select three team members to go back to one specific incident from the past. She stresses that it is highly likely that all of us will be needed to flashback in order to succeed. She hands us each a copy of the brief and gives us one hour to allocate the tasks. She warns us again that this will be an 'all nighter' and that our national security depends upon a quick result.

'Jesus! ' says Shauna as she reads the brief. You can always tell when something is really bad if Shauna restrained herself from using the more colourful swear words.

'Good God.' Andy added, looking stunned.

'This will be no mean feat. We will have to select and plan very carefully.' Berni said quietly.

'They are asking a lot of us.' Brian said whilst shaking his head.

I was the last to speak, stunned by what I had read.

'If this is just the first part, then I'm glad I don't know what the second part is.' I said quietly.

'Well, I'm not going back again! 'Shauna said abruptly. 'My past is so fucked up, I'm not taking any of you back there, I just can't!' she said with conviction.

'OK Shauna, we understand. You stay here until you're needed. Andy said looking around at the group for agreement. Everyone nodded ascent and Shauna sighed with relief.

'I think we should avoid any emotive or problematic flashbacks and try to stick to something more concrete, something we can change which won't affect anyone personally.' Andy added. We all agreed.

'Relationships and personal crisis should be avoided at all costs, as we don't know what the knock-on effect will be.' Brian said calmly.

'That narrows down the field somewhat. Barry, what do you think? You've not said much.'

'You're correct Helena. That's because I think it will have to be me.' he paused. 'I have worked in Finance and it is possible that I could flashback to one of the business arrangements I have been involved in and try to alter something. This would hopefully mean that the outcome could be monitored without directly affecting people's lives. It would meet the target of the brief by demonstrating the power that *Watcher 22* can wield. There will, of course, be consequences, but this would be limited to the finance market rather than relationships or personal circumstances.'

'I think that Barry has come up with a brilliant concept.' Berni said thoughtfully.

'Yeah, we can test this fuckin' thing out without hurting anyone or causing emotional chaos.'

'If you're sure Barry.' I said, feeling grateful for his suggestion. 'It would mean taking two of us along, back to your past. We would be inside your flashback.'

'Yes I understand the implications and I think that under the circumstances I would like to choose the two group members who will accompany me. This is quite a personal thing. I do hope you understand.' he added carefully.

'Of course we understand matey. ' Andy said looking around the group, as we all nodded in approval. Everyone was so relieved to have a plan which seemed to offer the least intrusion.

'In that case, I opt to take Helena and Brian along.' he paused. 'Berni, Andy and Shauna will be monitoring us in the pod, alongside the medical teams. Their input will be vital as they know how this works and can sense danger or the need to be pulled out quickly. Does everyone agree?' We all nodded sombrely.

'I think I can speak on behalf of the group when I say how grateful we all are Barry. It's not easy taking two relative strangers back into your past, in fact, it's very brave. Not many of us would volunteer. So on behalf of us all, I'd like to thank you. And I can assure you that

Brian and I will be sensitive and discreet throughout.'
Barry nodded, looking slightly embarrassed as he
shrugged off the praise.

'You're a fuckin' star in anyone's books!' Shauna
said loudly and everyone laughed at her directness, but
also out of a sense of relief.

'I agree with the sentiment Shauna!' Berni added
whilst smiling.

'Sod this polite English banter! Now's the time for a
group hug, before they come back for us!' Andy said
somewhat urgently.

'You're bloody right Welshy.' Shauna said jumping
up and corralling everyone together into a group hug. It
felt good to be close again and we held on to each other
tightly. There were smiles and some cheek kissing and
friendly back-slapping between the men. None of us
had heard the door open.

'How very touching.' the Inspector almost snarled. I
couldn't help but feel there was a bit of jealousy here.
Maybe it wasn't much fun being up at the top, on your
own.

'Now if you can spare the time to brief me on your
decision, perhaps we can get on with the serious matter
of saving the world,' she said rather dramatically. Barry
winked at me. He was more than capable of dealing
with the Inspector.

The Inspector wasted no time in herding us down to the pods. All the equipment from *XP* had now been brought up to MI6. The old offices had been stripped bare and everything had been transported here. Barry had jotted down some suggested flashbacks of business deals he had been 'involved' in and the powers that be were analysing them, whilst we made our preparations. A decision was imminent. Cagney and Lacey accompanied us to a briefing room, which was close to the pods. We were seated in a circle, preparing for action. Berni, Andy and Shauna were briefed about their role. They would be working alongside the medical teams and psychologists. Their input would be vital as they had experienced the actual process and had the advantage of knowing us all so well. Also, Berni's intuitive skills, combined with Shauna's feistiness instilled confidence in us all. Not forgetting Andy who was great at keeping a cool head in a crisis. None of them would hesitate in pulling us out, for all the right reasons. The medics and the psychiatric team do a great job of monitoring what they see and analysing data, but in a situation like this, we needed more than that.

The Inspector's phone rang and we all fell silent. She nodded and although her words of agreement sounded positive, her facial expression was not quite as convincing. She turned around to place the phone back on the hook and seemed to hesitate, just for a moment. I looked over at Berni who had also noticed. Luckily Shauna was chatting away to Andy and plaiting the ends of her long curly locks. This didn't feel right.

'Right Listen up. A decision has been made. I'm afraid that Barry has no choice in this.' she glanced over towards Barry. He frowned and raised his shoulders unsure of what was to come. 'I'm afraid that they have thrown out your three suggestions Barry and having accessed your original *XP* personnel file. They have made their own selection.' Barry pursed his lips in annoyance, but you had to give it to him, he kept his cool. No doubt some plummy prep school training was serving him well. Shauna had not had the pleasure of such privileged schooling.

'What the fuck? Going through our private stuff without asking us! That's just bleedin' wrong and... '

'Silence!' The Inspector raised her voice, almost confirming her frustration. 'Barry, I would like you to know that I had no part in this, but 'they' can do whatever they like, as long as national security is maintained. I realise that this is an intrusion of your privacy, but this event has been chosen for a good reason.' she paused. 'Would you like me to run this by you in private first?'

Barry had lost his previous flush of irritation and now he just looked annoyed. He shook his head before speaking. Barry then took the floor to address us, every bit the professional.

'Time is short and as I have no choice in the matter, there seems little point having any private discussions. I take it the decision is final?' The Inspector lowered her head and nodded before handing him the file. He opened it and it was immediately clear that he recognised the chosen event. It was unusual to see Barry blush. He turned away for a moment. 'I accept this task, but I would not have chosen this particular event to share. However, I can see the logic behind it and I will of course comply.' The Inspector smiled and gave him an unexpected pat on the back. 'We should begin.'

'I have selected Helena and Brian to accompany me and assume that I may brief the other team members. That just leaves the staff, whom I assume will be briefed or already have been?' again the Inspector nodded. 'I would just like to say that I am not proud of many of the things that I have done, but I am not a coward. If just one of my poor decisions can be used to cancel out some evil threat, then maybe I can gain some solace from that.' Everyone clapped. We all knew that Barry was good at hiding his emotions and was ashamed of his past. This was a massive step forward for him. Even the Inspector gave one of her half smiles, never enough to show her teeth, but still, it was a good sign.

'Would you like Cagney and Lacey to leave the room?' the Inspector asked.

Barry paused for a moment.

'I think I would like them to stay. They have been alongside us for some time now and they are privy to the bigger picture and know our team quite well.' Cagney and Lacey seemed genuinely pleased by the decision and came to sit with us in the circle.

'Right. That's settled then. I'll leave you to brief your team.'

Barry smiled and nodded at the Inspector. He looked nervous, as anyone would when having their private life put on display, especially when you weren't particularly proud of your behaviour. It took great courage.

'I will outline the background and my involvement.' Barry began. 'In my defence, I have never set out to hurt anyone, money was my God for a long time and some of the decisions that I have made were callous and calculating with no thought for the individuals involved. I have hurt people who trusted me. I have taken their money knowing full well that the deals I had set up would ultimately crash. As long as I got my commission, I didn't care. I left a trail of destruction behind me and I never looked back.' Barry paused, looking around the circle at the lowered heads and flinching as some group members avoided his gaze. Berni looked up and gave Barry one of her encouraging smiles. He gave her a quick nod and then continued.

'I was working for a Finance Company in London and I was reasonably successful at representing my clients' interests and selling stocks and shares. I had many contacts and in the finance business, good tips are like gold dust. I got a tip-off about the subprime crisis in the US long before news travelled across the pond.' Barry paused for a sip of water.

'Just to clarify Barry, could I explain this to the Team, make sure we're all reading from the same hymn sheet.'

Barry nodded at Andy to go ahead, looking relieved to have a break.

'First off, investors from abroad put a lot of money into the American economy and as interest rates were low, it meant that Americans could get credit easily. Some people took out interest-only loans to buy houses as it meant that monthly payments were lower. So, the combination of easy credit along with an expected rise in house prices led to mortgages being given to people without checking their ability to pay. Some people took out loans that they would never be able to pay back, even without an interest rate rise. The banks allowed this to happen, by not adhering to any rules regarding income or placing reasonable limits on the amount borrowed. A lot of people mistakenly thought that they could sell or refinance their homes at a higher price later on if needed. More houses were built and supply exceeded demand, which means that prices fell. All with me so far?' Everyone nodded.

'I've seen a programme about this on the News. It was appalling.' Andy said heatedly.

'Steady on, know your audience.' Brian added, jerking his head towards Barry.'

'No, Andy is correct it was appalling. I make no excuses.' he paused. 'Would you continue Andy?'

'Of course matey. When people tried to sell or refinance their houses, they found they couldn't due to negative equity or mortgages that had been given to them on low rates which then rose. Once the mortgage rate went up people couldn't pay and they lost their homes and remained in debt.' Andy paused.

I looked around and could see from the sadness on the group's faces that this was something close to everyone's heart, including mine.

'I'll continue from here Andy.' Barry said directly. 'I know how awful this was, but I need everyone to understand, especially those I'm taking along with me. I want you to remember that home loans are often packaged together and converted into financial products called 'mortgage-backed securities'. These securities were sold to investors around the world. And this I'm afraid is where I came in. A lot of investors thought these securities were trustworthy and they didn't ask any questions about their value. From a conman's point of view, it was like manna from heaven. I got in before it all crashed and the banks collapsed. I had been tipped off that this may happen, but I kept shtum and went ahead with the deals anyway. Credit rating agencies gave the securities high-grade, safe ratings. I sold them to investors knowing that the economy could collapse and they would lose their investment.' Barry paused and looked thoroughly ashamed of himself.

'That was pretty shitty Barry.' Shauna said, her eyes flashing in indignation. I kept my eyes fixed to the floor, but could hear others muttering in agreement.

'But none of us are fuckin' innocent.' Shauna continued. 'There were times when I'd have sold my own mother for one skanky hit, if I could have found her that is!' Shauna said.

'We're not here to judge you, Barry. That was then and this is now. If we can use this unfortunate event to save lives, then you can feel vilified or a little less guilty at least.'

The mood in the group lifted and even Cagney and Lacey began to come around.

'That can't have been easy Barry. But Berni is right and we need to get back there and change it.' I said quietly. The door slammed signalling the Inspector's return.

'All done?' she asked.

Barry nodded. 'It's done.'

'Then we need to press on. Follow me and make it snappy.'

'Helena! Can you shut your fuckin' *Die Hard* maniac up?' Shauna said loudly.

'You can hear that?' I asked amazed that Flint had such power.

'Yes, we can all hear that I think.' Berni said and the group nodded in agreement, 'all except Cagney and Lacey.'

'He's a relentless bastard, I'll give him that.' Andy said as we walked down to the pods.

'A tactless bastard I would say.' Barry said wincing as the music faded away. 'I wonder you survived, having him as your Guide.'

'Dame Judi was a good match for him.' I added.

'Can we focus on the job in hand!' the Inspector said somewhat sharply. You could tell that she was feeling the pressure. She opened the door to the makeshift control room. It had all the equipment and staff at the ready. There was a large window which overlooked the pod where three beds and machines awaited us.

'Andy, Berni and Shauna please select one of the team to follow. Obviously, the better you know your team-mate the more help you will be.'

'I'm picking Helena if she'll have me. I know a lot about her and her past.' Shauna said quickly and I nodded in agreement.

'Best I go with Barry then, knowing a little about business and all that.' Barry gave Andy's arm a punch of solidarity and nodded.

'I was going to choose you anyway Brian, don't think you were the last resort. I understand a lot about you and your background. If you'll have me of course.'

'Delighted to Berni. We're on the same wavelength.' Brian said putting his arm protectively around her shoulders.

'Yes well, that's all very lovely. But if we could move on. Although you have an assigned partner, we expect you to observe the scene objectively, focusing on the interactions between everyone. I want you to watch your partners closely, but don't be afraid to advise us if you pick something else up. This particularly applies to you Berni.' she said turning to look directly at her. 'We know how perceptive you can be and the welfare of the team is paramount. This is a big operation and the preparation time is limited.'

We all nodded as the Inspector took yet another call on the landline.

'Send him in and quickly.' she barked before slamming down the receiver. The door opened and in walked Brown.

'Good to see you.' Andy said quickly filling the silence. He walked over and shook Brown's hand. I could see Barry cringing. There was no love lost there.

'Wouldn't have missed it.' Brown said nodding to the rest of the team.

'Will you be overseeing things?' Brian asked carefully.

'Of course, I was in charge of the relocation and I have checked the pods personally. This isn't something to be rushed into.' he said whilst flashing the Inspector an icy look. 'Normally we would take weeks to set up a group flashback, especially when we effectively have three clients flashing back into one person's event. Barry is very brave to allow this to happen and we have much to do.'

'Brown, can you brief Barry and the team? I have to report 'upstairs.''

It struck me as amusing, that however high up people rose in an organisation, they still referred to their superiors as being 'upstairs' as though they were on a par with God.

'Helena could you try and stay focused. That damn Guide of yours has a lot to answer for.'

For once I let this slide, after all Flint wouldn't hesitate in letting me take the flack for his behaviour.

'It's quite straight forward really. In his past, Barry met with two top investors and he made a deal that he knew would crash. This was a fraudulent transaction that went against the code of conduct. Barry knew this, and you all need to understand it as well. He benefited from this illegal deal and was paid a high rate of commission. The UK fund was then forced to close and bankruptcies and redundancies followed.' Barry hung his head in shame.

'We're not here to judge, and we're not going back as voyeurs, to witness this dodgy deal. We are going back to change it. We need to prove that we can change one small thing in the past, not like the team did before when the scar disappeared, I do know about that. But to show that the business sector and the economy can also be affected and futures can be changed.'

'So what does Barry do? He must have set up this meeting with a view to closing the deal. They'll expect it, those bankers will demand it won't they?'

'You're right Andy they will. Barry, we need you to switch portfolios. Our guys have researched a less profitable hedge find, one with mutual funds. It has a much lower return and would involve less borrowed cash for the investors, but it would mean that they would stay in business. You're a businessman Barry used to wheeling and dealing and I know you can swing this. I've brought you a copy of the new investment and want you to familiarise yourself with it. If they leave without accepting this deal, it's highly likely they will go to your competitor and simply invest with them and there will be the same outcome. This will not change history, for them at least. You can use whatever persuasive techniques you like and a smidgen of the truth, but nothing that you wouldn't have known then. They will have no knowledge of the tip-off that you chose to ignore.'

'You do understand what you're asking? It took me weeks to set up this deal with these clients. They are both highly respected and powerful businessmen who took a lot of persuading to come to the table. The return on the original investment was the only thing that brought them to the meeting. I was a small-time player and this was the big league.'

'But you weren't afraid to shaft them Barry were you?' Brown said somewhat harshly. 'It's not as though I'm asking you to play dirty, quite the opposite in fact. I am asking you to play fair. Time is running out here. If you won't do it then we'll just have to select one of the other team-mates and we will be less prepared. We know this is personal, but these are the breaks.'

Barry turned and hit the wall in temper which seemed out of character for him.

'Just give him a minute Brown, if you would.' Andy said standing between them.

'It's a lot to deal with, Brown. Maybe you just need to give Barry five minutes and let him read over the new deal and work out how he's going to play it.'

'I think Helena's right. I've done some shady deals in my time, not on this scale of course, and it takes some balls to change your game plan.'

'Time is not something we have a lot of.' Brown said in a clipped tone.

'Well under the circumstances, I think Barry needs a moment, if you want this to work he has to appear convincing.' Berni said firmly.

'Yes Brown, just sod off for a bit, and let him think.'

'I'll bring in some coffee.' Lacey said sensing the need to diffuse things, especially now that Shauna was piping up.

'Very well. I'll check the pods, again and return shortly.

Barry took his coffee to a quiet corner of the room and read the new investment package. He sighed heavily, it was not going to be easy. Meanwhile, we spoke in hushed tones whilst sipping our coffee. Brian looked over at me and half-smiled.

'I think we're going to have a job on our hands. I mean, how are we going to get the old Barry to switch deals? We don't have any real physical presence in the actual room do we?' Brian asked me quietly.

'I don't know, the time we actually changed something we had to come together and focus like we did when we broke the circuit that night when we escaped. We should push Brown on this and see what he has to say. They must have thought it through.'

'I think they just expect it to happen. As though it's easy, like we can just do it on demand. Last time it was the heightened danger and physical threat that drove us to react and quickly. This time we know in advance and it's a business deal, it's just not the same.'

'You're right. All of you are right. Brown needs to explain how I'm supposed to switch the deals. I know my old self. I was hard and cynical. I would never have entered into negotiations with this mediocre deal. Even if I am successful in switching the paperwork, that doesn't explain how the old Barry will accept it or sell it.'

'They haven't thought this through. It's nonsense. Last time was different as we managed to change the environment, which then changed the outcome. This time we are introducing a new deal without changing the characters.'

'Ah but that's where you're wrong.' Brown said haughtily as he walked back into the room. 'Let me explain.'

'What an annoying bastard.' Shauna said loudly. 'I don't know how you survived, having him in your head.'

'Tactless devil.' Brian added.

'He's relentless. Can't you make him stop?' Andy asked.

'I have no control over him, more is the pity and this time I don't even know why he's picked that song.'

'And quite honestly I don't care.' Brian added.

The music gradually faded as Brown made his entrance.

'Barry have you read that information about the new deal?' he asked very directly.

'Yes I have and Brown I have to tell you that the old Barry, would never have considered putting this proposal forward to the investors at this meeting. I have changed since then, of course.' Barry added. There was a faint crackle of static in my head and I made the connection with the song or I thought I did.

'That's where we have the advantage. I just wanted you to read the deal before explaining the next step. We're not complete idiots at *XP*.' he paused looking accusingly at Cagney and Lacey. There had obviously been some friction between MI6 and the company. 'We're trying a different approach and the team-mates who are going back with you will be pivotal to its success. Alongside those working here of course.' he added, noting Shauna's readiness to jump in. 'I'll be honest with you Barry, this particular procedure is still at the experimental stage as *XP* was closed down before we got much of a chance to trial it. But things are critical and MI6 have pushed us to produce viable evidence before they go to Phase 2. I can see their point, but you need to know the risks and there *are* serious risks.' Barry indicated for Brown to continue. 'We understand that, just as you said, young Barry would never consider selling this deal as the returns are nowhere near as lucrative. However, you did say quite openly that you are a different person now.' he paused. 'So, we're going to switch you.' again he paused. 'The question I have to ask Barry is whether or not you think you can do it.'

'Just to clarify what you are suggesting Brown. The word switch implies that I will basically 'switch' bodies with my younger self.'

'Wow! Like a body swap – like *Big* with Tom Hanks...'

'Correct.' Brown cut in and nodded as Barry absorbed the information.

'You lucky bastard!' Andy chirped in. 'How brilliant to have your young, virile body back!'

'Ah to be young again.' said Berni with a sigh.

'Well I'm glad it's not me, I was a wreck back then, and not just physically.' Shauna added.

'I must admit I'm happy where I am, the body could do with some work but...'

'STOP!' shouted Brown. 'This isn't a *Back to the Future* reunion party! Get a grip! Barry will return to his younger body in order to cut the deal. Nothing more. And now Barry, I'm afraid I must press you for an answer.'

'Brown, before I even begin to question how this is possible, I feel that you may have some misplaced confidence in my business acumen and sales technique. I am at best a charlatan, or at least I was. There was no master plan, no real underlying talent for salesmanship. Most of it was smoke and mirrors. I worked to fuel my lifestyle and only when it was absolutely necessary. Andy would have been a better choice.' Before Andy could chip in, Brown made it quite clear that Andy played in the little league and MI6 had demanded a high profile deal which would illustrate, beyond any reasonable doubt, that the past could be altered.

'Barry. I apologise for putting you under this sort of pressure, but time is of the essence. I need your verbal consent to continue. I understand all the points you have made. But ask again if you will go ahead with Operation Vice Versa?'

'I have so many questions. I feel certain that revealing any details about how this process works is top secret, as are the dangers attached to it. But how on earth can the *Watcher 22* program have been refined and developed to the point where a client in the present can enter their own body in the past? It's phenomenal!!! Just outstanding pioneering work…'

Brown tried to conceal a smile of obvious pride and put his hand across his mouth. He then shook his head in a bid to spur himself on.

'Barry I'm afraid we have little time. Perhaps once this whole thing is finally over we can have a 'conversation'.'

'I would like that Brown, very much. May I just ask, as my past and present self will both be putting ourselves on the line, is there a chance that I may not be able to switch back? The younger body would be exciting and I am a changed man…who knows perhaps I may not want to return.' he added smiling.

'That's as maybe, but it won't be your choice and we can only hold you there for a short period of time. It's more likely that we will struggle to keep you there for as long as we need to. We are working to a very tight timescale. I can assure you that you won't get stuck there, quite the opposite. This may be for the best, as the young Barry will be totally confused and horrified! Remember that he will be in an older body. He has not had your experience at *XP* and the flashbacks and revisits that you have had. This is not a flashback for him, it will be a very sudden and drastic change to his present life. It will be an enormous shock for him as he changes bodies and finds himself in the pod. Berni and Andy, you will have to help with young Barry once he arrives. Helena and Brian, you will be observing the deal and giving moral support to Barry once he has entered his younger body.'

'That would freak anyone out!' Shauna said, shaking her head.

'Charming!' Barry said then winked and smiled to let Shauna off the hook.

'Can I just ask, this young Barry, now in 'old' Barry's body, will he be sedated?' Andy asked.

'He will only be lightly sedated I'm afraid and that means that we will be relying on you and Shauna to monitor him.'

'What! He's going to be overwhelmed by all this. We can only just cope and we've been through the program!'

'I've spoken to the experts and they think we can convince him that he's in a dreamlike state.'

'You mean *we* have to convince him he's in a 'dreamlike state'! He's zapped out of a business meeting and then blasted into a pod in an old wreck of a body!!'

'Yeah... I know it sounds a big ask. I think the techie guys have developed a kind of radio wave that will make him zone out. They will blast it through his headphones. That combined with a light sedative should do the trick.'

'Dear Lord, I do feel this is a big ask of one so young.'

'Don't feel too sorry for him Berni, remember he is being prevented from making a profit out of the suffering of others.'

'Could we move along now? This is a tad uncomfortable for me, having my old sins scrutinised by the group.'

'Fair play to Barry. Let's get on with it now. There's nobody here who hasn't made a giant cock up at some point.' Andy said and patted the rather shaken Barry on the back.

'This is the order of play. Firstly, Helena and Andy will already be in the office before the meeting has started, Older Barry will act as a kind of cuckoo and shunt young Barry out of his body to be sent to the pod. Older Barry will change the deal and then the Barrys switch back and you all come home.'

Anyone could tell that Brown was attempting to make it all sound straightforward.

'It's not 'just a bit experimental' Brown! It's about as experimental as it can possibly be!! I don't think you really know if any of this will work do you?' Andy said angrily.

'Look we have been put on the spot and they pressured into doing this just as you have. We're confident in our systems and confident we can get you all back. Young Barry will just think he's had the worst living nightmare of his life. But he'll get over it and who knows it may change him, for the better.'

'And if the radio wave of dream doesn't fuckin' work, then what are Shauna and Andy meant to do with young Barry? He could be mentally scarred, it's way too much to take in!'

'If push comes to shove we will increase the sedation levels, but this may affect his transfer back. The radio wave is our best option.'

'Oh yeah and that sounds easy. Brown, is this the only way we can show that past events can be changed?'

'Look Helena they want empirical evidence, data, tangible proof that something has been altered by your visit. If we're experimenting with this, then so are the competition. China and Russia don't have any boundaries when it comes to experimentation. This is the safest and quickest flashback we can do in the time we have been allowed. I can't stress how vital this is. Proving that we can return to the past and change history could be one of the most significant breakthroughs of the 21st century.'

'Not too much pressure on us then?' Andy said and then patted Barry on the shoulder.

'Jesus James and Mary – this is goin' be one hell of a ride! Do you think…?' Shauna's question would never be answered, as in barged the Inspector and her face suggested that a storm was brewing.

'I clearly said ten minutes. Where have you been? They are all waiting for you.'

'You told me that I had to explain and get consent. That was rather a big ask in ten minutes Inspector.'

'Stop this namby-pamby nonsense and get them in place, NOW! There are lives at risk!' Cagney and Lacey jumped up off their seats and split us into two groups.

'Helena I'll be watching your back, no fucker will mess with you.' Shauna said, giving me a rare hug.

'Brian, I will, of course,do the same and will be keeping a watchful eye over all three of you.' Berni said with a slight shake in her voice.

'Bazzer, you know I'll be on it …'

'Enough!! This isn't The Waltons! Time to separate and get on with it. Cagney and Lacey stay with the observers in the control room. Brown accompany me to the pods to get these three wired in and prepped up. Come on, Move it!'

Everyone scrabbled around to follow the Inspector's instructions. The tension seemed to crank up a notch, as we went our separate ways. Just before I left, I caught Berni's eye. I'd seen that look before, it was one of fear and uncertainty. I must admit I thought we'd finished with all this delving into the past stuff. Berni turned and nodded to me in agreement, she was picking up my thoughts which was a great comfort as we headed back into someone else's past.

'He's such a card isn't he?' Barry said as we were being wired up.

'I can only apologise.' I replied as the music began to fade away.

'At least we're all in one room and we've got our other team members batting with us. Not that I don't trust the Techies and everyone.' Brian added quickly.

'It's weird being sent back into someone else's memory.'

'Not as weird as it as for me, I can assure you.'

'Helena and I will do everything we can to help, you know that.'

'Thank you, Brian. It is rather embarrassing for me, to have you visiting my past.'

'Look Barry, you just need to pretend that we're not there. Not one of us would ever judge you, it's not as if any of us have had perfect lives.'

'Helena's right. Just focus on the task in hand and pushing the deal. Don't get distracted by us.'

'All you can do is to try and keep your mind on the job, goodness knows that's enough to contend with. Oh and one last thing, please try to avoid experimenting with your new body, especially in front of us!'

'Pipe down now you three. We need to fit the visors before we do the transportation.'

All three of us are now clad in the obligatory white suits and are lying on our beds.

'Last time I did this I was in a room on my own. This feels very different, not quite so terrifying somehow. Barry turns and winks at us both and Brian and I nod back reassuringly at him. They fit the helmets. We all know that we are now wired into the system and there's no turning back.

'Helena and Brian will go first and acclimatise in preparation for Barry's arrival.'

We lie on our beds ready to go. I'd forgotten how cumbersome the helmet felt and with its memory came the familiar grinding in my stomach, which was now becoming more intense.

Then came strange crackle and fizz which filled my head. This is it. I shut my eyes and prepare myself as best I can. I feel isolated, yet strangely calm, knowing that this time I won't be alone. Sure enough, I arrive in the swanky office, wearing the same T-shirt and jeans that we always wore. I look around, desperately searching for Brian.

'I'm over here.' Brian calls to me. I turn around and am delighted to see him and notice he's wearing the same attire.

'Thank God. Are you alright?' I ask, feeling concerned as he looks a little dazed.

'It always gets me this way.' Brian says, whilst shaking out his arms and legs.

'Looks like we got here just before the meeting starts.' I add looking around the plush office. I move over to the window, gazing down at a beautiful view of the Thames which sparkles in the sunshine.

'I'm just glad the room's so large. Shall we stand over by the hospitality area?' Brian asked, whilst pointing across to a well-stocked bar and coffee machine situated in the corner of the room.

'That's a good idea, Brian.'

We moved across together, which was good timing, as the rumble of laughter and excited voices were heading our way.

'Oh God, I suppose this is it!' Brian said, who was still not looking great.

'Don't worry Bri, just remember that they can't see us. I wonder when they'll switch the two Barry's over.'

'They'll be waiting for him to get the clients in I expect and get them settled. Reduce any damage to the bare minimum.'

'This is nerve-racking! At least in your own flashbacks, you know exactly what's going to happen next.'

'Here they come.' Brian said anxiously.

The door swishes shut and in bounces young Barry, clearly buoyant with the promise of success. It is just plain weird seeing him as a much younger man. He exudes enthusiasm and to be honest, he is actually quite dashing. As he addresses the clients, it is obvious that the combination of confidence and the luxurious surroundings are beginning to weave their magic. He makes the clients feel at ease and the buzz in the room is electric.

'My God he's good!' Brian said, whilst looking on in amazement.

'I'd buy anything from him!'

'Me too! He has charisma and believability. Amazing. And he is quite good looking.'

'Watch out he's coming over to fix the drinks.'

Young Barry moves effortlessly over to the hospitality area and prepares the drinks whilst still participating in the conversation, which had not yet turned to the deal. The clinking of ice marks his return to the desk and he continues with the lively banter, whilst carefully pulling out the business file.

This was the perfect time to switch the Barrys over. We knew that Control would be able to see what was happening through our live feeds. Suddenly, we could hear the familiar sound of clicking and crackling. Brian turns towards me and we both instinctively cover our ears, even though we know that the sound is on the inside of our heads. A stillness seems to wash over the room, albeit for a few seconds and then things appear to be in slow motion. We watch Barry closely. First of all, his eyes seem to glaze over and then he closes them and seems to be shaking his head. As the crackling sound abates, Barry seems to shudder and shake a little and then his eyes open.

'Is he in there Helena, is that our Barry?' Brian asked edgily.

'I think it must be and if it is I'm sure he will signal us in some way.' I answer quietly, unsure as to whether Barry could hear or see us.

Barry opens his eyes and judging by their saucer-like appearance, we feel sure that the switch has taken place.

'He isn't getting long to adapt to his new body.' I whisper to Brian.

Barry looked over to the corner and winked. 'He can see us!' I said happily.

Luckily one of the clients was banging on about his recent trip to Thailand, which gave Barry a little time to acclimatise. He looks down at his hands and rubs them together, obviously enjoying the feel of the young, taut skin. Next, he pats his flat stomach and looks down at his fit, muscly legs and flexes them. His eyes only glance over his gentleman's area and he raises his eyebrows and aims his wink toward Brian. The side of his mouth curls up in delight. He then subtly puts his elbow on the table and cups his cheek whilst using his left hand to run his fingers through his full head of well-groomed hair. His eyes gleam with excitement. It must be mind-blowing to be back in your young body, especially with an old soul. What an experience!. We are all so carried away with ourselves, that none of us has noticed that the conversation has stopped. The time has come for Barry to do his thing. I notice that he quickly removes the glossy folders and places them in a drawer. Barry grits his teeth, which helps him to focus and prepare himself for the task ahead. He fires up the old VDU (Visual Display Unit) and searches for the new proposal whilst distracting the clients with a tale of one of his past investments. This guy can multi-task.

'He's finding our new deal on that VDU, ready to deliver. He's a resourceful devil.' Brian said proudly.

'I just hope he can pull it off.' I said warily. 'These clients are typical sharpshooters with their flashy suits and braces. One of them is even wearing a red tie. It's like being on a set of 'Wall Street'.'

'If anyone can do it, he can. I just hope he doesn't run out of time.'

'God knows how young Barry is coping back at HQ, he must think he's having the worst nightmare of his life.'

'Jesus Jones! Does this bloke ever give up?' Shauna exclaimed loudly, before realising that not everyone could hear Flint's less than subtle song choice.

'You have to give Helena some credit, for putting up with her crazy Guide for as long as she did.'

'He is certainly persistent I'll give him that.' Berni added.

'What on earth are you three talking about?' Brown asked, looking bemused. 'If it's not too much trouble could you apply yourselves, lives may be at risk here!'

'Keep your hair on Brown! There are some things that you don't understand and...'

'We are more than ready to help with Barry.' Berni interrupted Shauna before she could launch into her offensive.

'Right. Well as you can see, Helena and Brian are now in the office and we are preparing to switch the Barrys over. His vitals are good and things look stable. We just need the doctor to agree. Shauna looked nervously at Barry's recumbent body and felt the icy fingers of fear clutch her stomach. She was secretly rather fond of Barry, despite his posh accent and classy background. Underneath it all, Shauna always believed that he'd understood her. Barry was taking a big risk. He could lose everything and be stuck in the wrong world, in the wrong body.

'He's a tough character Shauna, you have to be when you work in business if you want to succeed.' Berni was trying to reassure her.

'And don't forget he had to fight like hell with his alcoholism. You don't survive AA without digging deep and finding some true grit.'

'That's right Andy. Barry has had some challenging times in his life. I'm sure he can pull this off.'

'We need silence now.' Brown said curtly. 'The doctor has given us the green light.'

The room fell silent. The only sound to be heard was the buzzing of the computers. The screens became animated and flashed excitedly. The three team-mates could only watch through the large glass window, as Barry's body began to twitch and his closed eyes fell into REM. Andy watched the monitor which showed the office setting, whilst Berni and Shauna focused on Barry in the Pod. There was a flurry of activity as *Watcher 22* was loaded and the transfer progressed.

'How long will it take Andy?' Shauna asked anxiously.

'I think it will be quick if they can get it to work.'

'I can tell that it has worked Shauna.' Berni said quietly, whilst pulling at Shauna's sleeve. 'Look! We need to get into the pod, in case he opens his eyes, before the radio wave or whatever it is starts to take effect. He'll be terrified!'

'Brown! Brown! We're going in. Is it safe, now the transfer has taken place?' Shauna raised her voice in panic.

'Calm yourself, Shauna. Listen to me carefully. You may enter the pod, but please remember that you must not disturb Helena and Brian who are in the same room. That could ruin the whole thing. You may comfort Barry if he comes around, but otherwise, just observe. Understood? We do *not* want him to wake up. There's a lot at stake here. Berni, I want you to oversee things and keep Shauna under control. No loud voices or fast movements. You must be very quiet. I am trusting you. Do NOT let me down.'

Shauna nodded meekly and Berni assured Brown that they would follow his instructions to the letter.

'Andy, do you mind staying here and keeping an eye on the monitors? If things start to deteriorate it will have an impact on all three of them.'

'Yep. Am happy to do it. Not that I don't trust these Techies, it's just as I have actually been back there, I know a little bit more about what to look out for.'

'Yes, yes. Just get on with it.' Brown said clicking his fingers impatiently. He was clearly under immense pressure. He kept pushing his finger against his ear, indicating that he was receiving messages through his earphone. Meanwhile, Berni turned to Shauna.

'Just a word of advice Shauna, we need to keep calm, very calm and very quiet. Whatever happens, all three of our friends are relying on us and they will be affected if we make any mistakes. We both just need to be very careful not to wake any of them up. Hopefully, Barry will not come around, but if he does he's going to be very frightened and rightly so. Waking up in your older body, in a white suit and visor, twenty years in the future would be terrifying for anyone. We can work this out together Shauna, but I need to know that you can handle your...' Berni paused.

'Big gob! Shauna interrupted.

'Well, yes. I wouldn't have put it exactly like that…'

'Could you both just get in there if you are going!' Brown shouted. And without further ado, Berni and Shauna eased open the door and walked into the room. They made their way over to Barry's bed and sat one at each side. Barry was lying still, at least for the time being. Shauna cautiously glanced across at Helena and Brian, who also seemed to be having a peaceful trip. The hissing of their breathing tubes and hum from the computers were the only sounds in the room. Shauna shuddered and turned her attention back to Barry. His body was twitching, but his eyes remained closed. Berni sighed with relief, before looking over to Andy through the large picture window. Andy raised his hands and moved his head to one side indicating that things were progressing, but slowly.

Suddenly, a red light flashed angrily on Barry's monitor. Shauna dug Berni in the ribs, managing not to blurt out any expletives. Something was changing. Barry seemed to be getting distressed. His heartbeat accelerated and the twitching intensified. Shauna stood up and caught Brown's eye. He nodded, realising that something was wrong.

'Oh God! What's happening Berni? This isn't fuckin' right!'

'Keep calm, Shauna. Let's just hope it's a blip and he drifts back off.'

The monitor continued to flash and Barry's heartbeat was erratic. All of sudden his eyes flashed open and he began straining to sit up.

'Brown!! Hurry up! Barry's coming round!!'

Brown shot into the room, accompanied by one of the doctors.

'I was hoping it wouldn't come to this.' Brown said, obviously flustered.

'Shauna, lean over so that he can see you through the visor. Just try and reassure him, as best you can. Berni, I need you to move to one side and let the doctor get to the breathing equipment. We will have to increase sedation. We can only hope that it doesn't affect the other Barry whilst he's doing the deal.'

The doctor adjusted the mix of gases which would send Barry off into a light sleep.

'He's drifting off! Thank God. He looked bleedin' terrified!!' Shauna said, still rubbing his arm gently.

'That will give us a little more time. But this is a dangerous game we're playing. There's always a chance that we could lose them both.'

The monitor returned to normal and Berni gently eased Shauna back into her seat. Andy tapped on the window, anxious about what had gone on.

'I'll tell Andy. You stay here.' Brown said abruptly before going back to the control room.

Berni and Shauna resumed their bedside positions, clearly relieved that things had settled down.

'He was so scared, poor bastard. 'Shauna said quietly. 'It would have been easier if he could have been prepared or briefed in some way. '

'It wasn't possible and how on earth could you explain it all in time. He wouldn't have been able to take everything in, things happen so quickly. I feel that in this situation a little knowledge would have been a dangerous thing. Hopefully, we will be able to transfer him back before he wakes up again and he will be none the wiser.'

'Berni, what you are you really thinking?'

'What do you mean?' Berni said turning towards Shauna.

'I just get the feeling that you might know what will happen here.'

Berni sighed. 'No Shauna, I don't know how this will end.' Berni paused. 'But you are right, my instinct tells me that we are playing a very dangerous game. We are interfering in history and this shifts the delicate equilibrium, the balance that provides stability...'

'I know like *Back to the Future?* That sort of thing.'

'Is that a film Shauna?'

'Yes! Of course, it's a bloody film and...'

'Well this is real and my deepest fear is that we are meddling in things we know nothing about. Why do you think they are so worried? If it could have been done before, then it would have been done before.'

'Yeah but maybe it has been and we just don't know about it.'

'I think that's extremely unlikely and ...'

Andy tapped on the glass and moved towards the door. He opened it very carefully.

'He's only about to bloody do it! You might want to come in here and watch this!'

The Great Pretender
Freddie Mercury

'Well Brian, all I can say is that Barry, young or old, is one impressive dude.'

'Cool as a blinkin' cucumber. He certainly knows how to play the clients.'

'Does it make you wonder if the young body, old soul combo is the perfect mix? I mean just look at Barry. The firm athletic body of a young man, but the experience and confidence of the older Barry and he is clearly having a great time!'

'You may just have something there… hang on a minute Helena, something is happening.'

Barry had left the meeting table and indicated for Brian to move over and keep an eye on the two businessmen.

'What's up Barry?'

'Listen Helena, I think that the program may have gone on the blink back then, back at HQ. It was only for a few seconds, but I could just feel myself drifting. Are you in contact with them back at the pods?'

'No, but they can see us. I'm sure it's just a blip, Barry. You seem to be doing brilliantly.'

'Well, I have been rather lucky so far and the whisky chasers may be helping. I think I may have swung it, but

SUE L. CLARKE

I need to get them to sign or none of this counts for
diddly squat.' Barry paused. 'Helena I can feel you
staring at me and looking surreptitiously at my rather
lean young frame. Don't think that I haven't noticed.'
Barry said, raising an eyebrow and leaning toward me. I
felt myself blush and looked down hiding a smile. 'I
must admit, I am rather splendid even if I say so myself.
I think there's fire down below...'

'Whoa! Steady on there Barry! Too much information.
I think you need to take care of the job at hand.'

'That's a rather unfortunate turn of phrase.' I said,
managing to control a giggle. What on earth was I
doing? I shrugged my shoulders whilst shaking my head
to snap myself back into the moment.

Fortunately, Brian signalled for Barry to return to the
table.

'Toodle pip. Let's hope that they sign up and seal the
deal.'

I couldn't help feeling rather relieved as Barry left to
try and close the deal.

Barry filled the clients' glasses with very generous
measures. One of the businessmen, whose complexion
had started to reflect the strength of a good whisky,
thumped his fist down on the table.

'I like your style Barry, I can see that this deal is a
runner, in the long term that is. There is no doubt in my
mind that it will be lucrative and a good solid earner.
But something isn't quite right here. It just feels a bit off.
Quite honestly Bazzer, it's just plain dull. We live in the
moment you and I, we all do. We are risk-takers and
you of all people Barry, normally push for high returns

on short term investments. This deal is solid and stable, but not really your style Barry boy...'

'I have to agree. Is there something you're not sharing with us? Something that you're keeping for yourself. Something sexy, something exciting, something a little more risqué?' the other client said, clearly feeding off the buzz of the moment.

Barry paused and slowly placed the heavy-bottomed glass down on the table. 'You couldn't be further from the truth.' Barry said in a measured tone and slowed the pace down beautifully. He even managed a sneaky wink across at Brian and I. He was one of the best manipulators I have ever seen and I've encountered a fair few in my time. The charge in the room seems to abate to a mere fizz, as Barry turned to his clients. He fixed his gaze upon them and intensified his pitch.

'In all honesty, you are both correct, but you disappoint me a little. Our success in business is all about timing. We are not a group of money-grabbing lowlifes, desperate to make a quick buck. I know only too well that we have clawed our way up, taken risks and played the market. However, I have put away those childish things, I am a man now, a fully-fledged entrepreneur. I can only speak for myself of course.' he paused. 'It is as simple as this, I now feel ready for deals that have a little more sophistication, a little more class. I want to build my reputation, now that I have raised my head above the bloody parapet. At times I admit I have traded hard and dirty, as I know you both have. I've even had to bow my head and tread gingerly away from disaster and ruin.' again Barry paused. 'My finances are, for now at least, in good shape. I love to gamble and thrive on the thrill of the chase, but my inner compass is guiding me back to the safety of our shores, away from Uncle Sam. I say this not to persuade you, but merely to share my opinion with you. It is only a gut feeling but I for one, do not want to be forced back to the very beginning. It was a long hard journey, clawing my way up to this point and I don't want to fall back down. Right now I am happy with my portfolio and I intend to play it safe and remain in prime position. I am confident that others will not be so lucky. I am not trying to sway you, merely inform you of my intentions which I trust will remain strictly confidential. It is your choice of course. Gentlemen, I must follow my instinct, but I understand if you decide to venture elsewhere for more excitement.'

The clients seem less cocky now and looked to each other for reassurance.

'How do you know all this and where does....'

'I have said all I am going to say on the matter and I am not at liberty to continue with further discussion.'

And with that Barry opens the desk drawer and retrieves the folders, he then splays these dramatically across the desk. He leans across to switch off the VDU. His confident air is appealing, but I know him well, albeit in his older form. The 'tell' is the small ruddy circles of pique that have risen on his cheekbones. They are beginning to fade, as Barry moves in for his parting shot.

'Sorry to play the killjoy chaps. There are plenty of risky deals with the promise of a quick return. But I fear that the promise is an empty one and some of our fellow investors will come unstuck. Maybe not right now or next week, but in the not too distant future. Of this I am certain and if I am wrong the market will still be there and we can all jump straight back in.'

The lights flickered. Had Barry said too much?

'Dear God, is this some sort of divine intervention?'

'I can tell you feel strongly about this pal. I've known you for a long time. I think I'm gonna take your word on this call. You've never let us down and if it is time to stand back and be boring, then I for one am in.'

'It's not desperately exciting, but we mustn't forget that the risk should never outweigh the potential return.'

'Well Barry, I think we have both been won over for now at least. But next time Barry boy I will be looking for something with a lot more oomph.'

All three men then raised their glasses to seal the deal. Barry began printing off the paperwork ready for signatures.

'This could be it, Brian!'

'He's brilliant, I'm blown away. It takes some nerve to keep your cool, especially under these bizarre circumstances.'

We watched in awe as the clients signed the new deal. They were fairly tipsy by this point, but even so, it was a massive achievement. Had Barry changed the course of history? It was overwhelming, we didn't dare to contemplate what the implications might be for all mankind. Could Hitler be replaced and if so would all the millions murdered still be among us? Could we undo the development and dropping of bombs on Hiroshima and Nagasaki? Could war be prevented? My mind was in a whirl. I could see that Brian felt the same.

The papers were signed and the clients left noisily. We all stood together waiting to be returned to the pods.

'Young Barry is going to be pretty pissed off when he returns to his own rather splendid young body.'

'You've really enjoyed yourself haven't you?' Brian said smiling at Barry.

'Yes, I have. It's been a blast to have a young and energetic body which responds to the merest whim. It's not wasted on me though, I have the advantage of age and experience, a perfect combination – a young virile body combined with a wise old brain.'

'You lucky dog!' Brian said, clearly quite jealous.

'All good things must come to an end.' Barry said wistfully.

'Hopefully, we will all be back to our old selves soon, quite literally in your case Barry.' I said smiling.

'They do seem to be taking their time about it.' Brian said nervously. Just then the lights flickered and we braced ourselves for transportation. Again nothing happened.

'You don't think we're, well... stuck here do you?'

'Calm yourself, Brian. We've done this many, many times and there have never been any problems, now has there?'

'Helena's quite right. It must be hard to get the timing exact, especially with all three of us to transport. Anyway, I'm in no particular hurry old boy.' Barry moved back to his desk after refilling his glass. 'I may as well leave young Barry with a blurry memory of today's events.'

'I thought you were on the wagon Barry?' Brian said sternly.

'I am. But young Barry isn't. Let me have a little fun, we'll soon be home and dry and I mean dry.'

The lights continued to flicker and it became obvious that things weren't going to plan and as darkness began to fall Brian and I began to panic. Barry was clearly in the mood to enjoy his newfound youth.

'I'm sure it's just a glitch in the program. We just need to be patient.'

'But what if it's not and we're stuck here, with the 'little ole wine drinker' getting slaughtered.'

'All in the line of duty my friends! Chill out, we'll soon be back in our pods and our bodies soon, worst luck.'

The night passed slowly and dawn brought an array of office cleaners, Barry waved them away from his door and they left nonplussed. It was clearly not the first time they had been turned away by Barry. And then in the distance, we could all hear music.

'Oh God! Not the interminable Flint with one of his sardonic ditties.' Barry said in a slurry voice. The music grew louder and I concealed a smile.

'*Stuck in the Middle With You.*' by Stealers Wheel. Barry convulsed into giggles, joining in loudly with '*Clowns to left of me, jokers to the right, Here I am, stuck in the middle with you.*' The lights went out and we were plunged into darkness.

It seemed as though everyone was starting to celebrate, even Brown. To all intents and purposes Barry had sealed the deal. But how quickly things can change. The pats on the back and the excitable hugs stopped as quickly as they had started. The cork remained in the champagne bottle, once bubbling with anticipation. Shauna was mid chest hug with Andy when it happened.

It was only later, when checking the reports from the Techies, that a massive power surge was identified. This blast of power had many outcomes including the loss of Server 3 for six and a half minutes. All clients were disconnected from *Watcher 22* for that period of time. The lights flashed off and the IT screens powered down. An eerie silence spread across the room, punctuated by a few gasps of despair as the implications for the team members were realised. Shauna held on to Andy even more tightly as her legs buckled. Andy began to guide her gently towards the room where Berni had been keeping a watchful eye over their friends.

The flickering lighters made it feel like a surreal Barry Manilow concert, without the sad strains of *Mandy* to normalise it.

'Shauna, come on! Stand up now lovely! Lean on me and I'll get us in there. Berni, Berni where are you?'

'I can't see Andy. Hang on a minute, I'll get my bloody lighter.' Shauna fumbled in her bag and they then managed to light the way to the pods. In the darkness, Helena, Barry and Brian still lay in the same positions and appeared to be sleeping, but each monitor was blank. Berni stood at the end of Helena's bed, holding tightly to the rail. She didn't speak but watched Andy as he quickly moved towards Barry to check his breathing.

'Shauna check Brian, quickly!' Shauna stumbled over to Brian's bed and leaned over him, his breathing was shallow. She grabbed his wrist and felt a faint pulse.

'He's alive, Brian's alive, just in a deep sleep. They're all alive aren't they Berni?'

'Yes dear, they are all alive. That's not the problem. It's getting them back that's the problem. We have interfered with the timeline, the natural order of things. It's backfired. *Watcher 22* had already pushed the boundaries. This was one step too far and before you say it Andy, if it had worked and meant we could go back and destroy Hitler, then wouldn't it all be worth it? I understand that argument, believe me I do. Time is not so easily altered and just like ghosts, people can get trapped between time zones. I'm just thinking about how very scared they must all be feeling.'

'Shit Berni! Don't think like that. Andy, how are we gonna get them back? *Watcher 22* is down. We need Brown and we need him now!'

'I think he's gone to see the Techies, to see if they can sort out the servers and get us back online. Meanwhile, let's cover our friends up, as their body temperatures must be dropping without the aid of the breathing equipment and they could go into shock.' Shauna, Berni and Andy worked together to make their listless friends as comfortable as possible, but still the power remained off.

'Maybe Berni's right, maybe it was just too much, trying to change history, too much for the program I mean.'

'It was a big fuckin' gamble after all. Let's just hope these poor buggers come back in one piece and don't get stuck there.'

Andy shuddered. 'It just doesn't bear thinking about.' Again the lights flickered and there was a dull humming sound, as though the computers were about to come back to life. But to no avail.

'Brown should be back by now.' Andy said quietly.

'We stay together Andy, in case they start coming around, especially Barry if he's not in the right bloody body or whatever, you know what I mean. He might even need restraining.'

'Don't panic now Shauna. I'll stay here with you and we can watch them together. Brown will be here soon I'm sure, as soon as he knows something.'

'It could have been us... We nearly went and then Jesus H...'

'Stop that now Shauna.' Berni said calmly. 'Nothing has happened to our friends yet. Let's just keep them warm and make sure their breathing stays constant. That's all we can do for now. There should be enough of those gases in their system to keep them under for a while.'

'I hope you're right Berni. If anything happens to our friends, anything...'

'Look, their bodies are holding their own, for now at least, it's their minds we should be more concerned about…'

'You three! Over here.' Brown interrupted, his face lit up by a torch, which under any other circumstances would have been highly amusing, but not today. Andy, Berni and Shauna fumbled their way toward the scary flash-lit face of Brown.

'The techies say the system went into overload. *Watcher 22* wasn't designed for such complex challenges, especially with multi-transportations to the same time zone.'

'So what is it you're saying then Brown? Are they stuck there, trapped while their bodies remain here?'

'Jesus Christ! Is that it Brown? Is that fuckin' it? We need some answers man!'

'Look, we just don't know yet. It's probably just some glitch in the system. The good news is that their bodies and their life support have been maintained. It's just the connection that has gone offline…'

'Oh, that's all right then, just the connection with their minds, their souls, their thoughts! These bodies are just empty shells!' Shauna linked her arm through Andy's and Berni's arms, in a gesture of solidarity.

'Well, that's as maybe, but for now, that's where we are.' Brown snapped curtly. 'Continue to watch over them. That's all you can do for now. I have to get back to Systems.' Brown flicked off his torch and left.

The faint beep of the life support monitors marked time for the next few hours. Occasionally, the system seemed to reboot and they were thrust into the full glare of the electric lights. But before they could adjust, the lights would flick off again. This happened repeatedly and each time it became a little more irritating. But nothing changed. Their friends remained alive, like Sleeping Beauties, deep in a sleep that they could no longer awaken from. The time dragged and in the end, they decided to take it in turns to watch over their friends. Andy offered to take the first shift, whilst Helena curled up on a visitor's chair and covered herself with a hospital blanket. Berni followed suit whilst Andy paced the room like an expectant father, this would be a very special delivery if he could just get his friends back. Occasionally, he would adjust the covers or check the heart monitor just to feel as though he was doing something. But nothing changed. After an hour he looked over at Shauna and Berni who were still sleeping. Shauna's arms were crossed, a clear statement of defiance, even in a sleep state. Berni snored gently and Andy noticed the line of a frown above her eyes, which he had never seen before. It didn't look like a particularly restful sleep for either of them. There was so little that they could do and Brown had not returned. No one had been in to see them or their sleeping friends. Andy walked to the door with fresh resolve. They were being left out of the loop. It was time for an update.

It was then that Andy realised. They had been so stupid. He ran back into the room, abruptly rousing Shauna and Berni.

'Fucking hell Andy! I nearly had a heart attack! As if things weren't stressful enough! What's happened? Why did you wake us like that?'

'Shauna! Berni! There's no one here. It's just us!'

'Don't be so fuckin' daft!' Shauna pulled herself up and threw off the blanket whilst Berni roused herself slowly.

'You two stay here. I'm going to find Brown or someone who can sort this out.'

Shauna rushed out of the room and was faced with the same emptiness as Andy. Deciding that it was probably due to a meeting or an early tea break, she went towards the double doors which led into Systems. The doors were locked. Shauna rattled them, but they were security doors and there was no way to penetrate them. Panic rose up from her stomach and she could hear the familiar sound of her heartbeat throbbing in her head. She called out for Andy and Berni, her voice catching in her throat. It seemed like forever before Andy's arms encircled her. He tried to reassure her as he guided her slowly back to the arms of Berni who cuddled and stroked her like a child. Andy stood at the doorway of the pods, for once at a loss for words.

After what seemed like a very long half an hour, the music and lights came on simultaneously.

'Thank God!' Brian said before exhaling loudly. 'I thought we were all goners or stuck in this unholy past, which I don't think Barry would have been that bothered about.' Brian added shaking his head in an annoyed manner. 'Come to think of it, this journey was originally meant for one, are you sure you didn't...'

'For God's sake Brian! I'm not a complete bastard. Of course I didn't, I wouldn't jeopardise people's lives just because I've been lucky enough to rediscover my libido and have the energy to use it. I'm disappointed in you Brian.' he paused, ' Helena please tell me that you weren't thinking the same thing?'

'No, well I don't know anymore. Like the song says, I just want to find my way home.'

'Good old Flint, never fails. They'll be working on it back there, no doubt about that. Our bodies are safe in those pods and it'll just be a computer glitch. These things happen all the time...'

'Look Brian old chap, I don't want to dishearten you, but we have no idea how long this is going to take. It's not like tracking a parcel from Amazon or losing a

Word document. This is complicated stuff and when we signed the disclaimer we knew, well we all knew about the dangers.'

'I'm just glad that Andy, Berni and Shauna are back there, fighting our corner. And while you may be happy in your new virile body Barry, you *know* we have to get back and the sooner the better.'

'I do understand Helena. However, I simply refuse to waste this precious opportunity. I have made a decision. Please hear me out. I am going to venture further afield. And before anyone interjects...' Barry holds his hand up in the air to silence any rebuttal. 'I only want two hours which I think is more than fair. Should the system be repaired before this time, which is quite frankly, highly unlikely, then it would not be an unreasonable delay on our return. Surely you wouldn't deny me this? Just two hours out of a whole lifetime. We could be stuck here for days, maybe weeks, maybe forever. Who knows? I just don't want to waste this chance. Surely you can understand that?'

'You're a bit of a selfish bastard Barry aren't you, I mean underneath all that well mannered, hoity-toity façade.'

'Hang on a minute, Brian. Before we all end up saying something we might regret. Let's think this through. If *Watcher 22* goes back online Barry and you've whistled off to God knows where, to do God knows what, you could miss our opportunity of going home.'

'Helena I do understand...'

'I haven't finished Barry. If you miss the opportunity to return then you may have to stay here forever. Have you thought about this properly Barry? Back home it's extremely unlikely that MI6 would let you leave Headquarters and rejoin society. I would hazard a guess that they would keep you sedated with your young mind trapped in your old body. Your real body would have to be maintained in 2018 and your family and friends would suffer a loss as though you have died. Secrecy would be their top priority, along with keeping you out of circulation. But more than that Barry, don't you think we should stick together like we always do?'

'I think we should take a vote, as potentially it could affect us all.' Brian said curtly.

'I agree. But before we do, would you allow me the courtesy of explaining myself. I don't think that's too much to ask.'

'Alright but make it quick, is that OK with you Helena?'

'I suppose so. It does detract from our original plan, but then who knows what will happen, so go ahead.'

'Thank you.' Barry pauses. 'Before drinking took my life over completely, I did develop a strong and loving relationship with a lovely young lady. We were a great match and happy in our own company. We had only been engaged for a year when it happened....' The lights flickered almost willing Barry to continue. 'It was not long after this very day,' Barry signals around the office, 'my life changed forever and drinking became my new God.'

'Barry I'm not sure you can change something else in the past. When we changed the contract earlier, *Watcher 22* stalled, if you do it again, who knows what will happen.'

'She's right Barry. I don't think you should try and change anything else, but if it's just to see her again, your fiancée, maybe you could see her from a distance then…'

'I feel that I need to finish the story first. Her name was Margaret, not Maggie or Meg.' he said fondly. 'We got engaged and began searching for our dream home. She loved the countryside and riding was her passion. We both worked in the City, we were both young and energetic…' Barry stood up as if to emphasise his youthful physique. 'We could both easily cope with the commute and then if little ones came along they would have a wonderful time in our rural idyll. It was all planned out so beautifully, I could not have been a happier man. And then everything changed, in the blink of an eye. It was just a skid, a patch of oil probably from a farm vehicle. A country lane, a late-night drive. Three weeks after this very day, Margaret was killed in a driving accident. It was instantaneous, impact with old stone walls often is.'

'That's awful Barry. I'm so very sorry. I thought it was going to be a nostalgia shag or something like that…'

'Brian that's not like you! You've been spending too much time with Andy!'

'That's OK Brian, I would probably have assumed the same thing in your position.' Barry paused and bit his lip. 'I just want to see her, just one last time. I won't speak to her. Just look at her. I'm sure that you can both understand. If you were given the opportunity wouldn't you do the same thing?'

'I think I can speak for both of us and say that we do understand…' my turn to pause. 'But Barry what can you achieve by just seeing her, except to renew the pain. You can't warn her Barry, it's too risky. I know you'll want to. I would be the same, but that's not why we're here and who's to say that when we get back, the contract that was changed here will still stand. You could go through all that and nothing changes or we get marooned here. Brian and I don't exactly have a body here, by the way. In case you hadn't noticed, we're just like shadows. It would be a disaster for us, like being one of the undead or something.'

'Helena's right Barry. Painful and frustrating as it must be for you. Let it stay in the past, where it has to stay.'

'I'm afraid that's where we disagree. You see I don't need your permission, being the one with the body. I don't think you can stop me.'

'Barry! I'm shocked! You know this could affect every single one of us. I thought we were a team!'

'Doesn't our group mean anything to you Barry? Being a team player, looking out for one another? You're lucky Shauna isn't here, because she'd kick your arse.'

'But you see she wouldn't Brian. Because, as I've already mentioned she would also not have a body. I think I've inherited some of young Barry's selfishness and its quite empowering. It feels rather good.'

'Really...well bully for you. If you think Brian and I will condone this then you're wrong. I can understand it, of course, but it's the bigger picture Barry, the consequences of your behaviour. It's not just about you.'

'I think at this moment in time, that's exactly what this is about and I'm not missing this chance. Who knows if I can change this, then I could marry Margaret and the drinking would never have started. We may even have children. I promise I will come back, but I really must go now and see my beloved Margaret for the last time.'

'Barry, please! I know you won't be able to stop yourself from speaking to her and warning her. Any one of us would want to do the same. But you will be risking our lives and there's no guarantee it will work.'

'You repeat yourself Helena. Thank you for the advice, but it's time for me to leave here. You can't follow me even if you want to, as you may miss the window to return and I'm sure that you want your bodies back. I will take my chances and in two hours I will be back here in this room I promise.'

'You selfish prick! The old Barry would never have risked the welfare of the whole group for his own end. We do feel sorry for you, but this is wrong Barry and you know it!'

'That's as may be my dear chap, but frankly, I don't give a damn. Toodle pip.' And with that Barry swirled his silk-lined jacket over his shoulder and left the office. It was as simple as that.

Berni, always the voice of reason, comforted Shauna and looked across to Andy.

'Something has changed. I can feel it. I don't think we've been deserted. I think something is coming. We need to sit tight for now and just remain calm. We're safe and for now, so are our dear friends. They are alive, but just not with us right now.'

'How can you be so sure Berni? Why have they locked us in here in this room? Where the hell is Brown?' Andy paced up and down, impatient for answers.

'Trust me, something is coming, I can feel it.'

Andy walked up to the locked door, with the red sign still denying any chance of exit.

'We're trapped, just as Helena, Barry and Brian are trapped. It's a fuckin' nightmare!'

'There are times in life when you just have to sit it out. I feel sure that help is coming. Remember that in history, as far as we know, nothing like this has ever happened before. It's an unknown quantity, there is no simple solution when lives are hanging in the balance.'

'Do you think they're just containing us? Trying to lock down the situation, hold it in stasis while they decide how to proceed? Is that it Berni?'

'That's it Andy. Exactly it. They don't want us wandering around and to be honest we are better remaining close to each other, albeit in this highly anxious state.'

'I just hope that they're OK stuck back there with Barry, he's a bloody loose canon. He could just sod off somewhere and leave Helena and Brian stranded.'

'There is always that possibility Shauna, but we are their Guardians just now and that's all we can focus on. No point in considering 'what ifs', not now. Hang tight, something is coming our way!'

'It's a fuckin' mess! How did this happen Berni? We're like soddin' Guinea pigs or lab rats. I bet they're watching us from afar. I just don't understand, we're trapped in the biggest, most highly advanced Comms unit in the world and no one is communicating with us. It's shite, the whole thing. Is anything happening Andy? Andy, what's going on?'

'Hang on a minute Shauna, I can't hear for your babbling. Wait! I hear something. Quick come on over to the door!'

Berni and Shauna needed no second invitation, they rushed over to the locked door and stood just behind Andy.

'Can you hear it? Listen....'

Berni was the first to speak. 'Someone is coming. You're right Andy. Let's stand clear, away from the door.'

They all moved back slowly as the red light went off and within seconds it turned to green. Brown was the first through the door.

'Stand clear you three, make way, make way!'

'All right Brown, keep your hair on!!' Shauna muttered as they all moved to one side, expecting a mad rush of techies on the scene. Andy looked across at Shauna and Berni, with a look of incredulity, as Brown stepped to one side to allow just one man through the doorway. The door slammed shut behind him.

'Is this it? The entire rescue team?' Andy blurted out as the man walked swiftly over to the flickering computer screens, carrying a Laptop bag and pulling out one of the swivel chairs as Brown turned to face the remaining members of the team.

'Pipe down and listen carefully to what I am about to say.' he said somewhat curtly. 'This is Nathaniel Hawks, one of our leading experts, he's been briefed and has signed the Official Secrets Act., that was the delay. He doesn't work directly for MI5 or MI6, but we use him on occasions, well on occasions like this…'

'You mean when you're screwed and no one has a fuckin' clue?' Shauna butted in. Brown sighed in response.

'That's not helpful Shauna, seriously let's all move back and leave Nathaniel to do his work. He needs peace and quiet in order to concentrate. Nathaniel if you need anything we'll be just over here, back with the other team members and…'

'No Brown, actually I would like all of you to sit behind me. I may need input and the window of opportunity is beginning to close. I do have the technical expertise, but all of you have experience and may see things or think of things that can help.'

Brown was clearly irked at being contradicted and after a slight inclination of the head and thin-lipped inner sigh, he signalled for the team to pull up their chairs.

'I know your team has already used the service pack, that's the common or garden pre-released patches. But this calls for something else. This fix will be a little more complex as this bug is a nasty swine and it will take a very special software patch to mend this and push the update through to the device drivers.' Whilst Nathaniel was talking he had managed to restart the computer and display the black operating screen with the familiar white font. Nathaniel then unzipped the laptop bag and switched on his laptop. 'I've already downloaded the patch, don't ask me where I got it from, just don't ask.'

'Just a quick question, Nathaniel, if I may?' Brown glared over at Andy, but Nathaniel had already nodded his assent.

'It's not online see. The computers, they well that was the problem I think they went off-line.'

Brown raised his eyebrows.

'Fair point matey. But for this, we will be working in offline mode and we can update the patch without accessing the server. It's a tad more complicated than that, but we will soon know if it's worked. It could be as simple as a common virus or missed update and that's what we're hoping for, but I have brought a little something as back up.' Nathaniel lightly tapped the keyboard of his laptop. 'And then, and only then, will the fun begin.'

'It's all above my bloody head!' Shauna muttered under her breath.

Nathaniel clattered away on the keyboard, refreshing the screen and occasionally leaning back to swig from his water bottle. Andy kept looking at his watch and Berni frequently went back to check on their team members. But nothing changed.

'It's a bit of a bastard Brown. I'll give you that. No wonder your people were struggling

Is it deliberate, some kind of targeted sabotage, a cyberattack?'

'Hard to say right now. What do you make of it?'

I honestly can't tell, not yet anyway. I'm waiting for this reboot then we shall see. I've in-putted the fix that I brought along, now we just wait and see if the patch works. Nothing more to be done here.' And with that Nathaniel stretched out his arms, swivelled his chair around and addressed Shauna. 'Would you take a turn around the grounds with me?'

'What the f…'

'She means yes, that would be lovely.' Berni quickly interrupted. 'Take the nice man's arm Shauna and stretch your legs.'

The time dragged interminably, but Berni was glad of some light relief from Shauna. Brown busied himself answering endless phone calls and Andy went back to watch over their three sleeping friends. Berni decided to join him and they sat together, their silence punctuated by the comforting regularity of beeps from the machines. Both of them began to drift into a troubled sleep, the most uncomfortable kind when you are sat upright with your chin on your chest. The peace was broken with a flurry of activity. Nathaniel darted into the room followed by a super-charged Shauna.

'He's only gone and fuckin' done it!.'

Brown pushed past the excited couple as Andy and Berni roused themselves and slowly stood up.

'Look at Helena's trace! The red light has now gone to green. She should now come back to you.'

'And the others Nathaniel?' Berni asked quietly.

'I was told to…'

'Look we didn't want to risk all three at once. We decided to try and bring Helena back first. She is the most experienced and can update us about the situation.'

'So the other two just hang in fuckin' limbo!! Brown you callous bastard, never giving a shit about the whole team.'

'Shauna, this isn't the time.' Berni said quietly, putting her arm around the furious Shauna.

'Quiet now you two. Helena doesn't want to wake up to all these shenanigans.'

Everyone quietened down. Helena was the most important person right now.

The bleeping and flashing grew faster, signalling Helena's return. Brown gently removed all the wires and tubes as Helena's eyes began to flicker open.

(MI6 HQ)
Control room
It's all coming back to me now
Celine Dion

39

Chapter

It's true what they say about your hearing coming back first, well it certainly was for me, unfortunately. Perhaps more people should be made aware of it and then they may choose their words more carefully. It's not too pleasant hearing your team discussing your possible demise. I think it's their sadness that's the hardest to bear and the choked snuffles and thin reedy voices as their hope starts to ebb away. None of this is our team's fault, I can tell that they have been poorly informed or in the worst-case scenario, nobody really knew what the outcome would be. One thing I knew for certain, each one of them was fighting our corner. I was so relieved to be away from the office and that arrogant little shit Young Barry and his selfish older self. He could stay in stasis or wherever the hell he was, but Brian, well I desperately wanted Brian to come back home and soon. According to the team, this was not yet the case. I was the only one to re-enter this hazy existence, so far at least.

Then it happened. A fizzy crackling, like mountains of space dust being poured into my head. A flash, a crack and suddenly I am back! Pinpricks of light danced

250

across the darkness and at last, I knew that I could open my eyes. My tongue felt swollen and my mouth was sandpaper dry. I had never felt like this after my previous revisits, something must have gone very wrong with the program. Gradually, I managed to ease open my heavy eyelids and the world zoomed in and out. I felt a gnarled knot tighten in my stomach, a wave of trepidation, something was wrong, very wrong. I tried to find my voice, but the signals from my brain couldn't seem to connect to my mouth. It was a similar feeling to that of being very drunk, detached and blurry.

'Helena, Helena... can you hear me? It's Berni. You're all right, you're back at HQ with the other team. Just take your time my dear, you've been away for quite a while. Don't try to rush the process. Just take deep breaths and get your bearings a little while we check out Brian and Barry.'

The very mention of Barry's name made me fight even harder to come around. I knew what I wanted to tell them, but I couldn't find my voice. No sooner had I grasped what I wanted to say, then it dissolved and drifted away, tantalisingly out of reach. I decided to close my eyes, maybe it was visionary overload and I should concentrate on making the verbal connection. I could hear Berni's dulcet tones, broken only by the jagged interjection of Shauna's caustic comments. Then I felt a weird sensation. Someone was rubbing my feet. I managed to half- open my right eye and to my surprise, I saw Andy doing the good deed. He was unaware of me watching him. I took this opportunity to give him the once over and noticed how tired and drawn he appeared. We must have been away for longer than I thought.

Suddenly, the atmosphere changed. The voices went quieter. Something was amiss. Never one for being left out, I was determined to bring myself around. Time to channel my overriding curiosity to push myself into consciousness. On command one eye flashed open and stayed open, after adjusting to the light, I began to look around. Then I saw them. Barry and Brian, lying still on adjacent beds. There had been no effort to raise their heads onto pillows or remove any of their wires. No one was rubbing their feet. The machines beeped slowly, no sign of any awakening. My eye then rested on a flustered looking Brown. I heard Shauna's voice before I even managed to focus on her.

'What do you mean, they're not fuckin' ready? Who's not ready? Barry and Brian can't speak!! So they're not telling you they're not ready! You mean you're not ready? Nathaniel, help me out here! You've managed to start bringing Helena out of it, can't you do the same for the other two, for Barry and Brian?'

I could just make out the stranger's face as he turned his head to one side looking very uncertain.

'Nathaniel, who's not ready? You? Because it's not these two poor buggers!'

'I only follow instructions Shauna. I was told to bring one of them back and if that was successful only then to focus on the other two. It made sense to me.'

'It was your instruction Brown wasn't it?' Shauna paused. 'I wonder…. would it be Brian that you focus on next?? I bet it fuckin' is. Are you even going to bother bringing Barry back…'

'Shauna!' Brown raised his voice. " We are all under tremendous pressure here. Nathaniel, please continue with your work. Nathaniel looked peeved and made a point of brushing against Brown's shoulder as he left the room.

'Aren't you going with him Brown?' Andy asked curtly. " We need to spend a little time with our team-mate. And before you say it, we know you record all the conversations, so it's not as if you will miss a thing. A little courtesy would go a long way right now.'

Brown sighed. ' There are a lot of questions to be answered here…but before you jump down my throat Shauna, I can see that Helena needs a little more time to come around. I'll give you ten minutes after that she's all mine.'

I smiled as Shauna showed Brown a well-deserved look of repulsion, 'If you had been through this process like we bloody well have, you'd be less of a shit…'

'But we are grateful for the time we have, thank you Brown.' Berni intervened in an attempt to smooth the way. I felt relieved. Right now I was the one with questions. I signalled to Berni to raise my pillows and everyone fussed around the bed. I felt much better being upright.

'Thank you, my friends.' I paused. My voice was still slightly hoarse. 'When are they going to bring the others back?'

'I don't know whether you heard the new bloke Nathaniel saying that he's onto it now. Anyhow Helena, what the hell happened back there?'

'It's obvious that something went wrong Helena. Are you able to tell us?'

I signalled to Shauna to pass me the water and sucked keenly through the red stripey straw.

'We don't fuckin' know anything from when we lost the signal. Figured something or someone was up to no good. Bet it's that bugger Barry, Brian is solid.' I smiled in agreement, before trying out my voice. It was crackly but usable. I decided to stick to the bare essentials.

'At first, Barry wanted to leave. He did well with the deal and managed to change the contract. But then he started enjoying his…' I indicated my head and circled around the body area.

'Yeah, we get the idea, felt the rumble in his jungle.' Shauna said knowingly.

'Yes, something like that.' I managed a smile. 'When the system failed to return us back here immediately, it started him thinking. The opportunity arose and he decided that he would take two hours out, away from everything and go out into this new world.' I took another drink. 'We talked about his body remaining here and the young Barry's distress and about what that would mean if he didn't return.' Andy glanced over at Barry's dormant figure. 'Barry had been in a relationship, he wanted to settle down. That was before he began drinking. The love of his life, Margaret, was killed in a car accident. The accident was three weeks after the date when we arrived. So when we arrived there, she was still alive. Barry wanted to see her one last time. We warned him that it may change nothing and also that we might all be stuck there, as Brian and I have no physical presence, it was a huge risk.' I took another drink, this was hard work. 'He pointed out that he was the one with the body and he didn't need our permission. He had made up his mind. Then he left the room and Brian and I were stranded, too afraid to follow in case we couldn't get home.'

'What a selfish fucker he turned out to be!'

'I can imagine it would be a great temptation.' Berni added wistfully. 'We shouldn't judge him too harshly…'

'Well, I bloody well can.' Brian's gravelly voice came from the neighbouring bed.

'He let us down badly. I'm just so glad to be back. What happens now?'

'Brian! Thank God you're back and...'

Brown interrupted as always.

'Ah, excellent. Two out of three Nathaniel. Very good. You know what comes next.'

Nathaniel met my eye for a moment, he looked uncertain and strained.

'I have warned you Brown, this is a very small window of opportunity. If Barry has moved from the designated zone then...well, I'm not sure how this will work.'

'Get on with it man!' Brown barked his order and Nathaniel left the room.

'It's Barry's own fault if he's disobeyed orders. You all know this to be true. I suggest you form your witches circle or say a few prayers or whatever your little group does when you want something to happen.'

Brown left the room and Andy and Shauna moved all three of the beds together. All eyes were on Barry. We waited in anticipation, not so much for his awakening, but desperate to know which Barry would come home.

Even though only four weeks had passed, it seemed like an age. Barry had woken up, only to be instantly whisked away by Brown under the keen watch of Nathaniel. We had been debriefed, then sent home and ordered to take some much-needed R & R. After a period of rest and following the inevitable reinstatement of the internet, we had all been in regular contact by text and email. Things were gradually returning to normal, young people were back to banging into lamp posts whilst staring aimlessly at their phones and drivers in cars have resumed their phone habit of pretending to lean on the window with their phone held against their ear. The phone boxes were slowly being removed and the frequency or rather infrequency of the post had gone back to normal. The local shops and supermarkets had a short reprieve and an increase in sales, due to online shopping being defunct. Sadly now you could feel the shift, the isolation and detachment of the so-called 'social' media returning. Face to face communication, and text free evenings became a thing of the past again, sliding silently into the distance, for better or worse. Personally, I felt it was for the worse. The young people I had spoken to had started to enjoy face to face meetings and the joy of letter writing, freed from the domineering lure of texting and keeping up with Facebook, Instagram, etc. Cyberbullying simply disappeared down the same sewer it had crawled up from and the continuous phone checking had ceased. Life had become simpler and less intense. Communities were just starting to spring back to life, partly as people had no choice. If you needed food or anything at all, then you quite simply had to get off your backside and go get it. Word of mouth meant something again and plans were rarely altered, people meeting 'just to chat' had become the norm. Gossip and social media nonsense had been sent back to whence it came. Our young people had a respite from the helter-skelter pressure of instant communication and I think they secretly liked it. But that's all over now and back we are, cemented inside the digital slapdash and chaos of daily life.

I am heading down to London for one of our get-togethers, this time it was being held at Berni's house. Barry had only been released by M15 a week ago and we were all desperate to see him and find out, well find out which Barry had come back. Barry had not been mentioned in the debrief which, although thorough, had focused more on our confidentiality and ways of easing back into normal life. There was little information about what had been achieved and when we asked about Barry, Brown simply used his pursed lipped expression, accompanied by a nonplussed frown and shake of the head. We can only assume that the experiment failed and although history *can* potentially be changed, it must have righted itself on our return. I was so relieved that we had all made it back in one piece and excited to be going to one of our group reunions. Berni's party theme is based on the film *Mama Mia,* fortunately, the costumes were reasonably straight forward. There had been a little friction between the boys about certain roles, but we finally nailed it. I have the part of Meryl Streep (Donna) which fortunately meant that cut off dungarees, a white shirt and sandals would suffice. Shauna was the ideal fit for Sophie, minding her language of course and Berni wanted to take the Julie Walters character, Rosie. Barry was perfect for Harry, the character played by Colin Firth. Andy agreed to be Sam, the Pierce Brosnan character, despite the dreadful singing We had a conference call to work out the Brian dilemma. Although Brian would have been quite happy to play Bill-the Swedish adventurer, the group decided that for balance we needed him to be Sky, played by Dominic Cooper. After all, Brian was the youngest man in our group, not that young of course, but a match in age for Shauna. At least this time everyone could travel easily in costume, there had been some flack and funny looks when travelling to the Wizard of Oz party.

My journey was smooth and uninterrupted, partly because I always chose the quiet carriage. I arrived at Berni's house half an hour early, knowing that she wouldn't mind. We hugged and chattered away in her country style kitchen, whilst she made tea in a teapot, complete with tea cosy. I sensed an air of trepidation, Berni seemed a little distracted.

"Is everything alright Berni?" I asked

She shrugged my question aside, but I could tell that she was uneasy and I knew why. Everyone felt the same. This would be our first meeting with Barry. He had not been in touch with any of us directly, a message about the party had reluctantly been sent via Brown. None of us wanted his involvement, but we had started this thing as a team and it seemed only fair that we should be reunited and at least get the chance to find out what had happened. Had he even met up with Margaret? The doorbell broke my concentration and Berni disappeared to let Shauna and Brian in. Berni took their coats and I could hear the strains of *Money Money Money* drifting in from the dining room. Great! I was so glad that Berni was happy to get into the spirit of things. Next to arrive was Andy dressed as Sam, looking strangely handsome in a crisp white shirt and smart jeans, complete with a brown belt. Not to be outdone Shauna then made her mark. After rummaging in her bag she turned around and after bending down for a few moments, turned around proudly sporting a blonde wig. She was wearing a lacy white dress and white satin ballet pumps. She looked amazing and there was more than one admiring glance from the male contingent. Brian looked the part too, in his cut off denim shorts, trainers and a low cut patterned shirt. He even wore a wooden beaded necklace, which was perfect.

'I resisted the fake tan, it just wasn't me.'

'Such a bloody wuss!' Shauna chipped in. 'I just used that cream that you put on, not all over though, just where it shows.'

'You look perfect!' I whispered in her ear, mid hug. 'Stand with Brian and let's have a photo before you get dishevelled and before…'

'Yes before the laddo arrives.' Andy interrupted and as usual said exactly what we were all thinking.

'Don't know why the fuck he was invited! Nearly got the lot of us wiped out. Such a selfish bastard.'

'Well, you all look splendid.' Berni interrupted, always the diplomat. 'Andy do the honours would you and take a snap of the happy couple. Aptly the strains of *I have a dream* drifted gently in from the other room. There was a glimmer of attraction as Shauna and Brian stood face to face, holding hands. It was heart-warming to see them both so happy and healthy with just the faintest gleam of attraction in their eyes.

'That's a cracker.' Andy said happily, showing us all the photograph.

'Before we sit down to eat, could I ask everyone to put their phones in this old cookie jar.' Berni asked firmly. 'I think we have all had enough of the interruptions and stress that these devices can cause.' Everyone agreed and put their mobiles into the large glass jar which she carefully placed on the old Welsh dresser. 'Excellent now follow me into the dining room.' We all obeyed and the music hit us as we walked in and we formed a circle, holding hands and swaying and singing to *The name of the game*. It was lovely and a group hug sealed the moment. There was laughter and mayhem before we reformed the circle for *The Winner takes it all*. A slightly slower track which made me reflect on the year that we had all had. Shauna was hitting the high notes like a true professional and Brian was also playing his part.

How quickly things can change. The sharp rapping of the brass fox, door knocker, brought us all back down to earth. Sharp glances were exchanged and the circle of joint hands became broken. Berni made a soothing gesture and shot a warning glance at Shauna, before turning down the music and making her way to the front door.

'Maybe it's just an Amazon delivery.' Shauna said, trying to lighten the mood. 'From before the crash, they're always bleedin' late.'

There was no escaping the tension in that room. All we could hear was a muffled conversation that held few clues. I was so relieved that this 'get together' was being held at Berni's house. If anyone could control the group dynamics it was Berni.

'He's a cheeky bastard even showing his face.' Andy said, whilst turning to fill his glass.

'Practically left us for dead.' Brian added whilst walking over to get some ice from the plastic pineapple.

'Think we all need a fuckin' drink!' Shauna said nervously. Brian caught her hand and with a silent shake of his head, guided her away from the drinks table. I had a long slug of my Bacardi and coke, this was going to be very, very difficult. Shauna and Andy could both be volatile and I was surprised that Barry was brazen enough to come, but then again hadn't he shown a very different side to his character when he deserted us? Fortunately, *Super Trouper* was the next track on the CD, and everyone smiled and nodded knowingly. Berni entered the room, avoiding everyone's eyes as she gestured for Barry to enter.

There was a moment of toe-curling silence. A feeling so awkward, that no one could make eye contact. This was our team, close-knit and loyal until Barry had chosen to put himself first. Now the prodigal son returned and someone had to break the ice. The obvious choice for this would have been Berni, but she was as dumbfounded as the rest of us. Luckily the Welshy cut straight across any formalities and dived straight in.

'Hello, Barry you old bastard! I'll give you credit, you have a nerve showing your face around here and if it wasn't for...'

'Thank you, Andy.' Berni paused. ' I think it would be more appropriate for us to take a seat and listen to what Barry has to say for himself. This isn't one of the Nuremberg trials and I'm sure things aren't as clear cut as we may think.' Berni then gestured for everyone to take a seat and turned the music down.

'Thank you, Berni.' Barry said quietly, nodding ascent as Brian offered him a can of coke. I could see Shauna sneering at him, the telltale spots of anger beginning to appear on her cheeks. Brian guided her to the chintz settee and sat her down, holding her hand firmly, which I felt was a wise precaution. Andy leaned against the wall, possibly to reinforce his position in this tense situation. Berni and I sat side by side and even though it was a three- seater settee, we sat close together as if in need of physical contact. Brian positioned himself directly opposite to Barry and was prepared for confrontation.

Barry took a large gulp from the can of Coke, took a deep breath and gave a cursory glance around the room, clearly mapping things out. 'Good evening one and all. Thank you Berni, for inviting me. I don't deserve this opportunity to redeem myself and I thank you for allowing me to..,'

'Spare us the posh claptrap Barry! We all know what you fuckin' did...'

'Thank you, Shauna.' Berni interrupted. 'I think we should hear what Barry has to say for himself, after all, we have had to wait a long time for this.' She indicated for Barry to continue and shot Shauna a warning glance.

'I messed up. I know I have. I put my own selfish feelings above the safety of the rest of the group and I do, most sincerely, apologise. I know this was a terrible mistake and I beg for your forgiveness. I came here today to stand before you and face each and every one of you, I take full responsibility for my actions and..."

'Not good enough matey is it? You put the lives of team members at risk, left them there, knowing they could be trapped there forever, unable to return without you! Didn't you?'

A cold chill descended on the room. Barry looked down at his feet and nodded his head.

'I did and I am ashamed of my actions. I know that the damage I have done to the team is probably irreparable. But I have to try. Only a coward shirks facing the truth head-on. I am truly sorry.' Barry paused.

'Look Barry, what you did was quite honestly abhorrent and seemed out of character somehow. You were always such a trusted and loyal member of our team, a little....'

'Up yourself...'

"Thank you, Shauna, a little domineering at times, but you would never have put any of us in harm's way. You need to tell us why you did this and what happened. If you can't do that then I feel our friendship is, as you say, quite irreparably damaged.' There were mutterings and some nodding of heads.

'I understand. All I wanted to do was to see my beloved fiancée once more before she died in that car accident. Wouldn't any of you have done the same? Maybe I could have saved her, married her, changed things...anyone of you here would have done the same thing! Come on! You know I am speaking the truth!!'

'And did you? Did you see your fiancée, did you change things? Prevent her death and live out a happy life?' Brian asked quietly, without looking up.

'No. No, I didn't. I couldn't, the program blocked my contact. She couldn't see me, couldn't hear me, I couldn't touch her or warn her.... I tried God knows....'

'We do understand why you tried this Barry, to see your fiancée, maybe even save her. I think I can speak for all of us who, in the same position, would have been tempted. It was just the mercenary way you cast off your friends, friends who had risked their lives with you back at XP when we were trapped in that program. This was us Barry and you were willing to sacrifice two of our team for your own self-serving purpose.' Berni's voice cracked with emotion. I took her hand, squeezing it gently for reassurance.

'Yes. I did all that. I did and I put my hands up. I deserted the team and I knew what I was doing. I showed weakness and arrogance and I deeply regret it. I don't ask for forgiveness, just understanding.'

'Early days boyo. Steady on there. If you had met your fiancée and changed the future, we would be sat here at our little reunion minus Helena and Brian. But you would be just fine. Have you thought about that?'

The sound of silence.

'Yes Andy, I have thought about it, many times and words fail me. I ask only for you to consider my position with fairness.'

'I think that may take a little time, to be honest. There is a lot of anger in this room. We have heard your explanation, Barry. You have to understand that until now we were unaware of the outcome. Brown refused point-blank to tell us what had happened to you. So maybe now we know, we need time to think about your take on events and work out how to move forward.'

'That's more than fair Brian, I respect your decision. Is that how you all feel?'

The group nodded in agreement. All except one member of course.

'That's all very Oprah and supportive and I'm sure it fits in with some fuckin' namby-pamby psychology. I'm not so sure that time is a 'bloody healer.' Funny how no one is asking the real question, the most bleedin' important question?' Shauna now had everyone's attention.

'I know you are all thinking the same thing, so don't stare at me like I'm a weirdo!' I could feel Shauna's temper starting to rise. 'OK, so I'll do it! Is it you Barry, the middle-aged version, both inside and out? Your body is obviously, but how would we know if the old you had stayed behind in that young body. This version of you could be a lie. The real you may be back there and the young one sent to us like a sacrifice, coached by your older self.'

'Don't be ridiculous Shauna! How could you say that? Of course it's me. I'm not some version of Tom Hanks in *Big*. Do you seriously think that *Watcher 22* and MI6 would accommodate such a switch and allow me to transport back, seriously? That's if it was even possible?'

'I don't know...Shauna has a point. We have just accepted you at face value. Not questioning if you are the version of Barry that was with us on the program and aided our escape.'

'This is outrageous!! I expected anger, accusations and some abuse, but not this! Not questioning my identity, It's me, Barry! Surely you can tell?'

'No actually, we can't. How could we possibly tell?'

'You make a good point Andy and I think before we begin considering any kind of reconciliation, we need to resolve this. You have broken our trust Barry and should be able to understand that we need to establish the truth before accepting you back into our team.'

'Stop pussyfooting around! You're lucky to be here at all Barry and you know it! Old or young. I think we should ask Barry some questions, ones that only the old Barry would know the answers to. Remember, young Barry would only have the information his older self could impart in a very short space of time. What do you think?'

The Team began nodding, caution had arrived rather late at the table and this very important question deserved an answer.

If anyone looked through the window into Berni's house, I think they would have been rather surprised at what they saw. The cast of *Mama Mia* was now all seated, with Berni at the head of the table donning her glasses which denoted the seriousness of the situation. The sunny mood, direct from the Greek Isle of Skopelos, seemed to have evaporated, but not in the heat of the Midday sun.

'Don't you think that MI6 checked me out and debriefed me? Brown was all over me like a rash! I have already been rigorously interrogated and even now my every move is monitored. I have to wear an electronic ankle tag, which is truly degrading.' Barry said as he flashed the anklet for all to see. This wasn't difficult to display as Barry was wearing shorts and it made me wonder why this proud arrogant man would want to show this particular badge of correction off. He could easily have worn light trousers to hide the device or argued the toss to change character. I shook away my doubts, determined that Barry should have a fair trial.

'I think it would be appropriate if we all took a moment to think of a pertinent question to ask Barry. Something that only the 'old Barry' would know the answer to. One question each should suffice.'

'That's fuckin' easy for me!' Shauna barged straight in as you would expect. "At whose leaving do did we dress up as film stars? And name the characters.' Shauna looked quite smug, but I felt that Barry would definitely have coached his younger self on something as obvious as this.

'Do I really have to list the names?' Barry sighed as we all nodded. He didn't look in the least concerned.

'It was, of course, *my* leaving soiree. I was dressed as Fred Astaire, Helena was Marilyn Monroe, Shauna was perfectly sublime as dear Audrey Hepburn and who could forget Andy's amusing rendition of Tom Jones. The reason I know all this is because I selected the outfits and the characters.' Barry paused, 'This is so tedious.'

Shauna looked irked and the dangerous flush of annoyance was beginning to adorn her cheeks.

Andy was the next to ask and again seemed confident.

' Who was the top Guide selected by the clients of *Watcher 22*?'

Barry grimaced at Andy and flashed an impatient look up towards the ceiling.

'Is that your best shot Andy?' Barry paused and just for a split second he appeared to hesitate. 'Although it was a long time ago, I think the correct answer is Richard Burton.'

Again the old team nodded their agreement.

Berni was next, 'I came to the program a little later than others, do you remember what my special skill was?'

'nursery school children could guess the answer to this one.' Barry smiled, but seemed to put his head down. Something wasn't right here.

'Dear Berni you are of course a clairvoyant which is a gift, rather than your given birth name as Shauna once suggested.'

A flutter of laughter went around the circle. Shauna pursed her lips together, but her eyes seemed to be smiling.

'Who's next?' Barry drummed his fingers impatiently on the table. Brian seemed a little uncomfortable.

'Like Berni, I also came to the group a little later than the others. But I would ask you Barry, to name all the characters at Helena's party along with their real names.'

'Simple pimple. Do I have to?' again it appeared to me that Barry was stalling.

'Shauna was the wicked witch which is appropriate,' he flashed her a smile. 'Berni was the good witch, I forget her exact name, Brian was the lion, I was the tin man and dear Helena was Dorothy and lastly Andy was the scarecrow. Could we stop this now? I am feeling a little persecuted. I know I messed up and I have apologised. Surely you can tell that this is Me!!'

'Just one last question should suffice.' Berni added determinedly. 'Helena. Do you have a final question for Barry?' I had been thinking about asking an obscure question and then decided to opt for an easy one and see if Barry paused again.

'Barry here's an easy one for you, who were my Guides back at *XP*?' Andy sighed and Shauna could not hide her feelings.

'For fuck's sake Helena, that's not even worth a response!' A rumble of grumbling went around the table. I winked at Shauna and she frowned back at me. I was watching Barry intently, firstly a look of scorn crossed his face, but then I felt sure that he paused, just for a moment, whilst everyone was groaning.

'Dear Helena you insult my intelligence once again, your Guides were the inimitable Dame Judi Dench and the wonderful Alan Rickman, God rest his soul.' And with that final flourish, Berni rose from her seat, switched the music up and began bringing in the food.

Everyone ate and chattered, those that could drink alcohol did so and the mood in the room lightened. Tales of past adventures and updates on future plans were shared alongside the meal. I just couldn't shake off my scepticism. Barry was doing an admirable job, whichever Barry he was. As we cleared away the dishes, I shared a moment alone with Shauna.

'What the bloody hell are you up to Helena?' she asked in her most direct way.

'I asked an easy question on purpose...'

'You feckin' well did, but why?'

'Did you notice Shauna, that there's just a very slight pause before he answers?'

'Now you mention it, I did notice him looking down, there does seem like some sort of delay. What the hell is going on? Do you think he's the young Barry Helena? Is that what you're saying?'

'I really don't know, but something is slightly off..."

'I agree with you Helena.' Berni said quietly as she entered the kitchen carrying a tall stack of plates. 'Something doesn't ring true. At first, I thought it was nerves or embarrassment about what he has done, But this is Barry and those aren't qualities he normally displays.'

Andy barged into the kitchen with Brian, clearly the worse for the wine.

'Hey you three, come on in, it's time for some dancing!' he linked arms with Berni and Shauna and escorted them into the dining room. 'Come on Helena.' he added with a wink.

The table had been moved to the side of the room and the chairs were now pushed back against the wall. Brian switched the volume up and ABBA's songs filled the room. This lightened everyone's mood and we danced our way through a wide selection starting with *Thank you for the music* and going right back to *Waterloo*.

Finally, it was time for the last song. We formed a circle and put our arms around each other's shoulders. It felt so good to be reunited with our strange family, we had faced so many serious challenges. Strains of *Knowing me knowing you* filled the room. The circle got tighter and I had made sure that I was positioned next to Barry. As the track came to an end we all gave our hugs and kisses as we had done so many times before, sometimes not knowing if we would ever see each other again. I turned to Barry and we hugged, Barry always chose the European way of kissing on alternate cheeks. He seemed a little hesitant, so I pushed through and kissed him anyway. Maybe I was wrong about him, after all, he felt and talked just as I remembered. I shrugged my shoulders and shook my head ready to hug my way around our circle of friends. Shauna was next and grabbed me in a big bear hug swinging me around and just as I came back down to earth, I looked across at Barry and that's when I saw it or thought I saw it. A tiny glint of light flashed from behind Barry's ear. It was very fast and could well have been a trick of the light. Maybe it was a reflection from the light or a glass. I looked across at Shauna, but she was mid hug with Brian, a very long hug as it turned out. Berni caught my eye, she knew, I could tell. Andy was heading my way for his farewell hug and I clung tightly to him.

"Steady on there Helena, we'll see each other again very soon. With my head on Andy's shoulder, I cautiously looked across at Barry and he flashed me a cold stare. There was no light behind his eyes. There was just a glimmer of a smirk before he turned Berni around and kissed her on both cheeks as he had always done.

Faintly, ever so faintly and far way in the distance, on the very edge of hearing, came the strains of an old favourite and I knew that Flint was still alongside me. helping me from whichever world he now finds himself in.

I walked across an empty land
I knew the pathway like the back of my hand
I felt the earth beneath my feet
Sat by the river, and it made me complete
Oh, simple thing, where have you gone?
I'm getting old, and I need something to rely on
So tell me when you're gonna let me in
I'm getting tired, and I need somewhere to begin

Somewhere Only We Know
Keane

Printed by BoD™in Norderstedt, Germany